ALL THE TREES
IN THE WOOD

Stephanie Percival

CONTENTS

All The Trees in The Wood

CHAPTER 1

I don't know the exact moment Daddy disappeared, whether night or morning. They said he had stumbled into the river whilst drunk. I'm not sure I have ever truly believed that. I am certain that *she* had something to do with it – the woman I saved – the woman who owes me a life. And here I am again, back to the place where it began.

There are no tell-tale signs of the house that was here. The glade appears empty. No shards of white plank, no remains of the wood shed, no guttering or glass an archaeologist might document. Now it is just a space interrupting the wood. The ground smoothed into hillocks and dips. The trees look familiar though and I pat a trunk, grateful that some element of my old home remains.

The space looks smaller than it did, and besides the obvious change in my perspective due to age, there is new fencing bordering the area. The barrier increases the gloom. Behind the planks lurk modern houses; their gables and upper windows peering at me.

I feel hot and uncomfortable. I drank too much wine with lunch and the glade is airless, thick with the stench of wild garlic and sap. A cloud of midges shifts with the shadows. I sit on a fallen tree trunk to catch my breath and steady my thoughts. This might have been the exact place where our piano once stood. On the ground is a round pebble. It is the sort of trophy my mother would have placed on a ledge to ward off evil spirits and surround us with protection. I smooth my thumb over its surface marvelling at the swirl of amber through it, a part of me hoping it had once adorned my window sill. Looking upwards into the crisscross of branches above me I imagine lying in my childhood bed. My head is heavy and the trees spin above me, as if I am at the centre of a carousel. There is no breeze but the branches sway and I can hear the leaves muttering. The murmurs sound familiar.

"What ya doin?"

I nearly fall off the log.

It takes me a moment to regain my balance. The shadows fuse and separate, making it difficult to focus. But gradually from across the glade a figure emerges.

It demands again, "What ya doin here, Missus?" as if the space is more his than mine.

"I used to live here," I tell the boy. His head is too large for his skinny body and I cannot guess his age. "Shouldn't you be at school?" He chuckles. Although he looks odd, he doesn't appear threatening.

"I knows things ... I knows things about the witchy house."

I never referred to it as that, but I know what he means. There was always whispering in the village about the superstitions associated with my old home. "Do you live nearby then?" I ask, indicating the houses across the fence, looking for a gap which he might have crawled through.

"No," he sneers, "I live in the wood." I guess he must dwell in one of the shacks on the edge of the forest. "What you got in your hand?"

I unclench my fingers revealing the pebble. He leans towards it sniffing and then wipes his nose on his sleeve. I catch the scent of him; fern and forest floor, and I wonder whether he does indeed sleep in the wood.

"You shouldn't keep it. It belongs to them."

I was going to put the pebble in my pocket as a keepsake, but the stare from the boy's black eyes, makes me drop it.

"You got a fag?" He leaps onto the edge of the trunk making it shudder. He is wearing muddy plimsolls. Close up his skin looks leathery and ingrained with dirt. I shake my head, regretting I no longer smoke, thinking it might mute the muddle in my head.

The boy is pirouetting on the log, balancing without difficulty.

"Where did you sleep then?"

I try to work out the layout of the house, orientating myself by identifying trees which had once been familiar. "I used to look out of my bedroom window at that tree," I indicate an elderly oak with a Cyclops's eye which greeted me each morning and watched over me as I slept.

Suddenly the boy leaps from the log. He is so light I think he might fly. He departs saying, "Nice to meet you, Missus."

Then he is gone, melting into the undergrowth before I have a chance to ask his name.

Once he's left, the quietness returns. The ache in my temples is getting worse making blotches across my vision. The press of migraine which has affected me most of my life, hovering. I close my eyes and wait until the dizziness subsides. But the past prickles in as specks in the darkness behind my lids, liquid with tears.

Echoes in my mind hum, becoming louder, accompanying the throbbing in my head. I think about the boy's question. What was I doing here? The trees about me do what they have always done and murmur a response, but I'm out of practice interpreting their wisdom, and the only word I can identify is; Lorelei, Lorelei, Lorelei. And then I understand; it is because of her that I am here.

Lorelei. I had given her that name. That's what I thought she'd said when I found her. We'd been living down in the valley then. A farmer had lent my parents the use of the barn for the band to practice, so our caravans were parked in a nearby field. Perhaps it was an orchard; I remember blossom and odd little apples like gargoyles.

At five years old I was left to my own devices, so long as I kept the caravan in sight. The frost was hard in January 1976 and made the world an ice palace, turning water to glass. My head was full of images from a book of fairy tales. Daddy had come across the tome in a charity shop. Within its hard grey cover, fables from around the world were concealed, waiting for me to turn the thick cream pages, dusty with age. The cover was etched with lines, deep enough for me to trace with a fingertip and try and make sense of the patterns; trees, goblin legs, spying eyes and fairy wings. The book enthralled me, and now the imagery was reflected in the real world. Icicles glistened from the eaves of the farm buildings, ruts were filled with shiny rings, the orchard trees bore silver pods linked with chains of spider web.

In the corner of an adjacent field was a trough. The water had frozen and I was using the surface to try and emulate the illustrations from the book. With a stick I'd gouged talons and wings, maidens hidden in the trunks of trees, high mountains and stars. As I drew, the ice croaked and creaked as it absorbed the strokes I made across its surface.

But then there was a different sound. A cry. A distant whimper from near the river. I wasn't meant to go down to the treacherous banks alone. But the call was out of place in the bright morning, I thought an animal could be in trouble. I also considered the willow trees might have summoned me.

I crossed a strip of pasture towards the river. The scene looked like one of the drawings from my book. The exposed roots of the willow were claws clasping a strange creature. I made my way to a shallow bank where cattle accessed the water. Each animal print had a circle of ice within. These cracked as I stepped into the tracks, my Wellingtons sinking down into each muddy hole so I moved with the exaggerated pace of giant's footsteps.

Creeping closer I glimpsed a shape of white draped on the bank below. Trails of willow branch moved through the water allowing sunlight to flicker over the object beneath. The sheen of material resembled the surface of an egg. I wondered if something had been born within the roots tangled at the water's edge. More than ever, it resembled a picture from my book, with the black lines of root and bark and eddying water.

I stepped closer, my Wellingtons touching the water. I knew I shouldn't go further. But then the thing moaned. I waded under the willow, wavelets bumping rubber boot against my shins.

Now I was close enough to recognise the shape as human, or a being in the guise of a woman. I put my hand on her head and stroked the wet hair. I heard her speak her name. It sounded like, "Lorelei."

The legend of Lorelei was one of the tales in my book. An abandoned woman who sang to lure sailors onto the rocks below. I'd had to ask Mother how to say the word. Pressing my finger under the letters and saying them phonetically. 'Lo ... re ... lei'. The name was accompanied by an illustration of a beautiful woman singing on a rock above a river.

I took off my duffle coat. The toggles were tricky but I managed, and I laid it over her. She was shivering and I could not see her feet as they were swathed in material. Could mermaids exist this far from the sea?

Then I left her and ran to the caravan, shouting for Mother and Father, "Ma, Ma. Daddy, Daddy."

They were quick to respond to my call. It was rare for me to shout for their assistance. I was breathless as they asked what was wrong. I pointed to the river and stuttered something like, "There, over there, she's there."

They followed my pointing finger and I let them run ahead. Tom Hart, one of the band members, the one we called Woody, came out from his caravan, asked what was going on and we headed to the river bank together.

The two men lifted Lorelei and between them carried her back to our caravan. Lorelei's hair hung down in a silvery ribbon, her wet dress dripped a trail of sequin drops as she was moved. She was so pale, as if she'd been turned to ice like the rest of the world and was melting in the weak sunshine. The swell of her belly was exaggerated by the clinging of her wet garment.

Throughout her journey she kept murmuring 'Lorelei, Lorelei'. It was much later that I considered she might have been saying, 'Laura lied' or even 'You'll all die,' or perhaps that was my over fertile imagination and she had been asking, "Where am I?"

In the caravan she was placed on the couch which folded down into Ma and Daddy's bed. Ma's forehead was creased in a way I recognised; she turned to Daddy and said, "You know who she might be? Do you think it could be …?" I didn't hear a name but Daddy shouted "Don't be stupid! Not possible," and slammed his hand down on the side board so the whole caravan shuddered.

He and Woody went away before Ma said anything more. But she still had a frown on her face as she peeled the wet fabric up Lorelei's body and over her head, making her lift her arms as she did when she helped me undress.

The swell of Lorelei's belly was impossible to ignore. It had a marbled blue sheen and was so distended it looked ready to burst.

"Is she going to pop?" I asked.

"No," Ma replied, "But she is going to have a baby. Very soon."

"Find her a clean night dress Annie," Ma requested. I chose Ma's only pretty nightie. The others were utilitarian cotton. This one was aqua satin which rippled like water when I held it, reminding me of the place she had been found. We put Lorelei into bed, covering her up. I was allowed to pat her hair with a towel. As it dried the silver became a sheet of satin and there was a single stripe of black so it resembled a magpie's wing. She did appear to be the image from my book, Lorelei fallen from her rock into the river, transmuting to reality. I held her hand whilst Ma warmed soup for her.

"Who do you think she is?" I asked Ma, thinking she might tell me who she'd considered before. But she said absolutely nothing. I decided to tell her what I thought. "She's Lorelei." I said with certainty, stroking the long cool fingers. "Like in my book. That's what she's been saying."

Ma sat beside Lorelei and fed soup to her. She concentrated on lifting a spoonful of liquid to Lorelei's mouth. "Well, we can call her that for now," she said.

I was left with an expectation I would find out a proper name and history later. But I never did.

CHAPTER 2

Lorelei's baby was Archie and for a time he was like a brother. It was due to his request that I was back here.

Earlier I'd driven back to Broomstone. As I'd left the bypass up the hill to the village the air changed. Broomstone didn't follow the natural laws of the rest of the world, but had a microclimate which immediately sucked me inwards. Today was a sultry summer's day. The air conditioning in the car struggled and circulated hotness around until I felt a pressure in my lungs making me breathless. I found a place to park opposite the Linden Tree Pub and waited. Winding the window down allowed air loaded with the odour of sap to ooze in. I could feel its stickiness, thick with pollen, clinging to my skin.

The summer of 1983, following my father's disappearance - the summer of Lorelei's poisoning incident - had been similarly oppressive. It had made everything heavy: the foliage, flowers, even the bees buzzing had been slower. Storms continually threatened so the air crackled with charge. My body also betrayed me with swelling and budding which mirrored the verdant season. I had breasts where there used to be nothing, my body ached, my skin sweaty. Spots clustered my face mingling with the freckles.

I'd arrived too early for my meeting with Archie this morning, so had sat in the airless heat of the car, thinking about my childhood. I'd felt uncomfortable, my armpits sticky. My trousers, too thick for the weather, created damp discomfort around my groin. I wiped my forehead expecting to feel the eruptions endured by my thirteen year old self, but only discerned, under the slick of foundation, the craters they had left.

I'd clicked the key in the ignition. This had been a bad idea. I should not have come. Looking out of the fly specked windscreen towards the tower of the church, the huddle of cottages around the green and the brush of forest glimpsed in the distance, I knew this would be too painful. I turned the key, but before the ignition caught there was a knock on the roof.

It made me start.

I had not seen Archie Libani for years. It had taken me a few moments to identify the features of childhood turned middle-aged. We'd gazed at each other for several seconds. Still the same silver blue eyes, still the same ash blonde hair. He was gesticulating and saying something which I found difficult to hear as if hampered by the dense air and the weight of time.

I finally realised it was simply, "Hi Annie. Good to see you."

I clambered out, wiping my hands on my trousers before an awkward handshake-embrace type of contact where all the wrong bits of us touched or brushed together.

I'd grabbed my briefcase from the passenger seat, glad to have something to hold in front of me. We had been in contact via e-mail. Through our communication I gathered he'd returned to Broomstone to convert the old manor house, his former home, into a hotel.

"Well, you haven't changed a bit," Archie had told me.

I hadn't thanked him. Even though he had probably meant it as a compliment I didn't regard it as one. I'd tried to leave the girl with the nickname, 'Stinking Annie' behind. Today, I'd dressed with consideration. Had my hair styled, applied a mask of make-up. I thought I could escape that childhood Annie. But not here. Here the past clung to me like bramble barbs.

"You look well," was my feeble response at small talk.

"I'm not too bad. Plans for the Hotel are coming together."

Quercus Hall was the biggest house in the village. The place Lorelei had returned to after years away. It had the potential for a country house Hotel, with its history, celebrity association and a mystery factor which would draw tourists.

"You can come and see the Hotel later, but I thought we could eat and talk here first."

We entered the pub, into a low ceilinged white-washed room with beams. If there were any changes they were lost on me. I had never set foot in this place.

I asked for a glass of wine, promising myself just the one, as I was driving. Before I'd been able to take a much needed swig, Archie was saying "Well, what do you think then?" and had pulled from somewhere a cutting from a magazine with my name at the top of the article.

"What do you mean?" I asked, managing to get the glass to my lips and enjoying the richness of liquid in my mouth.

"You wrote this article about my mother. So, will you write a bigger piece? A book perhaps, a biography?"

I had written the piece a year ago, on the fortieth anniversary of the celebrated album, 'Dryad,' which had made Lorelei a star. I remembered how long that small editorial had taken me to write. The difficulty I'd had in gaining any information about Lorelei's past, her family or her music. I didn't want to disappoint Archie but it was unlikely there would be enough material for more.

I looked at the flimsy sheet lying between us. It had obviously been folded and unfolded many times.

"Archie, to be honest with you, this piece was a struggle. I didn't find out much about your mother's past history, I couldn't even track down her parents. My Ma helped with the bit about the music for the album but wouldn't say much about the band. She said there wasn't any bad feeling about Lorelei's sudden rise to fame but I'm not sure I believed her."

Archie nodded and scratched his neck. He looked at me as if expecting me to continue.

"I did some research locally but nobody wanted to talk about her. I think you were away at the time. I came to Quercus Hall but was sent packing by one of Lorelei's nurses. I drew a blank trying to get in touch with Roderick, Rosa wouldn't answer my calls and I received a curt response to a message I sent Cedric.

Unless you've got lots of information, I don't think there's much mileage in it."

I thought Archie was going to speak, to make some excuse for his step-father and step-family. He scratched his neck again and looked downwards. He seemed to be observing my empty wine glass with disapproval. But he just asked, "Do you want a refill?" and I nodded.

Whilst he went to the bar, I visited the rest room and freshened up, powdered my sweaty brow and reapplied my lipstick. Looking in the mirror I supposed that the Libani family dynamics might have changed significantly during the intervening years. But I had my doubts. Beneath Archie's adult facade I had begun to detect the spindly child I had known. The slight tremble as he picked up his glass, the tapping foot against the table leg and the trace of eczema on his neck, were things he had been unable to conceal. Equally, he could probably see through my camouflage to the gauche girl I had been. She appeared to be getting more conspicuous the longer I was here. I scowled at her in the mirror. After applying another coat of lipstick, I went back to the bar.

On my return Archie finished his conversation with the barman and sat down again. He looked animated, "I've had a chance to do some thinking since I came back here to help look after Mum. I found all sorts of bits and pieces. A crate, for instance, with photos and scraps of paper with lyrics. Not a diary but notebooks. Oh, and some little sketches as well."

"So, how is Lorelei?" If the internet gossip was anything to go by, she was in a long-term coma.

"Well, she is hardly able to communicate or move from her bed ... But she does have lucid periods. That's when she told me where the boxes of her keepsakes were. I gathered she wanted her story written and she mentioned you by name."

"Really?"

"Well, I thought so."

"So, you'd like me to have a look?"

"Well, not if you're not interested in writing the memoir.

Mum wouldn't like that. You must agree to it, then I'll let you see the stuff and maybe you could visit Mum, perhaps talk if she's well enough. I expect she thought of you because you were here from the start and when she had her incident and because of this magazine article." He poked the sheet of paper with his index finger; it shed dusty particles and flopped like a dead moth's wing. "But if you're not up for it I'll find somebody who is."

I turned the glass in my hands. My fingers were pale against the dark wine. The liquid was the colour of congealing blood and clung to the sides of the glass as it moved. I was aware of the absence of metal on my ring finger, a recent occurrence. A band of even whiter skin showed where it had been. The finger felt light, as if at any moment it would lift from the glass. I thought of Archie's mother, her paleness, her frail beauty. I knew I should be the person to tell her story. After all I had found her; I had given her a name.

"You'd be paid of course."

That made me look up. Whether Archie noticed the pound signs flicker in my eyes I doubt, but I needed money. Especially now Jay had left and I was on my own.

Archie was scrutinising me and I wondered how long I had been day-dreaming. I noticed another glass of wine had been placed in front of me. He might already have asked me a question because now he said, "That's the other thing I want raised. Her poisoning. That never had a satisfactory conclusion. I'll never believe it was attempted suicide. I thought you could look into that too. I want to know the truth."

I shivered. I did not want to know the truth about that. I thought I knew what had happened. A flush spread to my face, a cloud of guilt making me uncomfortable.

"I appreciate your confidence in my writing abilities, Archie, but my writing doesn't earn me a living. I mainly write obituaries and amateur dramatic reviews for the local paper."

"Well, maybe this is the start of something better."

My glass was empty again and I felt a bit giddy. The room was warm. Glimpsing past Archie's shoulder, I could see the beech tree in the centre of the green, its outstretched limbs dense with unfurling buds. It was older than all of us. A witness to everything that had passed. I was reminded again of 1983 and feeling out of my depth. Trying to swim along a tide of adolescence. Dealing with Daddy's disappearance. Not arguing with my mother. Covering up my spots. Being cool.

As Archie and I ate our sandwiches there was no conversation. My thoughts were a tangle of memories from long ago and the recent past which merged into a jumble under the haze of wine. Neither of us was ready to share the intricacies of our lives over the past thirty odd years.

We finished our meal. Archie paid. I told him I needed to clear my head which was true, and I would think about his proposal. I intended to take the old track beside the wood up to where my childhood home had been.

Archie gave me a warning, "Don't be surprised by the changes. It's hardly recognisable." He added, "Come to Quercus Hall when you're done. Tell me what you've decided."

....

The start of the track not only had a way marker sign stating I was now on 'The Broomstone Forest Walk,' but the hedgerows had been trimmed, undergrowth cleared and the surface tarmacked. It had an air of respectability it had never had before.

At the edge of the wood though, the track became as muddy and rutted again as I remember, and although to my left the trees remained unchanged, on the right instead of fields stretching as far as the eye could see, there was now sturdy fencing and the slant of rooftops. This estate had sprung up after 2003 when I had last visited the cottage. Around the time Ma had moved to a flat in town.

I'd continued along the track averting my eyes from the new buildings, concentrating on the dense woodland to my left. Seeing the foliage budding in variegated greens and breathing in deeply, my senses were filled with the impression of home coming. The path climbed slowly so I could feel my calves pull with the exercise. Further ahead the trees became denser, their branches peppered the sky line with five o'clock shadow over the summit of Broomstone Hill, mimicking the dark clouds building above.

I almost stopped as I neared the glade. My heart was beating fast; not steadily, but a twitchy, racing rhythm that made me pause and gasp for breath. I felt myself stumbling as if I was approaching the cottage on a cold January night to the sound of my parents' final argument, (I did not know that then). I shouldn't have been out on that foul evening, but had been hanging around Quercus Hall spying on the inhabitants. As I'd left the village it had started to rain, gobbets the size of pebbles sheeting down to the accompaniment of thunder. Water streamed through the skeleton forest, making the tree silhouettes darker when a fork of lightning threw everything into relief.

By the time I'd nearly reached home, my clothes were wet through. Approaching the cottage the worst of the storm had cleared but there was a breeze which made the porch light sway, squealing as it moved. The scrape of metal against metal was accompanied by words being hurled from inside the cottage. The sound of my parents arguing was not unusual and I'd shivered, partly because of my wet clothing but also because I did not want to disturb their battle. The argument was in full flow. "Bitch! How could you be so stupid?" I heard the thump of furniture, the cottage walls trembled. I would not be able to sneak back in, so I'd hunched under the canopy of the wood store and put my hands over my ears. I did not want to hear, yet words seeped in. 'Bitch' and 'Stupid', were what my father resorted to most often. His temper was usually alcohol induced, though there were other things that made him mad; not getting his own way, losing at cards, being asked to do something by my mother. I suspect he also hit her, but the evidence didn't show, the blows carefully placed to remain hidden. The verbal battering had increased over the past few months. I thought this coincided with Daddy having to go cap in hand to the Libanis and work as a gardener at Quercus Hall.

Today my feet moved forward and I sank down onto the log in the centre of the glade, and tried to quieten the quaking of my body. Once again I'd returned to the foundations of my early life, my formative years. And I couldn't help but start to stir the silt of those memories.

CHAPTER 3

When Lorelei arrived, it was as if I'd opened a new chapter in my fairy tale book. It was exciting having her around. We renovated an old caravan for her. The dilapidated Romany hut had been my play house but my parents took paint brushes to it, and Ma made curtains. Woody refurbished the joinery inside. Afterwards it was magical, standing out like a bright jewel amidst the ramshackle caravans that were my home. But Lorelei had that affect; she was the central star in our bland world.

After the first night she had stayed in her own little house, I climbed up the steps in the morning and opened the door, just as I had done when it had been my own play place. She was not there. I went in and lay along the crib smelling her perfume on the pillow.

"What are you doing here?" she yelled at me. I hadn't seen her enter, and her presence startled me. She continued, "You scared me. You can't just be coming in and out. Didn't your mother teach you to knock before you come into someone else's space? Get out. In a while you can come back and knock properly and if I feel like it I might let you in."

I scrambled away feeling chastised. But I didn't sulk for long. I had been given a life lesson from my idol. When I returned I knocked very clearly on the door and was relieved at the bright, "Come in, Sweetie."

I cannot remember details of the days I spent with Lorelei; they were hazy, like the perfume of summer fields. I suppose we talked, or I asked questions and she answered, but the week before the arrival of Archie I was in her presence as often as I could be. In my life I had never previously classified the solitude

I experienced as loneliness, but I recognised it now against the landscape of someone to define it. I know now that when Lorelei left I became lonely again, never really achieving a connection with any other thing. It was as though in saving her life we had become entwined in some way.

Archie arrived in the night. I was woken by a bash on the door and Ma's voice.

"It's started."

"We'll come now."

Ma shook Daddy awake. "Get off, woman," he slurred. But they both got up and left the caravan; Daddy still grumbling about being disturbed from his sleep. I sat up and peered out through the curtains. Ma was knocking on Woody's door presumably to let him know what was happening. Lorelei was bent over moaning, the noise animal and alarming. The Land Rover roared and rattled. From my watch post, peering through the caravan window, I saw the vehicle carrying her away, one rear light blinking.

It was impossible to sleep again, trying to work out what was happening. Ma had told me they would have to take Lorelei to the hospital to have the baby, 'When the time was ready.' I guessed that time was now.

Before Lorelei arrived, I had told Ma that I wanted a sister. I dreamt of a girl just like me who I could play games with, chat with, have adventures with. My sister would be Snow White and I would be Rose Red. I remembered a day when Ma had said, "Put your hand on my belly. Can you feel your new sister kicking?" And I had been able to discern a movement under my palm within my mother's stomach.

"That's my sister?"

"Yes, she's growing inside me."

I did not question how the baby seed had got there, I just accepted that I had asked for a sister and now I would have one. Things were like that in my early years. I wanted something and it would be given.

My sister never arrived though. Ma went away one day and

the next returned looking grey instead of her usual bright self. From that moment things changed; I was saddened that I didn't have a sister, and I'd not always get what I asked for. Ma was more often cross with me. Instead of singing as she did her chores, she was silent. I never heard her singing around the caravan again. Until Archie arrived.

It was early morning when Ma and Daddy returned. They giggled as they entered the caravan. I was pleased they were in a good mood because they often shouted at each other, and the caravan would rock when they argued.

But there was no sign of Lorelei, and thoughts of my lost sister made me wonder if something had happened to Lorelei's baby, although Ma appeared happy. Instead of feigning sleep I couldn't resist asking,

"Where is she? Where is she?"

Ma came over to my bed and rested her hand on my forehead. Her hands were always cool and it was calming.

"Don't worry," she said, "Lorelei is fine. She's had her baby in the hospital and is going to stay there for a day or two where she can be properly looked after."

I was sleepy so it took me a moment to take this in. "The baby?" I said finally, as Ma continued to stroke my hair away from my forehead.

"She's had a baby boy."

I was momentarily disappointed, "I wanted a sister."

Ma laughed, "Well you'll have a little boy to play with and look after. His name is Archie."

"Archie," I repeated. It sounded like a nice name.

....

A day later, I woke up to shouting. "Yes, we *have* got to go and collect her."

"How come we've suddenly become midwives to a woman we don't know?"

"You know why."

"Not that again, she isn't who you think she is. Your sister has gone."

"I don't want to talk about that now, we just need to go and get Lorelei, like I promised we would."

"And you want me to drive ... Petrol is expensive, you know."

"Well, if you had a better job and didn't drink all your money away it wouldn't be a problem keeping a promise to a friend."

"Bitch!"

"Ow!" I heard the slap of my father's hand hitting mother. Then she was by my bed clutching her cheek. "Come on Annie, we're going to get Lorelei and Archie from the hospital."

I was ready in a few minutes and climbed into the back of the Land Rover. It wasn't comfortable as I'd roll around with every bump and hillock that we encountered on the frosted ground. Daddy drove us, looking ahead stony faced and grumpy. Ma was silent as well, a red mark on her cheek, neither of them happy like they'd been the previous day. I was; my breakfastless stomach churning with excitement, pleased to be included in the reception party.

The hospital smelt strange, with echoing corridors that had peeling paint. I didn't like it. Trailing behind Ma and Daddy with a teddy Ma had knitted as a present, we finally found Lorelei on the second floor. The ward had little cubicles dividing each mother with her baby. Lorelei wasn't in her bed but was gazing out of the ward window at the town below. I could make out the tops of trees, and chimneys and steel posts but the pane was too high for me to see what interested Lorelei. She was looking down as though something of vital importance was happening at ground level.

Only as Ma cooed over a cot did I realise the worm inside was the baby. Archie. He was tiny and so white his skin revealed lilac-blue veins beneath, giving his complexion the luminescence of pearl. His hair was a halo of silver against the blue bedding in the cot. "He looks like a fairy child."

"That's the ash blonde colour of his hair," Ma said, "It's unusual." Lorelei said nothing but kept her vigil at the window. A look flicked from Ma to Daddy to Lorelei and the baby.

"What's wrong with his leg?" I asked, noticing Archie's right leg was twisted so it looked like a branch that Woody would make into a walking stick.

Ma pulled me to the side, crushing me against her. "He's got something called a club foot. You mustn't say anything about it ... Understand?" she whispered at me.

"Yes," I said, not sure why it couldn't be talked about. It looked rather special, like a picture in my fairy tale book.

"Well, shall we get going?" said Ma in her too bright voice, the one she always used if something nasty was going to happen.

Lorelei turned but didn't say anything. She didn't reach to take Archie but let Ma carry him. Daddy and I hovered like spare parts as we were ushered out of the building by a nurse.

It was only when we'd got back to the caravans that I realised I'd put the teddy bear gift for Archie down in the hospital and forgotten it.

"Oh, Annie ..." said Ma in her tired voice.

"He can have one of mine!" I said, without much thought.

"That will have to do then," was the reply, as Ma busied herself settling Archie and making mugs of tea.

In my tiny corner of the caravan, I had three toys on the bed; a knitted teddy bear with the kapok stuffing spilling out and one of the bead eyes loose, (his nose was a large leather button, and shone like a bear's nose should); a rag doll, with yellow Rapunzel plaits and a plastic face, and a round roll of fabric that had a painted on cat's face and whiskers. It had lost its tail and ears. They stared at me out of the organs of vision that remained, *'How could you?'* They questioned me, *'Which one of us dare you give away, traitor?'* I grabbed the teddy, taking it over to the adults seated at the other end of the caravan. Lorelei was staring at her tea; Archie was snuffling in his crib.

"Here!" I said to Lorelei thrusting the woolly lump at her. "This is for Archie."

My action startled her and some tea spilt from her mug.

"Oh, that's very sweet," she said, but there must have been something wrong with her tea as she kept staring at it.

Ma explained how I had left the proper present at the hospital.

"Never mind."

Though I never questioned it, I didn't ever see Teddy again. After that Rapunzel and Cat never looked at me in quite the same way. Even now, I sometimes cry when I think about it. How I could be that disloyal to a friend?

CHAPTER 4

Winter merged into spring and Archie grew and became more interesting. He would smile back at me and try to copy the funny faces I made. He was often in our caravan, sometimes I was allowed to give him his bottle if Lorelei was resting, "Because motherhood is very hard," I was told. Occasionally a health visitor would come and say, "Just checking to see if everyone's happy," and I would take her to see Lorelei and Archie and wait by the steps to her caravan, until they'd finished.

"Bye, Annie," the health visitor would say as she left, and pat my head, "You look after them for me." The touch on my hair was uncomfortable; because my curls were too springy and touching them made them bounce annoyingly. I always meant to tell the health visitor that I *did not* like her patting my head, but was always too cross to manage to speak and too keen to find out what she had said to Lorelei.

I'd rush up the steps into the caravan and Lorelei would be cursing and saying, "Old busybody. Why do people always interfere?" I had no answer for that and didn't want to appear nosey either, so would say, "Can I play with Archie?" and Lorelei would look at me with an expression of such peace that it reminded me of the statues in the churchyard. I'd feel a wave of contentment wash over me.

"Of course, you can, you're his favourite person."

One day when the health visitor left she said, "You should be at school Annie. I need to have a word with your mother before I go."

I wasn't sure that I wanted to go to school. It was a distant, strange idea for me. And as I went in to see Lorelei I was joining in her curses of the busybody running our affairs.

....

Now the season for festivals was beginning so the rehearsals started in the barn. Daddy and Woody would sit on hay bales; Daddy with his guitar, Woody with his bongos and wood block instruments. Ma had a keyboard with a special little stool. There was usually another girl, who lived with Woody. The girls were all skinny, with long straight hair, and they wore flowered printed dresses and didn't say much. Some of the girls hummed along in the background, but they didn't sing like my mother. It was Katrina that year and I liked her. Sometimes she would look after me when Ma was out and we'd go down to the field and make daisy chains.

When the band rehearsed, I would be perched on the ladder to the hay loft, and listen from there. But sometimes Ma would let me sit with them and I could shake a tambourine. I liked to sing some of the choruses as well and nobody told me off. Ma did most of the vocals although her voice was quiet and low, so when the others joined in you sometimes couldn't hear her.

One day, Lorelei came into the barn with Archie in a funny little seat like a tiny deckchair. She put her foot on it, making Archie bounce a bit.

Every session after that when the band were practising she'd come in and sit on a bale and watch Archie. If he started to get restless she would bounce his seat and he'd be happy again.

It must have been April when it happened. It was raining; soft gentle spring rain which drips and drops and makes everything green. I was watching the slide of water from the open barn door making a muddy puddle at the threshold, and thinking that it accompanied the music. They were practising one of my favourite songs about a bird searching for a home, and I was going to join in the chorus, when there was the most beautiful sound. It rang around the barn as if a magical spell was being woven. I expected to look up and see a mythical creature like a phoenix sitting on a hay bale joining in our earthly music. But when I looked it was Lorelei. She was standing up, her white hair flowing around her shoulders, haloed with a spill of sunshine through the rain clouds. She was wearing a gauze dress of pale green and looked beautiful ... and her voice was ringing out a perfect pure sound, as if a fountain had started to brim and catch the light. I looked back at the barn door and saw that the rain had stopped, the sun had intensified and outside I could see the end of a rainbow arcing over the barn and the caravans and Broomstone village in the distance. I ran to the door to see if I could work out where the end might be, so I could search for the pot of gold. But as the sun grew brighter the colours faded.

The music and song behind me had also stopped. As I turned I saw Ma and Daddy and Katrina and Woody staring at Lorelei, completely still, as if a statue spell had been made. Even Archie was quiet, watching Lorelei with big blue eyes as if he wasn't sure she was his mother.

They seemed to be still for a long time. Finally, Daddy said, "That was beautiful Lorelei. I didn't know you could sing."

"I didn't know I could, but I have a memory now of singing, of loving to sing. That song you just played reminded me of something." She shook her head as if she was searching for the memory but it was flying away just like the sad bird in the song.

"Well, you'll have to be in the band," Daddy said in an excited voice. "Do you play an instrument?"

"I don't know really, perhaps?"

Daddy handed her his guitar, and she took it and strummed a few chords but then shook her head, "No, that doesn't feel right ... let me try the keyboard."

Ma looked as if she didn't really want Lorelei to touch it but slowly moved away. Lorelei sat on the stool and put her fingers over the keys. She frowned. There was a moment when I thought she would say the same ... "That doesn't feel right ..." but then familiar chords started to float through the air. Not Ma's tunes of course, but other folk songs that were part of the band's play list.

Daddy started to play a few chords and then Woody beat the rhythm on the bongos. Ma stood in the shadow of the hay loft so I couldn't see her face.

Suddenly, Archie squealed and started to cry. I went over and rocked the chair but he didn't stop. "I think he's hungry", I said. "Are you hungry, Archie?" I asked him, like Ma always did when he cried. His crying got louder and his face redder. Finally, Lorelei came over.

"Would you like to give Archie his bottle, Annie?"

Of course, I did.

"I'll just go and fetch one"

A few minutes later she returned with the bottle. Archie was really screaming now and I thought it strange that Ma hadn't come over and picked him up and soothed him until his milk arrived. Then Lorelei handed the bottle to me and immediately Archie had the teat in his mouth there was peace again. Lorelei returned to the keyboard, "I'm a bit rusty," she said, "but it seems to be coming back. Shall we give 'Where have all the flowers gone,' a go?"

And that song about long time passing filled the space around me, with Archie's sucking noise accompanying the tune. Lorelei started to sing again and I don't think I have ever before or since heard that song sung more perfectly.

CHAPTER 5

That spring the audiences were bigger, I thought it was because the band was better with Lorelei doing the vocals. Now I realise that was not the only reason. Her beauty and sex appeal were magnetic. With Lorelei fronting the band, Ma took a less prominent role. When we practiced in the barn Ma always stood at the back. With her pale brown hair and dowdy clothes, she became invisible in the dusty light.

I would occasionally accompany the band to the gigs. Archie sometimes came with us or was left with Katrina. Ma appeared quite content doing backing vocals and harmonies, which added a new level to the music.

One evening we'd all retired to our caravan. Lorelei had returned after putting Archie to bed and I was tucked up in the corner. The adults sat around the table not yet made into Ma and Daddy's bed. They were sipping drinks in tiny glasses, a dark liquid which gleamed. Daddy and Woody seemed very happy. Woody had his arm round Lorelei and they kept kissing each other, right in front of Ma and Daddy; I was glad that Katrina was still with Archie so she wouldn't see them. Daddy counted out the money, splitting it into four even piles of notes. I had never seen the dealing out go on for as long. I was right. "Best takings ever," Daddy said, "I reckon we could get a record contract."

Woody nodded. "Maybe we should use some of this to get a demo together," he suggested, inhaling on a skinny cigarette and blowing the smoke in rings so they hovered towards my end. The smoke smelt nice. I felt sleepy, and the adults melted into a haze at the other end of the van; the words too, muted.

Ma said, "Well, I think we'd need some new material. I'll get on with writing something. I've had an idea for a conceptual album, 'All the trees in the wood' ... what do you think?"

There were murmurs of agreement. "I'll help if you like," Lorelei volunteered.

....

After that my adventures centred on the barn. I would make a den up in the hay loft and hide away before Lorelei and Ma started their song making. Another keyboard had been purchased and they'd discuss ideas first and then play a few chords. The music drifted upwards and I inhaled it with the dusty loft air feeling warm and comfortable.

From a random collection of notes something that sounded like a song gradually emerged. Each song belonged to a tree; the oak, the rowan, the silver birch, developing into something akin to my fairy tale book magical tales with a central theme.

Thinking back, I realise the composition had been one-sided. It was always my mother who began with a chord and a 'What about ...?' Lorelei would say, "Yes, that's a good idea," or "that sounds great." But it was only later I realised she contributed virtually nothing to the actual creation of the songs.

They'd get to a point where Ma would say, "Well, I think this is ready for a trial," and in the evening the band would practice it, make a few changes, and then if it went well it would be on the list for the next show.

One morning after a gig there was knocking on the caravan door, '*rap, rap, rappity, rap.*' It sounded urgent. Ma pulled open the door and Woody's voice said, "Wow, you've got to see this!"

He pushed in, whilst Daddy sorted the bed out so that Woody could spread a paper on the table.

"Band from the Barn. Brilliant Gig. Five stars ..." Woody

was shouting. "Woohoo we're going to be famous!"

He did a little jig around the limited space in the caravan. Then he came over to my bed, "Come on lazybones, time to get up. You'll want to tell Lorelei that she's made the headlines!"

Ma was still in her night dress, but came over and helped me dress in T-shirt and shorts. "Off you go" she said, kissing the top of my head.

Woody was already smoking one of his skinny cigarettes as I went outside. He was leaning with his back to the van, smiling more than I had ever seen him smile before.

"What's the big panic?" Lorelei called in response to our knocking on her door.

"You'll want to see this," said Woody.

Slowly the door opened to Lorelei blinking in the light. Woody shoved the paper at her.

"Says you're the best thing that's been on at the Stagedoor Studio all summer!"

As she read, the screwed up features of Lorelei's face relaxed into her usual beauty.

"Can I keep it?" she asked. Woody hesitated but said with a shrug, "Yeh. 'Course."

After that there was a buzz about our little site, as if we, like summer insects were having a bountiful summer. "These are our salad days," Daddy said all the time, though I had no idea what he meant, just that we were eating lots of salad, because we could forage for leaves in the hedgerows.

At the next gig, a sense of tension surrounded the band, like the atmosphere after one of Ma and Daddy's arguments, a sort of cloudiness and everybody grumpy with each other. Ma and Daddy had a massive row before we left, the usual one about Daddy drinking too much. Archie was being tetchy as Lorelei came out of her caravan, where Katrina was going to look after him, and she just shouted, "Shut up, Archie, you're making my head ache," as she came down the steps to get into the Land Rover. Woody grumbled about his drums.

At the venue Daddy said he needed a ciggie and Woody

obliged, the skinny cigarette was passed around, even Ma took a drag though she rarely smoked. "Not good for my voice," she'd always said. I supposed it didn't matter now she wasn't doing much of the singing anyway.

I had never seen so many people pack the room in the Stagedoor Studio, a big room next to the Stage Coach Pub. The noise they made when they applauded made the smog of smoke shift and the room seemed to sway. I felt happy. Standing at the back of the stage, Ma let me hold a tambourine and sometimes I'd shake it in time to the music. The tiny cymbals clashed together and then trembled. At the end the crowd shouted, "More, More, Encore!"

Lorelei sang, 'Where have all the flowers gone.' This time everybody else stayed quiet, apart from Daddy playing single strings on his guitar. The song sounded nearly as beautiful as it had the first time I'd heard it, but not quite, because of the shuffling and heat of the mass of people in the room.

It was a late finish, but though I whined to Ma, "Are we going home now?" she told me, "Hush. Daddy's got some important business."

The crowd had gone now, leaving a dense fug of smoke hanging above the floor.

At the side near the stage, I could see Lorelei, Daddy and Woody having a chat with a man. He was different from the other spectators. He had a waistcoat in a shiny material which gleamed in the dim light. It was like a Joseph's dream coat in vibrant colours but in the dimness I could only make out darker and lighter shades of silvery grey. He had a beard and a rather large stomach which pressed into the waistcoat buttons. Daddy was shaking his head and Woody saying, "No man, that's not how it works."

Lorelei was standing a little way back, looking beautiful. For the stage shows she'd usually wear a flowing silvery gown that you could see through if the light was behind her. Sometimes she'd wear flowers in her hair, but tonight she had on a garland made of leaves and ribbon which Ma had fashioned for her. Though she sometimes just had bare feet, tonight she was wearing little white boots laced with red ribbon.

"No!" said Woody. "Lorelei! Tell him won't you!"

Lorelei moved closer and said something quietly.

For a moment everything paused, the figures of the group were still; even the swirling smoke slowed. It was as if the music had stopped in a game of musical statues. Then Woody shouted, "You bitch!" making everything tremble and start again. He kept repeating, "Bitch, Bitch …" as he pushed past Lorelei, and came towards me and Ma. He did not stop, just said as he left, "She's stitched us up good and proper. The witch."

We left then as well. Outside the venue Daddy climbed into the front seat, but Ma gave him one of her looks and said, "No way, you've had a skinful. I'll drive." Daddy didn't even answer back like he usually did but handed over the keys and climbed into the back with me. Lorelei got into the front. The journey back to the caravan site was silent. Lorelei's gaze was directed out of the side window, I could see her face reflected in the glass and when we passed under street lamps I saw she was smiling. Beside me Daddy was looking straight ahead and he didn't put his arm around me when I leaned into him.

"Are you tired, Annie?" Ma asked from the driver's seat. I murmured, "Yes," and I nestled into my father's resistant side.

The light in Woody's van was on when we arrived back. I didn't know how he'd got home, but I could hear his raised voice and see his wiry body moving around the frame of the window like a scene being played out on a movie screen.

Lorelei went straight to her home, not saying good night to anybody. Katrina stumbled down the steps of Lorelei's caravan. She glanced back over her shoulder and tripped on the bottom step, as though something had scared her. I wondered who Woody had been shouting at in his own van.

But by then I was climbing the steps to our own caravan and quickly changed for bed. As I was falling asleep I could hear my parents talking quietly.

"She's leaving then? It's definite?"

"That's what she said. That guy from the record company made it clear he wanted her alone. And he's prepared to pay big bucks ..." Daddy gave a low whistle, presumably at the thought of so much money. "I don't know, it's so unfair, after all we've done for her."

"We don't own her," Ma said quietly.

I knew they were talking about Lorelei but I couldn't contemplate the idea that she might leave. Leave the band, that's what they meant. But I was wrong.

CHAPTER 6

School arrived. It seemed odd that I had to leave my home each day to go and sit in a room with lots of other children and then come back again. After a week I told the teacher that I'd had enough school now. "Thank you very much, but I prefer to be at home."

Miss Rowan laughed. "No Dear, you don't understand, you must come to school every day until you're grown up. You need to learn all about the world we live in."

I knew I shouldn't contradict her but I had learnt less in my week of school than ever before. I could read better than most, my writing was passable if not neat. I could sing well and clap in time with music and I understood about food and the natural world.

I was also different from the rest of my class mates. They appeared neat and tidy each day, whereas I wasn't a neat and tidy sort of person. My clothes were clean but old and ragged; my shoes unpolished. Most of my garments were homemade by my mother, a fact I hated now that I could compare them with the shop bought clothes of the other pupils. I also had an untidy face, with its odd little nose covered in randomly scattered freckles. My hair was wild, like a curly bush on my head. Ma had tried to plait it tightly on the first day but it managed to escape its bands, springing out in corkscrews.

It was also the cause of my first transgression. During my second week at school, I became the child who was picked on. The boys ignored me but the girls were unkind, taking offence at my clothing. I wasn't aware of smelling at all, but they took to chorusing, "Stinking Annie, Stinking Annie," when I walked by. Ma used wild garlic in her cooking, we called it Stinking Nanny. But it was only later I realised the nickname had originated even before I lived in the cottage surrounded by the wild garlic of the forest. I guess even then I must have carried a feral scent different from others. I ignored the name calling. But one day in the playground I could tell a plot was being hatched. A group of girls with shiny pony tails and patent leather shoes were instructing another lower ranked girl. I was playing on my own. I'd found a ladybird and was trying to encourage it onto my little finger. Then I could sing the rhyme 'Ladybird, ladybird fly away home ...', and make a wish. I liked the rhyme because 'Little Ann,' my namesake, was saved from the fire by hiding under the frying pan when all the others had flown. She'd hidden, waiting for her mother to return. This ladybird was tricky to manoeuvre along the hillocks of my hand. Suddenly I felt my head being yanked back and the ladybird flew away before I'd made my wish. My hair was grabbed and twisted. I fell down, my scalp burning. Looking up, the girl's face smirked at me. "You bitch! You bitch!" I cried out. The girl quickly ran away.

"I'm telling Miss on you," she called over her shoulder. And I couldn't understand why, when I was the victim, it was she who was going to tell on me.

I stood in front of Miss Rowan's desk trying to explain, "She pulled my hair and it hurt. So, I told her off." I rubbed the patch on my head which was still tender.

"But you used a very bad word."

"That's what my Daddy calls my Ma when he's cross."

"But it's a very rude and nasty word, Annie. You can't use a word like that in school or anywhere else."

I squirmed where I stood. I had already learnt I must stand and listen to Miss Rowan, even if she was talking rubbish.

"I'll speak to your mummy," Miss Rowan said.

After school Miss Rowan sent me outside to collect my mother from the gate. She always stood a little way from the main group of mothers waiting. I whispered, "Miss Rowan wants to speak to you,"

"What?" Ma asked.

I raised my voice so all the other pupils and parents heads turned. "Miss Rowan wants to speak to you."

Ma grabbed my elbow firmly and propelled me inside.

Now we both stood in front of Miss Rowan, I could sense my mother shifting beside me, agitated.

"Annie used a very bad word today," Miss Rowan said.

"What word?"

Miss Rowan's reply was a whisper, so I knew it was a very bad thing to say, like talking about poo and weeing, unless it was about a baby like Archie, then it was okay. "She called another girl a bitch."

"Annie!" Ma turned and looked down at me with such a fierce gaze that I thought I could feel it hitting my face. "Why did you say a thing like that?"

"It's what Daddy says sometimes," I replied. I wanted to ask why it was such a bad thing to say, but couldn't work out how to ask without repeating the dreaded word again.

"Just because Daddy says it, doesn't mean you should say it. Now apologise to Miss Rowan."

"Sorry Miss Rowan," I mumbled, looking away from their angry faces. I stared at my feet which were stepping from side to side. I needed a wee but I couldn't say anything.

"And you'll apologise to Charlotte tomorrow, won't you?"

I nodded down at my shoes.

"You can go now."

"I need a wee," I hissed at Ma as we left the room.

"Well, you'll have to wait," said Ma, striding ahead so I had to run to keep up with her.

My knickers were already damp by the time we got to the closet near the caravan where I could relieve myself.

"Oh, Annie," Ma said, shaking her head, when I asked for a dry pair of pants. "You're not a baby anymore."

....

Those early days of school made me crave Daddy's

storytelling in the evening. He'd squeeze beside me on my bed, and I'd cuddle into him. I'd tell him about the girls who picked on me because I was different to them. Daddy told me I was just special, like Pinocchio. He'd tweak my nose and say, "But you don't tell lies, your nose is too small." Daddy said my school mates were jealous of me because I lived in an enchanted place, not the boring real world that they inhabited. He always made me feel better. Sometimes he'd read a story from my book, other times I'd ask him to make one up. He'd often begin with, *"Not so very far from here,"* or *"Not so very long ago ..."* and I would be transported to a different world, but one that was within reach, where magical things happened. Daddy had a wonderful voice, melodious and expressive. I hated it when he shouted at Ma because then it became harsh as if he was turning into a wolf. But when I was nestled in my bed with his voice lilting a story I would often be almost asleep by the time he said, *"... and they all lived happily ever after."*

A few weeks after the 'bitch' incident, Miss Rowan stopped me at the end of the day. "I'd like to speak to your mummy, Annie. Go and fetch her in please."

I went to the school door but didn't leave immediately, I was trying to work out what I'd said or done. A few minutes must have past and I could think of nothing. "Annie, what are you doing here still? I asked you to fetch your mother. Now go on!" I had no choice now that Miss Rowan had caught me. I knew she was watching me as I crossed the playground to the gate where Ma stood, looking anxious. Most of the other children had left so it was only Ma standing there waiting.

"Ma, Miss Rowan wants to talk to you."

"Oh Annie! What have you done now?" But she didn't expect a reply, as she walked through the gate and made her way to the door where Miss Rowan was holding it open for our return. Once we were back in the classroom, standing in front of her desk like before, Miss Rowan began.

"She's very quiet."

There were a few silent moments before Ma replied. "Is that such a bad thing?"

"Well, no," Miss Rowan said but in a way that made it sound as if it was. "It's just that she needs to interact with the other children. She seems very independent and aloof."

"Well, she's had to be able to cope on her own. We wanted her to be independent. Surely that's a good thing?"

"Well ..." said Miss Rowan in that voice again, "Perhaps if you invited a child over for tea, she could make a little friend." She turned to look at me, "What do you say Annie, would you like someone to go home with you for tea?"

Ma was scowling at me, but it did seem like a nice idea, to have a friend to play with. I didn't have any friends to invite though. Miss Rowan had thought of that. "Daisy is a lovely girl. Why don't you invite her?"

The next afternoon, Miss Rowan came to the school gate with me and pushed my back making me move forward. I looked up at Ma, she was scowling but nodded. I approached Daisy. Her hair was mousey brown, her eyes washed out and small which reminded me of grains of corn.

"Daisy would you like to come for tea?" I asked and her eyes grew shiny and surprised.

Her mother answered for her. "Well, that's very kind of you Annie, but we have things to do today. Perhaps tomorrow would be alright?" I turned and looked at Ma who gave a tiny movement of her head. I took it as agreement. The arrangement was made.

The following afternoon Daisy skipped along beside me as we started for home. However, that didn't last long. The path over the field was rutted and Daisy started to complain. "Don't you have a car?" We did have the Land Rover but we rarely used that. Daddy always complained about how expensive it was. And why would you take the car when it was nicer to walk, rather than being thrown around on the back seat? I was going to tell Daisy this but then she was saying, "My shoes are getting dirty, my shoes, look my shoes!"

She was wearing pretty red shoes with buckles. The leather had been shiny and the buckles glinted until she had walked home with me.

"My legs are tired," she whined.

"We'll soon we be there," I told her, as Ma was walking a few paces in front of us. She always walked quickly, knowing I got easily distracted, so wouldn't stop.

"I've got a stitch, ooh it hurts," said Daisy starting to make a snivelling noise. We had slowed down; Ma was shrinking into the distance.

"Come on," I said, hopping from foot to foot, wanting to go on with Ma but knowing I couldn't just leave Daisy.

"I can't." Her lip was wobbling, and real tears falling on her cheeks. She sat down on the track.

"Ma! Ma! Stop! Daisy can't go on."

After what seemed ages, Ma turned around. She started back up the slope towards us the usual frown on her face becoming clearer the closer she came.

She looked at Daisy. Without saying a word, she handed a hanky to the crying girl. Daisy must have understood the scowl Ma gave her because she shrugged and got up and started hobbling along. Ma walked behind us as if keeping guard over our pace. I hoped Daisy would not stop again, otherwise I think Ma might have hit her.

"Is this where you live?" Daisy asked once we were sitting in the caravan for our tea. "This is like the caravan we have for our holidays, but it doesn't smell of the seaside." She wrinkled her nose. She drank some of her milk, leaving a white moustache above her lip making me giggle. "But you live here all the time?"

Ma had made jam sandwiches for tea. I'd helped forage for blackberries and liked stirring the huge pot until it was hot enough to set into jam. Then I'd covered the lids with little gingham cloth caps, so they sat on the shelf like 'pretty maids all in a row.' It was the final jar of last year's batch so was an extra special treat. Daisy nibbled round the sandwich and left the crusts on the edge of her plate.

She looked about her. "Where are all your clothes?"

I hurried to the drawer beneath my bed, "Here. Look." Daisy sniffed, as if they gave off a bad smell. "And you sleep here?"

I nodded. She picked up Rapunzel and flicked one of the doll's plaits, then dropped her back onto the bed. I hoped she wouldn't pick up Cat. She didn't.

"Let's go outside," I suggested.

"Okay," was the response, given with a shrug.

I wanted to show Daisy the barns and the den I had made in the hay loft, but she took one look and said, "It's too dusty. I can't go in there. I want to go home now."

I went back into the caravan, "Daisy wants to go home now," I told Ma.

"Well, we'll have to walk. Daddy's got the car."

I repeated this message to Daisy. "I want to go home," she whined.

So, we headed back to the village again. This time the walk was uphill but Daisy made no comment, just kept on, head down, without speaking. Me and Ma followed.

We walked past Quercus Hall, past the school and through a little lane lined with cherry trees behind the main village street. It led to a cul-de-sac called Cherry Tree Close. A row of houses curved in a line crowding the pavement.

"This is my house," Daisy said, stopping outside Number 2.

She pushed the bell on the door and waited on her own doorstep. It took a while but her mother came to the door, with a pinny on, wiping her hands on a towel.

"Hello my darling girl, you're a lot sooner than I'd thought you'd be. Did you have a nice time? I'd have picked you up if you'd phoned."

Daisy ignored us as she pushed past her mother and disappeared inside. I heard her say, "They don't have a phone. They don't even have a proper house."

Daisy's mother gave us a smile and said, "Thanks," before shutting the door in our faces. Ma turned ready to start the walk back again but I hovered for a moment, still hoping Daisy might invite me in. I wondered what it was like inside that 'real' house. Did she have a doll and a teddy bear? Did she have a fairy tale book like me?

"I want to live in a house, Ma," I told her as we made our way down the hill.

I didn't think she'd heard me as she didn't answer straight away.

"So, you want to live in a little box, cheek by jowl with all and sundry, everybody knowing your business, looking at your washing hung out on the line, hearing your squabbles and noticing the time you come in and out. And instead of opening the door to freedom you'd have to walk miles to get a bit of peace. You think you'd like to live in a house, but mark my words, you wouldn't!"

I couldn't think up the necessary argument to disagree, so just kept on walking.

....

The following day at school, I was aware of talking going on round me that I wasn't a part of. There was sniggering too. Daisy, having been a loner, was now the centre of attention. I didn't hear my name just comments like, "She doesn't live in a proper house … her raggy clothes are all crammed in a tiny drawer … and her Mum and Dad have a pull down bed … in the same room …" That comment brought the biggest laugh as if there was something wrong with it. Only then did I consider it might be inappropriate.

I kept hoping Daisy would invite me to her house for tea. I wanted to see inside that red front door, go up the staircase I had glimpsed, see the bedroom she did not share with her parents. But nobody from school ever invited me to their house and Miss Rowan did not suggest I invite anybody home with me again. When we moved to the house in the wood, I thought it could change but if anything, it got worse. We were older but there was still the whispering behind hands and laughter when I got too close; a hold of the nose and chant of "Stinking Annie!"

The autumn that I started school was a horrible one. Miss Rowan hadn't yet decided I 'needed a little friend.' I felt alone as I tried to contend with the day-to-day tedium of school and when I returned home I knew something concerning Lorelei was amiss and that troubled me. At the time Daddy and Ma were hardly speaking to Lorelei, though Archie was often in our caravan. I don't really know what went on, because I was out at school all day. One day, when I got back home, I went over to the Romany caravan and knocked. No reply. It sounded too silent. I put my ear to the door but could hear nothing. Though I had been reprimanded before, I turned the handle and pushed open the door. There was nothing and nobody there. I rushed back to our caravan, "Ma! Ma! Where's Archie? Where's Lorelei?"

"Oh, sweetheart, didn't she tell you? She's gone away."

"But when will she come back?"

"We don't know. She's gone to London. She might be gone for a long time."

My stomach felt hollow, I could feel tears on my face. Ma tried to cuddle me but I pushed her away. Why hadn't anybody told me Lorelei was going away? I curled up on my bed and cried myself to sleep. In the morning, though, it was still true. Lorelei had gone and taken Archie with her.

For days the pain was raw. I cried each day when I got home from school. Even Daddy's stories didn't comfort me. Our caravan seemed like a jail. I'd go out after my tea and sit on the steps of the Romany caravan and wonder where they were. Lorelei had told me Archie liked me best. Now I had nobody to play with.

I didn't like seeing Lorelei's van, it looked wrong without them. I started to stay inside our caravan. "Aren't you going to play outside?" Ma would ask.

"No," I would shrug.

"What about reading your book?"

"Nah, can't be bothered." I would huddle on my bed, holding Rapunzel flicking her plaits to and fro and thinking of nothing except that I was on my own. I had nobody to play with and nobody to visit. Occasionally, I'd pull the net curtains beside my bed and look out of the window. The gypsy caravan stood unmoved, its colourful paint too bright as if it was drawing attention to itself.

"You could go over to the little caravan," Ma would say when she saw me look out, but I resisted. It wouldn't be the same without Lorelei and Archie there.

"Where's Lorelei gone?" I asked more than once.

"She's gone to London to make a record. She met a record dealer at the big gig we went to; remember?" Instead of pausing in her knitting Ma's needles sounded harsher … *Tick Tack Tick …*

"What about Archie?" and before she could reply I'd ask, "Will he be alright?"

"He'll be fine … He'll be just fine." Ma always repeated it, as if she was trying to convince herself as well as me.

Through October and November, I came to expect Ma and Daddy would be arguing when I returned home from school. More than I remembered before.

"Well, he's told us that we have to move … building houses or some such."

"I don't want to go," Ma would reply. One afternoon I'd stood on the small step outside the caravan door, waiting for a moment, listening.

"He says we can live in the cabin house on the edge of the woods."

"No. I won't live there."

"Why the hell not? It's just a house. You used to live there, I know, and you've said bad things happened, but that was a long time ago. Things are different now."

"I can't live there." Ma's voice lowered to a whisper so I had to press my ear to the door. "It's cursed."

"Don't be stupid."

"You know what happened there, what they say about it?"

"That was long ago. We don't have many options. You might like being back there."

"How can you want to move back there? After what happened to my family."

"It was a long time ago. Your parents died in an accident … an accident. It wasn't because of some curse. It's just the people in this village have to link it to witchcraft."

I didn't know much about my grandparents. Only that I didn't have any. Ma had explained to me how she and Daddy had each had parents but they were old and had died before I was born. Though, I did recall a day when Ma and I were walking near the edge of the forest. She'd pointed to a fallen old tree. I'd looked at the scorched bark, the massive roots rearing up like a horned beast climbing up from the earth. I'd made to run towards it to climb on it, but Ma had grabbed my wrist so tightly it burnt. "You must never go near that tree! That's the place my parents died, your Grandparents."

"How?" I whispered, wondering if the root beast had eaten them.

"There was a strike of lightening and my mother was crushed by the tree, my father tried to rescue her and was burnt." Ma sniffled and wiped her sleeve across her face.

"You're not supposed to stand under trees in a storm," I said, repeating the rule I had been frequently told.

Ma gave a long sniff and then said, "But there wasn't a storm or any sign of a storm that morning. They were foraging for mushrooms in the dawn, just as they usually did … but they never came home."

I was going to ask more details about what had happened but Ma turned and hugged me to her too tightly, so my breath was squeezed out. I could feel the wetness of her tears on my head and she was muttering something that sounded like, "It was a curse, our curse …" Ma didn't need to tell me again, to keep away from that place. Now my ear was pressed and cold on the metal of the door. Ma was saying something in a very quiet voice so I struggled to hear, but I thought she said, "… and my sister. How do you explain that?"

I wasn't exactly sure that's what she said because I only had a vague memory of her ever mentioning a sister before.

"Look, Holly's death was a tragedy. I know how difficult that must have been for you. But time heals. And you shouldn't believe what the dumb people of this village say."

So, Ma had a sister named Holly. That was a nice name. It went together with Ma's name of Ivy, reminding me of the carol, '*The Holly and the Ivy,*' and the line, '*of all the trees that are in the wood, the holly bears the crown*'.

Ma was saying, "I don't think I can go back there."

"I think you're going to have to put your worries away. It'd be better for all of us. Especially Annie. Think about it. It'll give Annie a bit more stability. Nearer school. Her own room." My breath gave a little jolt, '*My own room,*' was what I'd been wishing for. It made me forget about accidents and curses.

"And what about rent?"

"Well, I'll have to get a regular job."

"Yes, that'll be the day."

I jumped as Daddy slammed his hand down on the table, "We don't have a choice. I'll go to the job centre tomorrow."

"What about Woody?"

"He'll have to make his own plans. Katrina's parents are loaded, he'll be alright."

As I pushed inwards through the door, the talking stopped. "Are we moving then?"

Ma was shaking her head; I don't know if she was saying no or just telling me not to ask the question.

Daddy said, "Yes, we have to."

"Will I have my own room?"

Daddy smiled, "Well, young eavesdropper, you probably will, but I don't know whether you're grown up enough." He winked.

I did a little dance around the caravan. "I am. I am!"

I had dreamt of living in a house and now it was coming true. I ignored Ma's concerns about whatever had happened in the house before. I ignored the idea of the house being cursed.

CHAPTER 7

And now here I am again, sitting in the place where the house had been. Once, I had dismissed the rumours as untrue. Not believing the story of what happened in the house when my mother lived there with her parents. The tale was told me by an unreliable source. But now my opinion has changed. I believe that Ma was right after all … the house was cursed.

My head is still thumping, as I begin to walk slowly back toward the village and Quercus Hall. The humidity is rising to saturation point, as though I am walking in cloud, moving across a time warp. With each step the past presses in on me. As I push forward I reminisce about the day of Rosa Libani's fourteenth birthday party. It is so clear that I imagine I am re-treading my own footsteps. Twenty-six years to the day. Rosa's birthday fell on the twenty-first of June. Even my too warm trousers concentrate the memory, because my party outfit had been similarly uncomfortable. I can hear Ma's voice chiding me as I fidgeted with my tights and complained. Ma said, "Count your blessings." And I would have responded, 'One,' not caring if Ma heard my insolent tone.

Since Daddy's disappearance five months before, my life had become measured out in blessings. Ma became obsessed with the idea that we had things to be thankful for. The pagan rituals of herbs over doorways, the crystals and special pebbles of my early life had been found wanting, so no doubt it was time for change. I wouldn't have included an invitation to the Libanis' party as a blessing. I didn't even like the older Libani children and, more to the point, they didn't like me. But Ma obviously thought it a big deal. I don't think she was close to Lorelei anymore, but seemed to hold her in high regard since she'd returned. And of course, we regularly got to see and look after Archie. We had dressed in our best outfits. I'd been allowed to wear my red shoes which pinched because I had grown since I last wore them. They quickly became muddy from the path. I look down at my current sandals; my toes are dusty with grime and I regret not changing into trainers.

As I walk, shadows within the wood stir; the cloudy light weaving patterns with the branches and their silhouettes. I keep thinking I see a grey dress or shawl move in the gloom but when I pause and look again, there is nobody there. I sense I'm being watched. Perhaps the strange boy I met earlier is following me. But the movement is slower and makes me think of the old woman who used to live in the forest. The one we had always called a witch.

Miss Dryden, like the boy, sometimes appeared suddenly, and I was never quick enough to get out of her way. I wanted to hide from her at first because she had a gnarled old woman's face and eyes like shiny sloes which seemed to look right inside you rather than at you. The first time I had met her was shortly after we'd moved to the wood, and she appeared in a rustle of grey, like a pigeon.

"What are you doing out here on your own, child?" her voice creaked.

"I live here."

"No, you don't, only the hidden creatures live in the wood."

"I live in the house at the edge of the wood," I retorted, trying to stand up to my full height, which wasn't tall, but then Miss Dryden was hunched over and no more than five feet.

"Oh, that house," she said knowingly. But she didn't continue, not like most people who would say, "You mean the witchy house," or, "you know what happened there don't you," or, "that house is cursed."

The problem was she didn't need to say anything. I know

46

she knew the history of the house and exactly what tragedy had occurred in my new home.

Often she had a basket under her arm and would be collecting toadstools and berries which made a colourful mound against the wicker weave. When she saw me looking she would say, "Don't you go picking any of these, some are very poisonous. Leave well alone."

"Why are you picking them then?"

"Well, you nosey little sapling, I need them for my medicine. Here let me show you." I hesitated about moving closer to her, she was so strange and gave off a bitter sappy odour. But for an hour or so she'd put up with me following her and would tell me the names of the toadstools and berries she was collecting, the ones you could eat and those that were poisonous. "Don't you be trying this. You must learn well before you can pick them yourself."

I would listen but I quickly gave up asking questions because she would always bark an answer at me. Finally, she would say, "Now run along home. You need to be careful in these woods."

I never dared to ask her exactly what I needed to be careful of.

Another time Miss Dryden appeared when I was lying curled up on a mossy bank. My head had started to pound and the trees were moving about me as if they were dancers. I'd put my hands over my head and shut my eyes to hide from them. "Little one …" a voice said, "… what's the matter?"

I opened one eye to see Miss Dryden observing me. I blinked up at her. "It's my head," I told her. "It hurts. The trees keep shouting at me."

"That's not the trees; it's your wires getting crossed." She sat beside me and lifted me into a sitting position. She smelt of the flora of the forest. I already felt soothed. "Come on we'll go and see your mother." I stumbled behind her, my head pounding with each step, tree roots and branches accelerating towards me and then moving, so I kept tripping.

By the time we reached the cottage I felt sick.

"What do you want?" Ma demanded as she opened the door to Miss Dryden.

"It's this little sapling, she needs medicine. I'll bring something by for her."

I awoke in my bed trying to work out where I was. My head still hurt, my vision blurred, so the Cyclops's tree eye kept winking and blinking at me. When I went down to the kitchen for a glass of water, Ma put her hand across my forehead and said, "I think we'd better see Doctor Birch."

A day or two later, I sat in the front room of the big house where Doctor Birch had his surgery. The room smelt of polish and lemons. The carpet was a pattern of flowers twisting in and out which made my eyes fuzzy if I looked at it. I was called into the little room that Doctor Birch used as his clinic. It smelt of something different that made me sneeze. The doctor prodded me with the cold stethoscope and shone a bright light in my eyes. He was so close I could see grey hairs tufting his ears and nose. He told me and Ma that it was living under the trees. They were setting off an allergy. "She has visions as well," Ma explained. Doctor Birch chuckled, "Well, that can be the nature of this type of headache ... A migraine, which is rather more than a headache ... isn't it Annie?" He patted my head.

I heard the words as, 'My Grain.' That description made sense. Like the lines in the logs that Woody worked with. Miss Dryden had said my wires were getting crossed. Doctor Birch's prescription was, "Sleeping for a while in a dimmed room is the best medicine."

When we got home, a bottle of rose coloured liquid was on the doorstep. Ma picked it up, frowning. In the kitchen she removed the lid and dipped her little finger in it. The frown remained on her face as she tasted it. "What is it Ma?" I asked. "It's for you to have when you start to get a headache," she said, "Just one spoonful though." The liquor was sweet and minty, and if I took it in time, it did help the headache to disperse.

Today, a bitter smell of wild garlic wafts from the dark interior of the wood. The flowers cast a grey glow under the trees like nuclear fallout. My nickname echoes in my head, 'Stinking Annie'. Our cottage always reeked of it. The pungent smell clung to my hair and clothes. No wonder I had been reluctant to attend the party because it would be noticed by the Libani children, and I would be taunted with the refrain, 'Stinking Annie, Stinking Annie.'

Even in the heat, I shiver at the memory. The sky is becoming darker and on that day too unshed rain had clouded the air; it felt damp against my face. We were caught in a downpour on the way home and even after everything that had happened, I still recall being upset that my tights were muddy by the time we returned. I loved those lacy tights. They were the one thing I owned which I considered pretty. But they weren't new and the crotch was an inch from where it should have been making my steps awkward. Today my trousers impede my stride in a similar way and my inappropriate footwear makes me hobble.

A spattering of rain drops fall, hardly distinguishable from thunder flies. The damp air intensifies the sound of traffic on the bypass throbbing through the trees. The ghost of a siren fills my head. There was a siren on that June day so long ago. It had reverberated through the wood. A cacophony of echoes as the sound bounced from branch to branch, trunk to trunk.

I would have stopped to listen and hitch up my tights. Whilst Ma would have told me to, "Get a move on, Dilly Daydream."

At the edge of the wood the track narrows back to tarmac path. As a child it had been a slippery strip of ground bounded by unruly hedgerow and ditches overflowing with nettles and cow parsley. At thirteen I had been the optimum height for the strands and streamers of overgrown vegetation to catch against me. I thought they singled me out to sting my legs and tease my frizzy hair; tickling my face with whispers of "Stinking Annie." Today, the hedge above and the thick scent of greenery in the air makes me claustrophobic. The effect of wine has long worn off, so the sense of nausea I experience must be due to something else.

I am glad to emerge at the edge of the village green. It is a traditional village, though as a child I had not realised this, it had just been the place where I lived. Where we finally had a proper house rather than a caravan which could be moved on at a moment's notice.

Cottages huddle round the edges of the oval green. Rather than the charm some might see; for me, the thatched roofs and warped beams only add to the impression of conspiracy. On one side is The Linden Tree and next to it a shop and post office. There's also a gallery. As a child I loved to spend time with Myrtill, the owner; seeing her pictures come to life. I wonder if she still lives and works there. From here the square tower of the church is visible to the north of the village. Beyond it, though screened by yew trees, the grave yard stretches to the edge of the woods where overhanging branches keep the graves in shadow.

The urge to run to the centre of the green and hug the beech tree still compels me. Just as it has always done. The tree is ancient and large, with several massive grey feet like a prehistoric creature. Once, at school we had measured the trunk. Seven children were needed with arms outstretched to encircle it. The memory of smooth bark against my cheek makes me lift my hand to my face. I'd said, "*I can hear its heartbeat.*" Miss Rowan had laughed. "Trees don't have hearts, Annie," she'd said. At the time I didn't believe her. I'm not sure I believe it now. I am like a compass affected by a magnetic pole; my steps have strayed onto the grass towards it.

I sit on a bench which wasn't here on my last visit. A plaque adorns it, inscribed in a scrolled font, "*For Lorelei.*" With a line of lyrics from one of her songs; "*All the trees in the wood sing your name.*" And though the air is syrup-thick, I can hear the beech leaves writhe above me and their movement whisper, '*Lorelei.*'

She was at the centre of everything and she still is. Because mystery surrounds her life, her poisoning and her part in my father's disappearance. I shudder, knowing I must write her biography. I take a deep breath in preparation. I am going to have to revisit that dark time.

CHAPTER 8

Though the humidity barely alters, the drizzle becomes heavier. I make my way to Quercus Hall. It is at the bottom of a steep gradient at the south end of the village. I can see the chimneys of the building before I get near the driveway. The house is set down in the valley so is initially viewed from above. The roof appears uniform with four central chimney stacks and four outer ones, all topped with terracotta pots. The slates on the roof are black and slick with rainfall. It is odd that such an ordered roof covers such a strange house. Like seeing a bowler hat from the top and then instead of a face, beneath lurks a grimacing skull writhing with creepers. Every time the front of the Hall comes into view it surprises me.

On the day of the party, I had been more confused than usual. For a moment I'd thought the whole household had come out to greet me, because in front of the building a crowd of people waited in their party dresses. There was also a large yellowish shape with a flashing light on top, as if they had bought a huge novelty birthday cake as a centrepiece. Something not beyond the Libanis' style or budget.

But in the millisecond it took me to realise the impossibility of being welcomed like royalty to Quercus Hall, I recognised the shape as an ambulance. Ma had already observed it and was touching her collar, and touching her knee and counting her blessings.

The faces of the party goers had looked dazed in the blue edged light. The palest of all was Archie. He had been dressed in a pastel shirt and grey shorts and with his almost white hair was camouflaged against the stone wall. I had to squint so he would not fade completely. As he scratched his neck, Archie's eczema-afflicted skin looked like peeling bark and I was reminded of a slender silver birch. Beside him stood Rosamunde and Rosalinde, his older step-sisters. They were a different colouring altogether, a cinnamon shade of hair and olive skin. Their demeanour was also in stark contrast to Archie's. There was no worry or concern in their expressions but half smiles as if fascinated by the activity in front of them. As usual I could not tell which was which. They were so alike people just called them Rosa, either collectively or individually. Just thinking of them made me pat my hair down. I always tried to train my unruly mane into something which would not differ so startlingly from Rosa's gleaming ringlets. Rosa wore matching blue bows in their hair. I would have liked a ribbon but Ma thought such things were frivolous.

Ma had leant down to me and asked, "Who is it?" I was as intrigued as she was but knew she would not enquire. I'd sidled up to Mrs Birch, the doctor's wife, who always knew what was going on.

"What's happened?"

"It's Mrs Libani, she might have fainted or fallen. We don't know what's happened just yet."

I returned to Ma and told her, "It's Lorelei." She twisted her fingers round the edges of her cardigan, kneading the fabric as she muttered, "Oh dear, that wasn't meant to happen. I hope she's going to be alright."

My stomach twisted with terror as I thought of the bottles of tonic Ma had made for Lorelei that I had carried to Quercus Hall. What had we done?

CHAPTER 9

When Lorelei returned to Broomstone, she had not only married a handsome ex-rugby player called Cedric Libani, but she had gained three stepchildren. One of whom was Roderick. He took after his father in looks; tall and muscular with smooth, golden skin.

At sixteen he dismissed me as a nuisance but I was certain I was in love with him. I took to hanging around Quercus Hall when I thought he might be there. After Daddy's disappearance the pull of the Libanis became even stronger. One day Lorelei found me lurking in the bushes. "Hello, Annie, are you spying on me?" I shook my head, embarrassed. "Oh, I know who you're spying on," she said with a chuckle and I felt my face turn crimson, and started to sob. Since Daddy had gone tears appeared easily.

"You poor, poor child. It's alright, I'm not cross. Don't be sad now. Roddy's not here at the moment ... but come and have a drink with me ... I've got a secret to share."

I was so excited by the thought Lorelei was going to confide in me that my tears vanished. I didn't for one moment consider why she would choose to share a confidence with me.

Lorelei gave me a glass of milk and a biscuit and I sat on the stool at the kitchen table, a smart oak affair.

When I'd gulped down half the liquid and put the tumbler down on the table, watching the slip of white slide down the glass, Lorelei grabbed my hand. She had strange hands; the long slender fingers were wrinkled, the joints enlarged. Her finger nails were uneven, the coating of pink nail varnish did not cover the pock marked surfaces. The skin was rough. It didn't seem at all surprising when she hitched her shirt up and put my hand against her stomach. The skin there was warm and smooth. "You wanted a sister, didn't you Annie?"

"Yes," I said content to keep my hand against the warmth of Lorelei's skin although I had no idea why she was holding it there.

"Your baby sister's in here," she said patting my hand against her stomach.

"A baby?"

"Yes, I'm going to have a baby. Your sister. You're going to be a big sister. Isn't that wonderful?"

The milk and biscuit curdled in my stomach and I belched. "I need to go now," I said pulling my hand away. "I think I'd better go." I slipped off the stool and ran home, my feet sprinting over the forest path, my head pounding with what Lorelei had told me. I was old enough to comprehend that if she was saying the baby was my sister, she meant its father was my Daddy. But he'd disappeared. I hoped Ma was home, I needed to ask her.

I hurried back home, trying to fathom what Lorelei had said. When I opened the front door, I expected to find Ma waiting for me, but she wasn't even there. I heard quiet conversation coming from Ma's room and then a giggle, just like she used to do when Daddy was here. Daddy's back! My insides jumped like a firework and fizzed in my head with happiness. But as the front door slammed shut behind me, the conversation in Ma's room stopped. A moment later, Woody walked out. "Hi Annie," he said, "Alright?"

I nodded at him, the firework feeling fizzling away. Daddy wasn't back at all. I felt like crying. Woody let himself out. Then Ma came into the kitchen, "Hello Annie." She came over and hugged me. "I wasn't expecting you back yet. What shall we have for tea tonight? Something special I think, cheer ourselves up." And she cooked my favourite soup with little dumplings on the top and it did make us feel better because

Ma sang her 'Happy song.' There was a piano in the corner of the room, I was never sure where it had appeared from. It was just there one day as if its mottled wood construction had materialised from the trees outside. Its ivory keys were yellowed but the sound they made under Ma's fingers as she stroked them was as pure as bird song. In the warmth of Ma's company that evening, I completely forgot to ask about Lorelei and what she had told me.

As I curled up on my bed I was soothed by food and music. Everything was going to be alright.

Ma must have heard the news about Lorelei's pregnancy, because a week later I returned to the cottage to be enveloped in a fog of steam which smelt of the forest. My hair instantly frizzed. On the table were the remnants of nettles and woodland flowers and forage. "What are you making?"

"It's a tonic for Lorelei; she's pregnant."

I looked at the muslin bag hanging over the basin; the plip … plop of liquid straining through resembled the drops of blood which dripped when Ma jugged a hare. The liquid was such a dense green it was almost black, like the blood of the forest.

"When I'm done, I'd like you to take it over to her."

Later, I had the task of carrying a basket, with a gingham cover, to Quercus Hall. Besides the tonic were muffins and a jar of crab apple jelly. I kept on the path as I walked, conscious of the shadows in the wood and the potential for a wolf to be prowling within them.

CHAPTER 10

The effect of wine at lunch with Archie has completely worn off. My footsteps sound harsh on the tarmac and echo from the high walls as I pass through the metal gates of Quercus Hall. I climb the wide arc of steps that lead up to the front entrance. Archie greets me as I step into the reception area. There is now a desk designed to fit discreetly into the hallway whilst not detracting from the spacious grandeur of the entrance.

A seascape covers one wall. In it a small boat is tossed by waves and covered with foam depicted like a creature's claws. It had always disquieted me as a child. Even though now I have actually seen the sea, it unnerves me with its potential for danger, as if the water might flood out of the painting, sweeping us all away.

The house layout has been modified so I am disorientated. The Hall had always appeared a chaotic convergence of rooms, as if the architect had merely added rooms on a whim, with no precise plan. It could have concealed underground passages and priest holes; I had never been privy to those secrets.

Archie ushers me into a back room I do not recognise. He must have noticed my confused expression as he tells me, "This used to be the original dining room but we altered it to accommodate the new Hotel kitchen and dining room. We've put in a lift up to a suite of rooms for Mum."

Huge windows give a view out over the grounds. Two cedars stand sentry-like on the edge of the grass, casting dark shadows. Rolling lawn sweeps, in parched yellow, down to the lake. It is not as lush as it once was due to the summer heat. From here only the faint copse of trees outlined in the distance gives any suggestion of the island that is at the middle of the lake. I know it is there though. It has the tug of memory about it.

The decor in this part of the Hall has altered, so instead of dark wood panelling it is white and light. Archie leads me through a stainless steel kitchen and then opens a door and sweeps an arm to show a large airy space, "And here is what we call our den." It is not like a den at all. It is bright with fabrics in primary colours and a wooden table in the centre. There is corner seating below the windows with scattered cushions, amongst which a cat the colour of lead mimics a pillow. "That's Rasputin," Archie says pointing at the cat. "Just shove him out of the way if you want to sit down there." The cat opens one eye as if he's understood Archie's words. I will not try to move him.

The room has the feel of a conservatory, lots of glass and patio doors which when open, lead to a terrace bounded with a shallow stone wall and stone urns. The geraniums planted in them look withered, like grotesque spiders with yellowing legs and multiple red eyes.

Archie's wife comes over to greet me. She hugs me before I am able to dodge out of the way. She doesn't notice my resistance. She is tall, her build athletic and skin tanned. Her bobbed blonde hair tickles my cheek as she stoops to embrace me. Although her face is attractive, my eyes stray to her neck where a scarlet birthmark blooms. I think it unfortunate she has been named Poppy, because the blemish so resembles the petals of that flower.

At my gaze she brings her hand to her neck so the mark is almost covered. I look away, realising I've been staring.

"Would you like a cup of tea?"

I nod.

"Do you remember the Hall well? Archie tells me you used to come here as a child."

I mutter a negative and shake my head because everything about the house appears skewed as if it has been reversed and we are on the opposite side of a mirror.

Poppy goes to make tea and the phone rings. Archie picks up the handset and answers. Then with an apologetic wave of his hand, he wanders from the room.

It is now I realise I am disorientated because what I know of the Hall comes from viewing it from the outside, looking in through the windows.

The reason was my crush on Roderick. He was exotic, probably a prince, and therefore part of my future plan. I would sneak out from the cottage in the evening and crouch beneath the window ledge occasionally peaking over to glimpse the wonderland inside. The drawing room, I presume, still exists on the other side of the house. It was vast. Our entire cottage would fit within it. The decor was gold and turquoise like a renaissance chateau, and if I was fortunate my prize would be sprawled against the cushions on the couch. At sixteen he was beautiful and languid with a nonchalance that could only be expressed by somebody without cares. He might be reading a book or listening to music or just thinking. But whatever he did, it was performed with a charisma that lured me to the lighted windows of the Hall. Much like the moths which bumped the glass pane beside me.

Roderick did not give me the time of day. If I happened to be in his company he relished teasing me about my clothes, my home, my parents. Yet I adored him. Occasionally he would grab my wrist and twist the skin with such ferocity I would be left bruised for days. This I would cherish like a priceless bracelet.

During term time he was away at boarding school, but returned for exeat weekends and holidays, which made these glimpses of him all the more tantalising.

Most of the Hall has a narrow pathway around it and the foliage on the wall provided good cover for a stalker.

The particular evening I recollected so well, had been etched into my memories. It was the weekend before Valentine's Day. I'd made a card, made tiny rose buds; added paper birds and ribbons. Slipping it through the letter box at Quercus Hall, I'd felt a buzz of excitement in my stomach, as it plopped into Roderick's realm. It makes me shiver to think of that evening. Because it was the night I'd heard my father's voice for the last time. I never saw him again.

I had crept around the perimeter of the Hall and finally found my prey lounging along the settee in the drawing room. I could see he was talking but not to whom. I gazed at his lovely mouth and imagined he was reciting poetry to me. In a daze I watched; spell bound. I was annoyed when I heard movement behind me, and was about to turn and say, 'Shhh'. But when I did look, I saw a line of figures moving towards the lake. Under scant moonlight they were only perceptible by a low murmuring and by the specks of light which undulated like an airborne serpent. There were about eight of them but draped in black they moved as one shadow. My attention drawn; I followed them down towards the lake. The light snake coiled and with the creak of oars and splash of water I realised they were heading for the island.

I hesitated, wondering whether to follow. But my heart won the conflict and I returned to my main purpose at the Hall's windows. I remained until Roderick finally stretched, got up and left the room. I circled the house several times but could find no sign of anybody. I was about to leave but saw the snake of lights materialising from the lake. I waited whilst they passed, trying to work out who they were, but they were amorphous shadows in the darkness. Finally, I dared move. Unfolding my stiff limbs, I stood up and began to make my way home.

As I reached the footpath by the wood the moonlight was brighter, but the mesh of tree branches splintered the light creating shadow patterns. A breeze had risen up and the trees made tittle-tattle noises as if they had secrets to divulge. A few rain drops fell adding to the symphony. I hoped I could make it home before I got soaked through.

My miniature torch made wan light waver over the rutted track and I had to concentrate on where to place each step. So, the noise of running footsteps towards me took me by surprise. I stumbled, dropping my torch. The light extinguished as is hit the ground. Shock and fear weighted my boots. I remained fixed. A person, coming from the direction of my house ran past. The figure was a shadow, swathed in a black cloak. She carried a lamp which illuminated her pale face making her instantly recognisable. As she passed me, her cape swirled showing the scarlet lining of the fabric. I thought of the tale of Red Riding Hood and expected a wolf to pounce through the trees behind her. She seemed to anticipate it as well, as she glanced backwards, so her footsteps stumbled and she nearly fell. After that she faced ahead and strode onwards. The first crack of lightening forked through the trees. Fat, cold raindrops struck my head. I remained where I was, wondering what I had seen as the lightening exposed her. I was uncertain whether it was just crimson of cloak lining, or if there was blood spattered across her dress. Because the hand gripping the lamp didn't have the pale fingers I associated with Lorelei. It was also stained red.

....

"Annie." I jump.

The cat meows beside me, striking out with a paw as if I have offended him. He leaps from the couch and then jumps up again and makes himself comfortable at the other end of the cushions. Droplets of blood bead on the back of my hand.

"Annie? Are you alright? You seemed to be miles away." Poppy is looking at me with concern. She hands me a cup of tea and I take it, the brown liquid eddying, the fine china chinking in my hands.

Archie comes back into the room. "Sorry about that. Had

to take it," he says, indicating the phone in his hand before replacing it, in its stand, on a bureau.

"So, Annie, will you write my mother's biography?"

The memories are becoming so clear in my mind that I have no doubt it is what I need to do.

"Yes. I'll do it."

"That's brilliant," Archie says, making a move towards me as if he might hug me. Luckily my tea cup prevents the action but a little more tea slops into the saucer.

Archie sits down at the table. "Where will you start?" he asks.

"I'm not sure at the moment but as we don't know your mother's date of birth or early history, I'll probably start it on the day of your mother's incident. When she was poisoned." Archie is silent for a moment. I'm aware I might have suggested the wrong thing, as he continues to stir his tea, the spoon tapping against china. Chimes echo into the corners of the room. "Will I be able to talk to her?"

"Probably ..." The stirring halts as he looks at me, "... but I'm not sure when. She's not had a good day today so we'd better not disturb her."

By the time I have finished my tea the scratch from Rasputin on the back of my hand has dried in a rusty line. As I stand up the cat growls as if I have disturbed him again. I ignore him and put my tea cup on the table.

Archie, realising I am making to leave, asks, "You'll really do it then?"

"Yes, but I've no idea how long it'll take."

"Well, that doesn't matter." He has reached out and his hand is squeezing my shoulder too hard. "You'll stay here of course," I must have given him a dubious look as he continues, "... as our guest."

Archie shows me out and I agree to return tomorrow and stay for a while whilst I start my research.

It is late evening as I drive out of the village. The leaden clouds have given way to steady rain. As I circle the green and the lane beside the church I observe, through the mizzle, a crooked tree, stark without foliage. It is only as I drive on I wonder if it was actually a hunched figure draped in grey. The rain begins to fall more heavily as I drive down Broomstone Hill. It specks my windscreen scattering pin-pricks of light. In my rear-view mirror I can see an outline of the village with its darker halo of forest trees. Amber spots of street lights glow from the old fashioned lampposts, as if they exist in a temporary world, hovering in limbo. I am pleased to reach the by-pass with its regular line of bright lighting and the swish of other vehicles.

CHAPTER 11

The return to my flat fills me with dread. But there is a flicker of hope that Jay will be there, although I know I shouldn't crave his company. I've tried to leave him so many times, and now he's left me, which seems somehow unfair. As if it is he alone who has declared that our relationship is over.

I hate this place. And the feeling is reciprocal. From the way the stairs up to the door creak and groan at my footsteps and how the key snags. As I force the door ajar, I feel its animosity. Inside the lights flicker and buzz before finally casting a yellow hue the colour of fly paper.

I had not had much choice of accommodation following my split. The whole atmosphere exudes a dampness tinged with the aroma of drain. I expect to find something dead when I open the cupboards. It is not a good place for a new start. Still, tonight I have a sense of change. I pour myself a large glass of red wine and look out over the shimmering town below, glowing pin pricks far distant, the possibility of a future, a light at the end of a tunnel.

One of those lights could be a street lamp on Broomstone Hill. A beacon on one of the paved streets on the new estate. The nights I had lived in the cottage had always been dark. The very inkiest blackness like fabric rather than air. In the hot spring of 1983, it had been smothering and I would lie awake at night trying to breathe. Anxious that Daddy had still not returned. Even the season before the atmosphere had been veil-like, draping itself over the wood. The trees whispering beneath.

I set my laptop up in the corner so I can continue to look

out of the window and I begin to write. That distant speck beckons star-like; to be followed, *'straight on 'til morning'*. Not having a specific beginning point with Lorelei, I start with events I know but for so long have avoided thinking about. It is slow work because the occurrences have a way of mingling so I have difficulty distinguishing between them.

I return to the dark night, after seeing Roderick, and running home towards the cottage. In my mind's eye, I remember the storm lantern on the porch with its wavering beacon, returning home when I should have already been in bed. I begin tapping away on the keyboard. Gradually I allow myself to go back … back to the days before Daddy's disappearance. They emerge like ghosts in the reflections of the window pane.

CHAPTER 12

Seeing Lorelei fleeing from the woods had not been the end of the occurrences that evening. It was the night my father disappeared. As I stumbled homewards, the rain became heavier with lightening forking through the trees making the trunks leap and the ground spark. The storm had rumbled away, as I arrived at the cottage. I was shaking, desperate to get inside. I was about to turn the handle but paused, the shouts were loud, the battle in full flow. I couldn't go inside. Fingers of cold permeated my clothing making me shiver. Dampness dripped from the trees and my hands were like ice. The arguing went on and on, longer than on previous occasions. So instead of shivering in the damp, cold night, I finally crept under the lean-to where the wood pile was stacked. Behind it was a room that Daddy used as his tool shed. I was a surprised when the handle gave and creaked open as it was usually locked; securely fastened with a padlock. It was one place I was forbidden to go, but tonight I didn't care. I just wanted to be dry. The must of wood and dust clung to me as I entered the room. But there was another smell, rich and peppery like sweat. The room was black and I dared not turn the lamp on. With the wind moving the tree canopy and the sky cloudy, it was dark, but moonlight occasionally flickered in through a window, so I could make out shapes of rakes and spades, a bucket. I jumped as a black shroud came into view. But then I realised it was just a coat hanging on a hook. I went towards it, thinking I would wrap myself in it to keep warm, but when I touched it I realised it was not a coat or work jacket but a silken, flow of fabric like a cloak. The lining was satin and smooth under my touch and I imagined it gleaming red. I shuddered, realising it was a cape similar to the one I had seen Lorelei wearing earlier. Why did she and my father have identical cloaks? I didn't like the sensation of the fabric which moved under my fingers like water, lifting and shifting as the moonlight made it ripple.

Then my foot kicked something, making me fall. I manged to grab the obstacle and work out that it was a backpack. Pulling open the top cord I smelt the familiar musky scent of Daddy, and my fingers pressed into the warmth of a sweater. I took it out and put it on, it was snug and comforting. There were other things in the pack; a bag likely to contain toiletries and a lumpiness at the bottom which might be shoes. I supposed Daddy kept a spare set of clothes here. As I moved to get up I knocked something else and the clatter it made on the floor made me start. I scrabbled around finally identifying a candle in a metal holder. From my position on the floor with moonlight flickering, I could make out illuminated spots on the floor. I leant down to touch one … wax. Spots of wax had dripped from the candle onto the floor, but the marks did not look white but a darker colour, possibly red. They made a circular pattern marked out on the ground. I couldn't make any sense of it as moonlight kept wavering, caught up in the tree branches and cloud cover.

After what seemed like an age, I crept out of the shed, hoping I could get back into the house.

Besides a steady drip, drip of water slowing but still falling from every tree and every surface, the glade was quiet. The angry words from the cottage had stopped and so I tiptoed towards the door. My father's work boots were on the step, so he'd at least removed those before going inside. As I entered, the house was hushed, no clue as to what had passed remained. But I knew. I crept up to my room and lay in my bed, unable to sleep. I listened to the noise of the wood outside whilst trying to work out why my father was so mean to Ma and what I could do about it. The trees dripped and shushed outside, making a comforting response but I couldn't decipher what they meant. Perhaps I dozed because I woke again to a thumping sound and then what I thought must be the click of the front door. When I heard nothing further I decided it was just the wind making the wooden house creak and moan. I must have drifted off again because the next disturbance was the sound of my parents making up in the usual way. My mother's low groans, my father's hushed endearments. It sounded different now I was upstairs in my own room, more muted and more easily ignored. But I did feel relieved that everything was back to normal and slept more deeply.

The following morning Ma was humming to herself as I went down to breakfast. I was surprised to see Woody sitting at the breakfast table a mug of tea cupped in his hands. His fingers exposed from fingerless gloves looked grubby and the nails were engrained as usual. Ma smiled at me. Her whole manner gave no indication of the argument last night or the nights before. "You look tired," she said, coming over and smoothing my hair with both her hands, looking directly into my face.

Woody got up and left with a quiet, "See you later," and Ma answered with a similar soft, "Bye then."

I waited until the door had closed and then asked, "Why does Daddy shout at you?"

"I'm sorry, Sweetheart," she apologised, but didn't answer my question. "Our silly tiffs shouldn't keep you awake. We'll try to keep the noise down if it happens again. Now let me make you a special breakfast. How would you like your eggs?" With that she turned to the corner where we kept the eggs and started breaking them into a bowl. If I thought she was a little firmer with the cracking and more vigorous with the beating that morning, I put it down to tiredness.

Ma had a scarf around her neck; this was a common addition after a big argument. I imagined if the scarf was removed I would see a necklace of purple bruises.

I didn't see Daddy that morning, I assumed he'd found some work to go to. His boots were no longer on the doorstep as I went outside. When I left the house I crossed to the wood shed and tried to get in, to see if I could fathom out the wax drops on the floor, but now the door was bolted and padlocked again. I climbed on a log so that I could peer through the window, but it was obscured with grime and I couldn't see clearly. I thought I saw the shadow of the backpack near the door. I shrugged as I went on my way. Forgetting about what must simply have been an accidental spill of wax, which I had made more meaningful in my distressed state last night. I continued deeper into the forest and did what I often did on Sunday and walked through the wood inventing stories where I ruled the realm. I was drawn towards the church on hearing the bell chime through the trees, and thought perhaps the Libanis might turn up, possibly even Roderick.

The path was muddy after the storm and several branches had fallen. Undergrowth had been pushed and twisted giving the woods an untidy appearance. I took the track to the back of the churchyard, by the edge of the graves. By the time I walked through the kissing gate, making sure I didn't touch the posts so I could make a wish, I could hear a hymn resonating through the stone walls. I wandered through the gravestones looking at names. I had to use a stick to clean the grooves of moss and lichen so I could decipher some of them. There were the ancestors of Dryden's, Birch's and Alderman's. Families I knew who had lived in the village for ever. One of the yew trees was so huge, spreading out fans of foliage, it made a den below its branches and I crawled inside to hide. My hiding place was quite dry but retained the scent of concentrated forest which I loved.

I was just getting bored with my lookout when I heard footsteps. Through the branches I could see high heeled black boots on the path. It was Lorelei. Making sure I was still concealed I peered out. Lorelei was framed in a frieze of yew branches. She was dressed in a long white coat, making her monochrome with her magpie hair. The pale skin and black shadows beneath her eyes only accentuated this vision. Across her shoulders she wore a cape of badger pelt. I thought it macabre and pulled a face recollecting when I'd first seen it. Ma had created it for her when we lived in the caravan. Lorelei arrived there one morning; her arms full of bloodied beast. She'd said it was roadkill; then demanded that Ma make it into a stole for her. I shivered at the memory.

I had taken my eyes off her and when I looked up I thought Lorelei was going to go into the church but instead she walked round it and continued into the wood the other side. I decided to follow.

Crouching beneath the churchyard wall, I could hear her conversing with somebody. I couldn't hear every word being said. I could make out, 'oak' and 'tree' and 'help' … perhaps 'owe' or 'never' or 'hurt' … I couldn't see her companion from my hiding place. The conversation gradually drifted away and getting up I realised that Lorelei had vanished deeper into the wood.

Organ chords were again audible from within the church, it would be ages before they finished and Roderick might not even be here. I decided I could come back later anyway. For now, I'd go to Myrtill's gallery.

The shop front had a battered awning, shadowing the window glass to mirror, so I could see myself reflected. As usual there was a new artwork on display. This one a gaudy collage, made from scraps of material and daubs of paint. It danced in front of my eyes like a festival parade. On Sunday the shop wasn't open but I rang the bell and a few minutes later Myrtill was at the door peering out to see who was disturbing her morning. "Hi there, Annie," she greeted me opening the door. "Come through, I'm out in the yard." She was wearing dungarees and had a woollen hat on her head, long dreadlocks snaking from beneath it. She held her hands out in front of her, they were dusted with soil. "Just been doing some gardening. Give me a moment."

The yard was a tiny square of cobbles behind the shop, but there was a shed along the back wall. Myrtill disappeared inside. She was tall and had to duck to get in. I went to the open door and glimpsed the interior. Myrtill was bending over a shelf of plants, feathery under strip lighting. There was a lovely aroma of garden, which was not the same as the woody forest smell. I thought Myrtill must be an excellent gardener as well as an artist. "What are you growing?" I asked.

"Herbs."

"They smell nice," I said,

"Yes, they do, don't they?" And she took a deep breath, closed her eyes and tilted her face up to the ceiling. The narrow dreadlocks swung round her head reminding me of a weeping willow. "Gardening is a wonderful thing ... wonderful," and she laughed. It was a long low gurgle that bubbled from deep inside her, like a deep underground spring, as if a secret was trying to escape.

After Myrtill had sorted her gardening, I followed her up the steps that led from the yard to the rooms above the shop. I loved visiting Myrtill; her home was more like a den, the air thick with the tang of paint, glue and dust motes. Ornaments and objects were jumbled on every surface. There was a pile of well-thumbed women's magazines as well. Their glossy covers were now dusty, but there was always an interesting article to read. In one I found a piece about Lorelei's album 'Dryad,' and a quote by Lorelei saying how the words and music had just flowed out of her, as if it was something just waiting to be written. I showed Myrtill but she just shrugged.

Sometimes I'd bring Myrtill a treasure I'd found in the wood; feathers, or fir cones, buttons from Ma's sewing case. I'd occasionally pilfer things from people. I'd once bought Myrtill a skein of embroidery thread from Quercus Hall and had been delighted when she had used it in a collage.

"Do you want coffee?" Myrtill was the only adult who

would have offered me coffee. I didn't really like it but I loved being invited to have some. She would give me a bone china mug to drink it from, so it was doubly appealing. Whilst I waited for her to boil the kettle, I picked up a tiny skull from the sill. It was as light and delicate as lace. I turned it in my hand, the shape like a knife, the beak sharp against my palm. "Magpie," Myrtill said when she saw me. I tried to imagine the tiny skull covered in feathers with its black bill, and beaded eyes.

Once we had our drinks, Myrtill showed me the composition she was working on. Today the easel she uncovered took my breath away. On it was a mosaic of black and white feathers, intricately woven to form a young woman's face. "Look carefully," she told me. "There are two faces. Do you see them?"

"Wow! Yes, Yes!" I said, because if I tilted my head I saw another figure emerge from the feathery collage, this time a hag. I kept tilting my head to and fro so the image flitted back and forth between the two. Hag and Beauty. Beauty and Hag.

"Do you like it?"

"I love it!" Most of Myrtill's work was abstract and I had difficulty understanding it, but this was simple.

"You know what inspired me to do this?" Myrtill waited for a beat, whilst I shook my head. "Lorelei. I saw her walking last week, and she reminded me of a magpie. She was wearing that badger cape."

"I saw her in the churchyard just now, and I thought the same," I said, feeling very wise.

"Did you now?" Myrtill said, but I wasn't sure whether it was in response to my having seen Lorelei recently or my clever thinking. "So, which one do you think is the real Lorelei?" Myrtill asked; "The beauty or the crone?"

"The beautiful one of course," I replied quickly. It was obvious wasn't it? Myrtill's next words were unexpected, and at the time I didn't give them much thought. "Don't be so sure … beauty can cover up so much wickedness."

As I left Myrtill's, I saw the Libani BMW circle the green, a dark headed figure in the back, and I knew it meant Roderick was returning to school. I'd got so tied up with Myrtill and her art that I'd missed seeing him. I cried as I walked back to the cottage.

When I returned home Woody was sitting at the edge of the glade, which I considered his work space. He was perched on a tree stump and a halo of shavings and sawdust surrounded him. An odour of scrubbed wood hung in the air. Pieces of varied shapes circled him, morphing into sculptures like patient pets.

He lifted a hand to me in greeting and then continued with his whittling. In other circumstances I might have gone over and talked for a while, but today I was aware of my tear streaked face so went straight inside and up to my room beneath the eaves. Lying on my bed I wrote about my misery at Roderick going away in my diary and listened to the scraping and tap of Woody's chisel outside, Ma's voice singing as she cleaned downstairs.

Later, I heard the whistle of the kettle and then Ma talking to somebody in the kitchen. I jumped up because it sounded like Daddy. But when I got to the top of the steps I realised it was Woody. I took a few steps down and asked, "Where's Daddy?" Ma and Woody stopped their conversation. Ma dropped a spoon on the floor and it clattered as she turned towards me. Her mouth opened and closed but no words came out.

It was Woody who told me, "Your daddy hurt your mother last night. I think he's staying away for a while."

That had happened before. Daddy going away for a day or two after an argument. Then suddenly returning, a smile on his face, a present of a bracelet or book, as if nothing had happened.

Woody reached out and took the scarf from around Ma's neck. A ring of black bruises gleamed against her skin. "He needs to come back and apologise I think. Don't you?"

I nodded and returned to my room. I hated that Daddy shouted at Ma, and hurt her. But I loved him. I wanted him to read to me. I cuddled Daddy's jumper I'd taken from the wood shed the previous night and took my fairy tale book off the shelf. I turned to the tale about Lorelei luring sailors to her, but the words were blurred by tears filming my eyes. Had my Lorelei lured Daddy away?

I guessed Daddy was still cross with Ma but would return later. In the morning I went to school as usual. When I returned Ma had the scarf around her neck. I asked, "When will Daddy be home?"

"I don't know Annie. But I think he must be very cross with me this time," Ma said as she made me tea. "He's punishing me by staying away."

"I want him to come home," I sniffled. It wasn't fair that he was punishing me as well as Ma by his absence. I stomped up to my room, leaving my tea on the table.

Ma called behind me, "I'd like him to come home as well." She stood at the bottom of the stairs, "We need to stick together Annie. Come and have your tea."

I paused, aware of my stomach rumbling. I made my way back down stairs and started to eat my stew. After taking a few mouthfuls, I paused, gravy dripping from my spoon as I lifted it; "What will we do if he doesn't come back?"

Ma stirred the stew in her bowl and finally answered, "He will come back Annie." She continued stirring, appearing hypnotised by the motion. Then said, "But I think if he's not back later tonight or in the morning then I'll have to go and tell the police that he's missing." That sounded drastic. But the longest he had ever stayed away before had been two nights.

CHAPTER 13

I awake slumped in the chair hunched over my laptop. Dribble is leaking from the side of my mouth and I wonder how long I've slept. I quickly wash, tidy the flat and pack a suitcase. The click of the door sounds happy as I step outside, as if it is quite content that I'm not going to be home for a while. The feeling is mutual.

I decide to visit my mother on the way back to Broomstone; it will not be a long detour. Ma's flat is in a small town called Stonewick, on the third floor of an airy modern block.

Her rooms are uncluttered, the only adornments a piece of twisted wood, a shell and a glass vase which catches the light and scatters rainbow spots across the room.

Ma is equally simply attired. She wears a long shapeless shift of blue without embellishment and is barefoot. I watch her feet move across the carpet, the long toes curling into the pile as if she is a gymnast preparing a move.

I'm never sure how Ma spends her time. She still creates her own clothing and there is an old fashioned Singer machine in the corner and a sewing box with the glint of needles, pins and silk thread spilling from it. A keyboard and guitar await somebody's touch in the spare room but whether Ma ever plays them or sings is something she never shares with me and I don't ask. I don't know if she goes out or if she has friends but she appears perfectly content. As though now she lives alone, without me or Daddy, she has finally found the balance and peace she has always craved.

She makes me a cup of herbal tea which tastes like straw. It is pointless to ask for a regular cup of builder's tea with sugar and caffeine just as it would be to request a glass of wine.

Between sips of tea, I tell her about my assignment. She nods a response, pre-empting what is coming.

"I need to ask you some more questions about Lorelei."

"Go on then," she says with a sigh, and she sits beside the window and looks out over the roofs of adjacent buildings and fiddles with the fabric of her dress.

"Where do you think Lorelei came from?"

"I've really no idea. I don't think anybody has a valid theory."

"Did you believe her? Believe that she had permanently lost her memory?"

"Yes. There was no reason not to. Her story was in the papers for a while and nobody came forward. Nobody recognised her, and she has quite distinctive looks."

"Could she have come from the woods?"

"What do you mean?"

"Could she have been living in the woods, like Miss Dryden, a complete mystery person?"

"Annie ... for goodness sake." She turns from the window and scowls at me. "You're an adult now, not a little kid. Lorelei isn't some sort of magical being out of your fairy tale book. She was a young girl in trouble, probably disowned because of her pregnancy. Surely it doesn't matter now whether she had amnesia or not."

"But you must have found out something about her."

"Nobody really knew her Annie". Ma turns away again. She is tilting her head as if trying to focus on the light and shade moving across the tiles outside. "She was a solitary person. You didn't ask questions about her, if you did she wouldn't answer anyway. I think she was as unaware of how she came to Broomstone, just as much as everybody else."

"So, you think the amnesia was real, you don't think she had another agenda?"

"If she did, I have no idea what it could have been."

"But she did use your music; she gained her fame because

of you, didn't she?"

"I suppose so, in a way, but I don't think it was deliberate or malicious, if that's what you're getting at."

My eyes follow the geometry of buildings displacing the horizon outside. I recalled the early days of Lorelei joining the band, when I had been a young child. Her voice was not soft and low like Ma's but was powerful and haunting. Even at six years old I recognised she was beautiful, and when she sang all the men in the room gawped at her. I wondered if Ma had been jealous but she always denied there had been any bad feeling between them.

"'Dryad' was your song though,"

"Songs don't have true ownership, Annie, they are like cats in that way, they seek out their home. True, I wrote the lyrics and music to a song that I called 'Dryad', but Lorelei made it her own. If I had sung it, it would never have been a number one record. I just didn't want that." Ma looks at me again. "Annie, I wrote 'Dryad' about Lorelei, it was her ode." That's something she hadn't told me before, but now it seemed obvious.

"Did you like her?"

Again, Ma avoids a direct answer, as she always manages to do to that question.

"I looked after her. Like a stray. A wild bird with a broken wing. She wouldn't let anybody get close. I always felt as though I was simply minding her until she was able to fly again."

"Do you visit her then?"

"No, never. She probably wouldn't be able to recognise me and I'd rather remember her beautiful."

"What about Archie? Wouldn't you like to see him?"

"Annie ... why can't you accept that I've moved on from Broomstone? That the Libanis have nothing to do with me; Archie is an adult, and Lorelei is damaged ... they're not part of my world anymore."

"What happened to our house?"

"I've told you before Annie. I was glad to move on to be honest. When they built the new estate our landlord was given a good offer. They didn't want a grubby old cottage with tales of witchcraft attached to it, adjacent to their wonderful prestigious homes." Ma almost spits the words out.

"So, you were against the building development?"

"Not really. It's worked out well for me. It's just I hate to think of the glade empty. Change is sometimes hard to come to terms with."

I agree with her.

I leave my mother's flat with only a scant amount of information about the things I really want to know. And I haven't even broached the subject of my father's abuse of her and Woody's regular presence. I will have to resume the conversation at a later date.

CHAPTER 14 - IVY

Ivy watched as her daughter left the block of flats. The curls on the top of her head bouncing, untrainable. Annie strode away with a purposeful stride. Ivy knew her daughter had always had too much imagination. Perhaps she'd been wrong to try to curb it, but she'd had no choice. She'd had to balance her husband's encouragement of it. He'd filled Annie's head with tales of enchanted beings, fairy fables and inappropriate ballads. Ivy was constantly aware of the book of folk tales he had bought Annie, the odour of which pervaded the caravan with a musty smell as if the characters depicted in the book were emerging like phantoms hanging in the air.

And then one had escaped from the pages, or that was how it seemed. And Lorelei or whoever she really was had somehow ended up entangled in the tree roots at the river's edge. Ivy shuddered, tried to keep her thoughts in the here and now. However Lorelei had ended up in the water couldn't be good. She might have been trying to kill herself or somebody else might have tried to murder her. Ivy couldn't shake off the possibility that Lorelei was indeed a magical creature, linked directly to her own family and what had happened when she was a child. She scratched her neck, feeling the raised tissues of scarring which still remained. A reminder of the disease that had nearly killed her and had taken her sister away. Ivy shivered; it was better to imagine Lorelei had escaped from the pages of a book rather than her own past. Ivy took a deep breath and tried to cleanse the darkness of her thoughts with a breath tinged with the patchouli scented air. In the real world, somebody should have missed Lorelei and should have been looking for her. But even after she became famous, nobody stepped forward to claim her as family.

'Why' she asked herself 'Why couldn't Annie leave it alone?' And now this stirring up of the past. Returning to Broomstone and dredging all that had settled. For a moment Ivy thought Annie might look up and see her at the window, so she stepped back a pace into the shadow. It seemed that Annie couldn't let it go. All these questions again and again. Round and round in circles. It didn't do anyone any good to delve back into the past. She was aware of her hands trembling.

Ivy stepped into the back room and sat at the keyboard. Her fingers straddled a chord of black keys, C minor; melancholy. As she pressed down, a sombre melody echoed in the room and she started to sing. Words formed in her head and she sang without thought, *'Don't meddle with the past. It breaks my heart and makes me miss you more.'*

It wasn't until a teardrop slipped and splashed onto the keys that Ivy realised she was crying. Perhaps she'd go and visit Woody, see what he said. She'd have to get the bus and walk to his caravan on the other side of Broomstone forest. But he always had a way of calming her. And maybe it was time for the truth … or some of it at least.

CHAPTER 15

I take the turn off the by-pass into Broomstone and immediately sense the bubble of tension envelop my car and suck me inwards. There is a point on the hill, around the milestone post when the mobile signal fades making the real world distant. I have put the '*Dryad*' CD into the slot in the car and the music mingling with Lorelei's voice is winding around me. As the car climbs the hill I feel as if I am being bound inside a cocoon. The timbre of her voice hypnotic, the words and melodies so familiar, as if they are stitched with my DNA.

Today a lump comes into view on the road; I have to swerve around it. A badger, knocked down by a car. I pull over and get out. Wrapping my fingers into the sleeves of my jacket, I manage to move it, thinking of the mess it will make if cars run it over again and again. I tug it onto the verge, holding my breath so I don't catch the odour from its damaged body. Its black and cream fur is matted with blood, staining the fabric of my jacket. People sometimes collect roadkill to use. I'd seen a programme about a woman recently, who'd made fantastic hats and fashion accessories from these animals. But Lorelei did it first, decades before.

It must have been just before Archie was born when Lorelei had come to the caravan one day with the dead badger in her arms. There was blood smearing its ivory fur and a smell of death about it.

"I found this on the roadside," she'd said, "I thought it would make a wonderful stole. You'll do that for me, won't you Ivy?"

Ma frowned. I thought she'd say, 'No.' I could see light reflecting from the badger's eye, making it wink at me. "You've got to, Ivy. It will be one of a kind," wheedled Lorelei. Ma got up, walking towards Lorelei. I shuddered as her fingers stroked the badger fur and she smiled, "Why not?"

I followed as they took the animal to the barn and proceeded to cut its belly and drag the entrails out. It smelt foul. I had a feeling of being drowned in blood and gagged. I moved to the barn door and hovered at the perimeter so I could keep a check on what was going on but also able to turn my head to take a breath of clean air.

Ma had got a bucket and was stringing the badger above it so the blood was running and then dripping into the receptacle below. *'Drip, drop, drip, drop ...'* It was mesmerising.

Ma wiped her bloodied hands on a cloth and said, "That's all for now, we'll let it settle, then clean it, cut it and line it." As they walked towards me, Ma's hands stained red, I realised Lorelei had done nothing to help. She had merely been an observer like me.

CHAPTER 16

I park in front of Quercus Hall, in one of the newly designated parking bays ready for guests when the Hotel is officially opened. I decide to walk back into the village before going inside. My head feels heavy, on the brink of migraine. The air is dense with pollen and potential rain.

Behind the row of lime trees at the edge of the green, I glimpse the red and white awning of the shop that had been Myrtill's. One look tells me 'The Gallery' has changed. On the door is a notice, *'Tarot and Palmistry. Your future revealed.'* A rack of postcards stands sentry. I spin it slowly and it creaks and flutters like a mystical creature.

Before stepping inside, I look in the window. The awning, much smarter than the old one, keeps the drizzle away. Crystals turn slowly catching the light, throwing glittering geometric shapes across the scene. I can see my reflection caught in the radiant shards within the window display. It vacillates between existence and non-existence. I turn the absent band on my finger and feel insubstantial, as though I am being absorbed into the past. Beyond my reflection I can imagine the hovering thirteen year old regarding herself against the back drop of a collage.

No bell sounds to announce my arrival, but the air is so thick with fragrance it sets off a chain reaction and all the dangling trinkets and shiny surfaces inside tinkle and chime. My skin prickles. I feel as though I am a fly treading on the edge of a spider's web.

As I turn towards the shop's counter, I realise she is standing there. She has materialised without me noticing.

"You're back then?" Myrtill asks, as if I have been away on holiday for a week and she's been expecting me.

I am surprised she's recognised me so quickly, but then I'd had no doubt it was her the moment she appeared. She is still tall and slim with balletic arms and angular cheek bones which give her the look of a jointed artist's mannequin. Her skin is a dark sheen. She's wearing a shoelace strapped dress in dull yellow with a tutu like skirt. The garment exposes a bony flat-chested décolletage. Her posture reminds me of a Degas ballerina. Her dreadlocks have gone though and her black hair is cropped close to her scalp.

"Well, my dear Annie, how the hell are you?" she asks in her sing song voice, and comes round the desk and hugs me. She smells the same. An aroma of herbs belonging to an exotic cuisine. I wonder if it is cannabis. Back in 1983 she had been arrested when, as a result of investigations following Lorelei's poisoning they found several plants in her outhouse. I think she was released with a fine and a warning. I sniff again but even though I am older I have no idea whether I smell perfume or pot.

"I'm good," I lie, finally answering her question, trying to avoid her scrutiny. She holds me by the shoulders making me face her. Her eyes are large and dark brown with an intensity which sees beyond my face and bores into my centre.

"No, you're not."

"I guess you don't have to be psychic to see that," I reply, one hand instinctively rubbing my empty ring finger. I look around the shop bewildered by the change and Myrtill still being here.

"It's changed a bit. Don't you still paint?"

"Tell you what; it's not busy, so why don't we have ourselves a coffee and a chat?"

Whilst Myrtill busies herself making coffee in the back, I wander through the shop, touching strings of feathers, beads and crystals; smelling candles and incense sticks.

We sit on high stools beside the counter.

"I still paint," she tells me, "But you can't make a living from it. I've diversified." She gives a gracious sweep of her arm so all the goods in the shop tremble and hum.

"And the fortune-telling?"

"Well, that's part of the package. I've found I'm rather good at it. Why don't you tell me about the break-up?"

I flinch at her perception, then realise, rubbing my empty ring finger, I'm not difficult to read.

"We found out too late that we liked each other but not enough to put up with each other's clutter and bad habits. Often he'd be going out as I came in and gradually that became the norm because both of us preferred it." I have no intention of telling anybody about the real reason behind the split - Jay's constant infidelity, his undermining of me. Or of my weakness in always believing he had changed his ways. Like Daddy with Ma; he was good at saying sorry, making up.

Myrtill is sympathetic but I can see in her expression that she doesn't believe me as I explain how Jay and I "had just grown apart." Although she frowns, she makes more coffee and listens. And then I find myself telling her about Archie's request.

"Do you want to stir up the past? It was all so long ago."

It crosses my mind that as the fortune-teller she should be the one who can see the reason for my being here, because I have no doubt that something, like a ley line or an elemental force has brought me back.

"Don't you know?" I tell her, fingering a dream catcher above me, so the mirror twists a reflection of my head, "It's destiny."

CHAPTER 17

When I return to Quercus Hall, Archie leads me up a set of back stairs with several twists, turns, steps up and down, so my overnight bag which I'd gamely said I could manage, knocks into the walls and paintwork. If Archie notices he does not say anything. As I follow him I notice he is limping, his deformed leg beneath the fabric of trousers will have grown, entwined like a tree branch; moving awkwardly.

We finally come to a long corridor which is at the top most part of the house. On the walls are pictures which make me pause. Framed behind glass are rows of moths, each with a pin through the body. They are such beautiful shimmery colours, pastel blue, violet and silver, with specks of red, purple, emerald shining like jewels, that I can imagine why people might want them adorning the walls. Archie realising I'm no longer following says, "Oh, you're looking at those horrible things. Had to find somewhere to hang them. It's Cedric's hobby. Killing and maiming things and calling it art."

The room I'm allocated is in what must have once been the attic. It is low ceilinged and gabled. In the centre is a double bed below a skylight, so I will be able to see the sky changing and the stars at night as I lie there.

There are two other dormer windows to the side through which I can see the expanse of lawn, the tree tops of the wood on the island, indicating the centre of the lake. Further away the countryside rolls and folds with wind turbines standing watch on the horizon. The room borders between hotel accommodation and a family room. Perhaps it is a more personal guest room for relatives and friends. I observe my reflection in the chevalier mirror and smile at myself. I am pleased to be considered a friend; I don't have many of them.

"I'll leave you to settle in. Make yourself at home and then come down and join us for tea." I thank Archie and listen as he goes away, his footsteps sounding uneven.

The room is sparely furnished and a smell of disuse lingers. There are two ornaments on a low shelf; matching carved bookends in the shape of 'R's'. I pick one up allowing paperbacks to slump on the shelf, a puff of dust released into the air. I trace the contours of the wood feeling it beneath my fingers as I had done many years ago. They had been a birthday gift to Rosa on their fourteenth birthday. Ma had carried them to the Hall and amidst the confusion of Lorelei's incident, I never knew if Rosa had actually received them. I recollected them being made. I had held the piece of wood when it was simply an unformed block. But even at that time I had stroked my hand across it and known what it would become. That's what Woody had told me anyway, "The carving is already in the wood. You just have to feel it. No, I mean sense it."

He continued to carve, the wood falling in curling locks to the floor, reminding me of Rosa's hair. I had been envious the block wanted to become Rosa's initial so asked, "Can I have a bookend for my birthday. An 'A'?"

"You could but there's only one of you and an 'A' is trickier because of its sloping sides."

A cloud of jealously engulfed me. They had their twinness which simply emphasised my isolation and also, if I'd had a name like Rosa not only would it make a suitable letter for a bookend but it would mean that I wouldn't have been called 'Stinking Annie' for all my formative years. I left Woody sitting on the tree stump carving away, and headed deeper into the wood sulking. I didn't need bookends anyway; I had few books. My prized tome of folk tales was so large it stood up by itself.

CHAPTER 18 - IVY

Woody watched from the steps of his caravan as a figure walked towards him. She had to lift her feet high up to avoid the rough ridged ground at the edge of the field.

She still looked graceful though. Gold in her hair caught the light even though it was a dull day. 'Why didn't I realise I loved her before. Before all the ugliness and unpleasantness?' he asked himself. He answered it as well … 'Because Ryan was always so possessive of Ivy, that if I'd got too close or said the wrong thing, Ryan would have thumped me.'

"Hey there," she called, her voice low and resonant. It had been the perfect counter to Lorelei's soaring soprano.

"Hey, lovely," he responded getting up and brushing down his jeans which were sprinkled with wood dust.

"Not at work today then?"

"No, took the last lot into the garden centre yesterday, so thought I'd have a bit of a break. We could do some foraging though."

"Okay," Ivy said, smiling. She enjoyed being here, finding leaves and fungi to make into a meal. It was a soothing occupation.

Woody grabbed a sack and locked up the caravan, "Never used to bother," he said, "Can't be too careful nowadays though. Things have changed." He pocketed the key and they followed a track into the woods.

Suddenly, a figure swung down from the trees and stood in their path.

"Hello, Ham", Woody addressed the skinny young man.

"Hello, hello," he replied, circling the pair in a skipping

dance. "Got a fag?"

"No baccy left," Woody tipped his tobacco pouch upside down to prove it.

"You?" Ham stopped in front of Ivy, staring at her.

"No, I don't smoke."

"You're her mother, ain't you?" he said pointing a crooked finger at her. "I saw her I did, by the old witchy house. You lived there didn't you? All gone now … All gone now." This he repeated with a whistle between the sentences as if it were a song.

"You mean Annie?" Ham nodded. "Yes, I'm Annie's mother. When did you see her?"

"Just the other day. But there's going to be trouble … trouble, trouble. All gone now. All gone now … but it's going to come back, everything's a'coming back …" Still whistling Ham disappeared into the wood.

"He's still making mischief then?" Ivy said.

"Ham's harmless, just one of the folk who lives in or round the wood."

"He seems to get odder," she commented, pulling her shawl around her, suddenly feeling chilled.

"Oh, he's alright. He just hangs about."

"What does he think he knows … about Annie, about me? Let's go back."

"He just likes to make stuff up. I wouldn't worry." Woody grabbed her hand, "Come on let's have a brew, you're getting cold."

The kettle made the whole caravan vibrate as it began to whistle. Woody made the tea in a brown teapot and poured it out into worn enamel mugs. He sat beside Ivy on the caravan bench seat.

Woody, realising Ivy was still stirring her tea without saying anything, said, "Look don't let Ham upset you. He really is harmless. He's helped me in the past too, moving things and cutting branches. He's just a bit odd in his ways."

"It's not just him. It's Annie as well. Stirring up things.

Things that should be left alone." Woody put his arm round her and she leaned into him. "Why did everything have to get so ... so ... complicated?"

"That's just the way things are. Look, why don't you stay tonight? Don't go."

The light was dimming, the tree shadows dark over the windows at the side of the van, the horizon becoming muted on the edge of the distant field.

"Okay, I'll stay," she said, kissing his hand.

Later, as they lay on the pull down bed, he stroked her hair and said, "Come and live with me. We could be happy here."

"I don't want to live in the woods anymore. You could come and live with me."

Woody chuckled, "That's the problem isn't it? I can't live without the woods and you can't live with them."

"And what would Annie think? She'd jump to conclusions, about how long we'd been seeing each other."

"Annie is a grown up ... she can think what she likes."

"Yes, but ..." Ivy shook her head. "What was that?" She sat up, trying to see out into the dusk.

"Probably just a tree branch, they sometimes tap the van."

"No, it was definitely somebody. It was a human shadow."

"More likely a muntjac making its way home. Nothing to worry about."

Ivy pulled the covers around her, worried about being spied on.

"I don't know why you're getting so coy. Nobody, not even Annie, is going to make a fuss about it even if they did see us together. We're free agents."

"You know how rumours start ... how they get misinterpreted ... how things end?" Ivy started to cry, "Oh god, how did everything end up in a mess like this?"

Woody had nothing to say, so just held her, watching the branches making strange shapes outside as the light finally faded. Wondering how long Ham had been spying on them.

CHAPTER 19

I make my way down to the den room later and find Poppy in the kitchen, oven gloves on her hands saying, "Just in time. I was going to call you down. Fish pie alright?" I nod as she bends to lift a golden topped pie out of the oven. The smell emanating from it makes me nauseous. It is so long since I've had a properly cooked meal, something other than a microwave 'pinger' or sandwiches, I'm not sure I'll be able to eat.

We sit at the table in the den, covered with a pristine white cloth, laid with cutlery and napkins on china side plates. Poppy says, "Sorry it's such a makeshift dinner." I wonder what they usually do. Perhaps they change into evening dress and sit either end of the vast table in the formal dining room, but that room has been revamped along with the kitchen for the Hotel business with small tables set out for guests. I gather there is a suite of rooms above, where Lorelei is looked after.

Archie clarifies somewhat when he says, "We usually just eat in here. I don't like the hotel dining room at all. Although we've made changes it's still ..." He shudders and stops buttering the roll he's taken. Instead, he grabs his wine glass and takes a slurp.

Poppy leans across to me so I think she wants to whisper in my ear. I move back a little, but Poppy continues in a hushed voice, "It's where the baby was laid out."

"What?"

"Lorelei was pregnant when she had her incident, about six months gone. Cedric had a coffin made and the baby was laid out."

I have a flash back to that dark oak panelled dining room and imagine a tiny coffin in the gloom. "Why would he do that?"

"I still have no idea," Archie says, taking another long sup of wine, draining his glass.

"That must have been terrible," I say, but think it might be a topic for the book. "You can't have been more than … what … eight?"

"Seven and a half, actually. It was horrific. She looked like a doll. Not one of those pretty ones but one from a horror movie. I had never seen anything so repulsive. And yet this thing had come out of my mother's belly. My mum who was lying in a hospital room wired up to alien machinery. They kept saying this thing was my sister. Then somebody shoved me and I was pushed forward, lifted up and told, 'Kiss your sister and say goodbye.'"

I shiver. The thought of that unformed baby lying in its coffin, and poor little Archie being forced to kiss it, is a thing of nightmares. And under it all I am questioning whether this was the child that Lorelei told me about. That she was my sister as well.

Archie gets up and replenishes our wine glasses. Only Poppy has eaten her fish pie. The meal is turning grey and congealing on mine and Archie's plates.

Poppy doesn't comment on our poor appetites, just removes our dishes and asks if we'd like coffee, which we both decline.

"Where's the baby buried … in the churchyard?"

"No. Don't you remember? She was buried on the island." The glass in Archie's hand is trembling. I wonder where they had interred her. It reminds me of something we'd found there a long time before.

"Do you remember when we all went to the Island … finding that slab? Well, you found it."

"Vaguely. Why?"

"Because I always thought it had the name, 'Lorelei,' engraved on the stone."

"That's ridiculous, Annie. Roderick said it was, 'Here lies …' or some such thing. It could never have had Lorelei's name on it could it? That was before she was incapacitated. And she's alive, not dead."

"That slab; it's always made me wonder."

"Wonder what?"

I don't continue, because I know I am being ridiculous.

"Wonder what, Annie?" Archie sounds cross.

"I don't know," I say lamely, "There was just something odd about it."

"You always did have too much imagination. Perhaps you're not the right person to do this memoir after all."

"No," I blurt, "I'm sorry. I am the right person. It's just I'm feeling a bit disorientated being back here again. I think I'll go up and jot some notes down. See you in the morning." I push my chair back and get up to leave.

"Make yourself at home," Poppy says, "Just ask if there's anything you need. Oh, and we're going to have a soiree tomorrow evening, so that you can meet some people."

I pause in the doorway and Archie sees my stricken expression,

"Nothing fancy, just a few guests who might remember something."

I gulp, my response sticking in my throat. I can't tell him I do not want to meet people at a gathering, after all that is why I've been invited here. I don't want to give him another excuse to sack me before I've even started.

"It'll be fun," he enthuses, and I suspect he's lying as I have never known Archie to be keen on company. "Poppy's renowned for her evenings," he finishes, so I know it is Poppy behind his new found sociability. She does seem the type who might have been to finishing school.

CHAPTER 20

I return to my room feeling restless. I get my laptop out, log on and type in the heading, 'Lorelei, the Mystery, the Truth.' As a working title it will do.

The white of the page below is instantly thrown into relief by the bold block words. It looks empty. That's how my head feels too. I haven't a clue where to start. But I think about what Archie said about Lorelei's baby being laid out downstairs. It is creepy. I don't even recall participating in the funeral, though I suspect Ma must have done. I get up from the desk and peer out of the window. From here I can just see the tops of the trees moving around. They're not like the trees where the cottage had been, they are so dark and dense that they huddle together as if to conceal whatever is on the island.

I don't like the island.

I am transported back to the day we visited. It was supposed to be a treat for my thirteenth birthday and my stomach was a swirl of excitement because I was going to spend the day with Roderick. Since Daddy's disappearance the Libanis had been kinder to me, I thought Lorelei might have encouraged them. The invite had been made by Roderick. That made it even more special … he wanted to spend time with me. The fact that Rosa and Archie would be there was of no consequence.

The day started bright but a strong wind blew in our faces as we headed across the lawn towards an avenue of topiary conifers. They were like illustrations from Alice in Wonderland and cast strange shadows as we moved between them. The bushes would once have been neat but were ragged with bald, rusted patches.

We reached a rough track which led away from the property down towards the lake. It was heavily rutted, with puddles of water. The scabby blackness of thorn bushes surrounding the lake at first concealed it. But then it appeared like a grey ulceration. Though breezy near the Hall, here everything was still as if we'd stepped into another realm. There was an odour of stagnation.

In contrast to the black banks and grey water the island in the centre stood out. It looked enchanted with its towering trees and lower evergreen bushes.

A rotting wooden jetty protruded into the water and at the edge, tied to a post, was a rowing boat. Its paint was peeling and the planks looked decayed.

"We're not going to use that, are we?" asked Rosa, as Roderick started unhitching the rope.

"Don't be such wimps," said Roderick. I stood a little straighter, I would impress him with my pluck even though my stomach was churning and my skin was tacky with anxiety. Rosa shrugged and both got into the boat.

Even though Archie weighed very little, with five bodies in it the rowing boat was low in the water. The oars creaked reluctantly and stirred the sludgy liquid. Roderick insisted on rowing. He was useless and caught the surface of water on each stroke, splashing me with stagnant droplets. I couldn't help but grimace and say "Oh!" as the cold pellets stung me. "Well, sit still then," Roderick responded and I forced myself to sit silently for the rest of the journey. We zigzagged our way to a pebble crescent of beach.

Roderick managed to direct the boat into the little bay and scrambled out leaving the rest of us to pull the boat high on the shingle.

"The path starts here," he said and was swallowed into the overhanging brush of bushes, as if gobbled by a monster's mouth. I watched Rosa follow. Even Archie with his limping leg hurried behind them. I hesitated. They all seemed certain but I was afraid of what I was walking into. Taking a deep breath, I pushed my way through and found the path. Things scuttled and rustled giving the notion we had disturbed a secret place. Brambles scratched my legs, catching my clothing, warning me about going further.

The season hardly appeared to have touched this place. It was like somewhere beyond the concept of time. Anything deciduous had been covered by swathes of ivy, moss and plates of fungi. Yew trees huddled in dark dips. No light penetrated the canopy of interlocking branches. The ground was uneven and furrowed. Troughs were filled with water, so in parts the island was like primordial swamp where things decayed, fell to the mud below and were transformed to the horrific beasts that local folklore suggested. I jumped as huge grey branches reached to me with tortuous limbs, and green backed amphibian logs opened their jaws. The others kept moving swiftly and I tried to concentrate to curb my fear.

Roderick seemed to know where he was going, definitely a prince on a quest. He strode ahead. I wanted to call, "Wait for me," but didn't care for a curt response. So, I moved more quickly, my trainers splashing through mud.

Finally, in a more open glade, they paused and I caught up, out of breath. We gathered at the base of a smooth trunked tree that threw twisted branches up to a sky we could not see.

"Where now?" asked Rosa.

Roderick unfolded a map. "There's a door. We need to look for some sort of building," he said, and folded the map back in his pocket. I wanted to view it to get my bearings but did not dare ask. I also wanted to know where the map had come from and what exactly we were looking for. Again, I knew I shouldn't ask.

We all took slightly different directions; I was pleased that Archie chose to follow me. He was only seven, and Ma had told me I must look after him if I was going out with the Libani children. I knew she didn't trust Archie's stepbrother and sisters. As I walked I noticed how thick with growth everything here was, very different from Broomstone forest at this time of year. Ivy as thick as some tree trunks wound its way around everything and across the ground. The space it spared was covered in moss and lichen making pavements of grey green. Then on the trees were plates of fungi in various shades of yellow, brown and black. When Archie bent to pick a tiny orange toadstool, I shouted, "No!" at him, so loudly, that for a moment I thought he might cry. My voice echoed; a wail of 'No, No, No,' ricocheting for several seconds. I wanted to halt it, as if it might rouse the island and stir its unseen creatures. We returned to the original spot and admitted we had found nothing.

"Let us have a look at the map," said Rosa.

Roderick shrugged, "If you must." He reluctantly handed the map over. They took several minutes whilst Roderick paced, occasionally sighing with impatience.

"Where did you get this from?" Rosa asked.

Roderick shrugged.

"You stole it, then," they chorused, "From Lorelei's bureau. The one we're not supposed to touch." They giggled as if that hadn't stopped them from looking in it.

Roderick shuffled his feet and looked down as he told them, "Actually, Lorelei caught me trying to get into the bureau. She told me if I wanted to find something I could take the map and look for the secret. The condition was that I had to invite Stinking Annie." He looked at me with unconcealed disgust. "I think it was her way of punishing me for snooping in her things."

The truth of his invitation, stuck like a bone in my gut. I wanted to scream but couldn't. I grit my teeth, determined not to cry.

"That's so ridiculous it's probably true," Rosa decided. "Anyway, I don't think it's a door we're looking for, I think it's horizontal, like a carved paving slab."

"Can I have a look?" I addressed Rosa. The girls sneered at

me and folded the map away.

Again, we spread out looking at ground level this time. Archie remained with me. I don't think he had any more clue as to what we were looking for than I did. Finally, I heard Rosa call. Archie and I found our way to them and discovered them in a different glade, looking down at a place on the ground. "What do you think this is?" they asked. I looked around me expecting Roderick to answer but he wasn't there, so I supposed they must be asking me. What they were pointing at was a circle of stone, about a metre across. It looked to be hewn out of rock, with three separate rings going down in steps. I bent and looked more closely. Archie copied me. "There's dead stuff in it," he said.

"I think it's ash," I told Rosa. A smoky odour rose, stinging my nostrils. It didn't look unlike the remains of our fire at home. I put my hand out and touched the silky flakes, bringing them to my nose. The ash was pungent, and horrible, nothing like the herbs we found in the wood and used for cooking. "Well, what is it Stinking Annie?" Rosa demanded.

"It is ash from a fire, but I don't know what's been burnt." My fingers tingled with the sensation I'd just touched the remains of a burnt creature.

"Look at this funny tree," Archie said, putting his hand on the branch of a gnarled hawthorn. The wood was so dark and his skin so pale, I thought foul sap might seep into him like an inky stain. I wanted to pull him away. The trunk was split into three, the branches crooked and lifeless. In places patches of grey-green lichen mottled the bark like scabs. I was reminded of an illustration I'd seen somewhere but didn't have time to consider where exactly or reply to Archie, because at that moment Roderick burst into the glade.

"What's going on? What have you found?"

"A pit for a fire," I replied.

"That's not what we're looking for. We're trying to find the slab."

The rest of us took that as the instruction to move on. I stepped away from the pathway to search. Brambles scratched and nettles stung my ankles as I scrambled around the undergrowth. I hadn't got very far, when Archie stamped his feet and said, "Here."

He was standing on an oblong of thick, yellowed stone, covered and almost hidden with ivy. "Shout for the others," I told him. His young voice carried through the trees. Whilst he called, I took the opportunity to start investigating, knowing the others would take over as soon as they arrived. I peeled the bristled fingers of ivy away from the concealed stone.

As I cleared it, I identified it as a gravestone slab, like those in the churchyard. I was beginning to reveal the cuts of an inscription on it when Roderick charged in and knelt down beside me, "Oi, let me," he demanded, elbowing me aside. I sat back on my heels, wondering whether the others thought it looked like a burial stone, but perhaps that's what they had been looking for. As Roderick peeled more of the vegetation away the letters appeared more clearly, 'L' and 'e' and 'r'.

"Does it say, Lorelei?" I asked, confused.

Roderick turned and glared at me, "No, don't be stupid." He swept his arm, pushing me back, trying to restrict my view.

"Does it say, 'Here lies …' I continued, thinking about the words used to mark gravestones in the churchyard.

"It says 'Laurel …' but I can't make out more." With that he got up and stepped away. "Come on, we've got to get back."

"What about the treasure?" asked Archie.

"What treasure? There is no treasure. This is just one of Lorelei's games. And I've found what I was looking for." When I was reluctant to move, Roderick grabbed the back of my T-shirt and said, "Come on Stinking Annie. Do you want to be left here?" That threat made me clamber up and follow behind the others. I definitely didn't want to be left here, but I did want to investigate further. Examine the engraving; check what the words really said. Roderick was never going to share the truth with me.

....

I get ready for bed and climb in knowing I will have difficulty sleeping. It's always the same when I sleep in a different place. I toss and turn and think of the story about the princess and the pea. Daddy used to tell me I was really a princess. I must have drifted off eventually, because I dream that I am back on the island getting caught up in a tangle of bramble, the barbs scratching my arms, leaving a trail of bloody dots. I come to a stone set into the floor, creepers and moss concealing it. Pulling at the iron ring, it creaks open. Steps lead me downwards, the air smelling of earth and decay. I am going to run away but then hear laughter. Looking further into a cavern I see Lorelei talking to a man. He has his back to me but as I approach he turns. 'Daddy?' They both start to laugh at me. I turn … run … waking up to the sound of rain smashing against the window glass above me and streaks of lightening making the furnishings leap and dance.

My arm hurts and I switch on the lamp and see that I have scratched myself, causing deep indentations on my skin. They're bleeding. I'm disturbed by the echo of my dream, disturbed at what I had appeared to have seen, as if my subconscious believes that my father could still be alive. It is ridiculous but up here in the dark attic room, with the crash of thunder and flashes of lightening, I feel removed from everything. I can't shake the sensation that there are things in this place, in the house and the village which are somehow not right. I slumber briefly and then am woken by rapping on the door. I sit upright wiping the grit from my eyes. "Who's there?" I whisper. The tapping continues. "Who's there?" I climb out of bed and tiptoe across to the door. I'm not sure if the sound is coming from outside the door. It might be above me or the noise of the storm. I hear somebody whispering, "It's me, it's me …" Taking a deep breath I pull the door open. Nothing. Just dense blackness, getting darker and darker towards the end of the corridor. But then there is a noise as if something is moving in the air. My skin prickles, as a breath moves over me. A final lightning strike illuminates the corridor. There's a shimmer stirring amidst the shadows and a cloud of dusty moths lifts from the walls.

I'm still asleep … I must be asleep. Purple blotches from the intensity of the lightening swim before my eyes. I put a hand to my head. Either I'm asleep or a migraine is beginning. But it doesn't feel like that. I close the door and then check the window to see that wind isn't hissing between panes and frames; but though the rain continues, everything is secure. I close the blinds, shutting out the retreating storm and get back into bed. I leave the lamp on. The unsettling sensation is familiar. I recall waking to the sound of knocking on the cottage door years before, a whisper of, "It's me,"wondering whether I'd been dreaming. Lying in my childhood bed with noises knocking and words permeating the air. Similar but separate from the trees tapping together around the house.

CHAPTER 21

After breakfast Archie says he'll take me down to the basement where he has stored his mother's keepsakes. "I've set up a little study space."

From the reception area we follow a flight of stairs down to another door which is propped open. The basement looks dark. There is a dank heavy smell as if no air circulates. After we've gone through the basement door the corridor widens and I glimpse a display cabinet filled with stuffed birds. I don't have a chance to examine it further as Archie is marching ahead, his lop-sided steps heavy on the stone floor. He switches on the main light. The space is large with brick pillars and nooks and crannies so the central brightness is absorbed and there are shadows and corners which remain a dense black.

Archie moves swiftly across the space, his limp not appearing to hamper him. He stops at a white washed rectangle which has been constructed as a make-shift room. He flicks another switch and an angle poise lamp illuminates the area. There is a desk with a wooden crate sitting on top.

"Well, this is it," Archie says, indicating the desk and then picking up a pile of papers. "You can work here can't you?"

How can I say 'No', when Archie has sorted all this out, and is paying me? It's the last place I want to be. At least this bit of the basement is brighter and still smells of paint.

I pull the top document out of the box, intrigued by a page of inky doodles. They look like pentagrams with words beneath that could be charms. "What do you think this is?" I ask Archie.

He shrugs. "Could be that Mum's a witch," he says. I stop and stare at him. "Oh, Annie," he says, "If only you could see your face. I'm joking … It's a joke." It is not until he slaps me on the shoulder that I'm jolted into motion and replace the sheet of paper.

"Look, I'll leave you to it. I'll get Poppy to bring you down a coffee."

"Okay, thanks," I respond, relieved that I won't be left on my own for too long.

I flick through a few more items in the crate. A thin sepia tinted page which looks as if it has been ripped from an encyclopaedia is the next one I pick up. It carries an odour of dust and decay. There is a photo of an etching and underneath words describing a summoning circle. Stone rings in the ground all with measurements of three and standing behind it what is termed a trifurcate tree. Bile rises in my throat and I stand up suddenly, the chair scraping on the stone floor. I need to check something. I pace to the furthest wall of the basement, my bones aching with dread as I see a copy of the tree on the page replicated as a mural. A trifurcate tree with two faces watching me through the inky lines. The image in front of me is a reproduction of the tree on the island. I recall the three ringed pit below with its burnt offerings and glance at the page; 'Summoning Circle.' Its description, '… a focus or channel for summoning a fiend or other dark entities …' My fingers again recollect the silk slick of ash from long ago, as if I am still branded with malevolent things.

I return to the desk. The paper is gripped in my fingers but trembles as if there is a draught. Then I notice it is my hands that shake. I'm unable to think about Lorelei or her life, unable to get started on the task I've been employed to do. I feel claustrophobic at being hidden down here, the paint fumes and dankness oppressive. All I can think about was the last time I'd been here. When I hadn't been invited.

CHAPTER 22

I had been to the Hall before. Before Lorelei and the Libani family had moved in. A time when it had been boarded up and silent. I never knew the people who owned it previously. It had just been a large decaying monstrosity. One with a rusting sign warning, 'Trespassers will be prosecuted.'

One evening, I'd followed Daddy and watched as he'd climbed over the wall. He was agile and had used the rope-like ivy stems to clamber over. I tried to follow him, but my hands kept slipping and I hadn't the strength to pull myself up far enough. After falling back for the third time, with grazed knees and a twisted ankle I knew I'd have to leave it. But I also knew I needed to get in and have a look. After all, why was my father climbing over the wall to get into a crumbling building?

As I'd already found throughout my life, if you think hard enough about something, it sometimes has a way of turning up.

At school the next day, I was loitering in the corner, alone as usual, when somebody crept up and hissed at me, "Hey!" At first I assumed they were not talking to me but the voice came again, "Hey, you, Garlic breath," so I knew she was trying to attract my attention. "Want to know a secret?" I didn't really, but it was a novelty to be included, even if it was by another outcast. Deidre Alderman. She was the second least popular girl in the school.

"Okay, what?"

"What you gonna trade?"

I shrugged. I had nothing. No secrets and no possessions

anybody would covet.

"Okay, well I'll tell you anyway." I guessed Deidre didn't have anybody else to share her secret with, and so I would have to do, trade or no trade. "And I'll come to your house for tea as payment." She said it as if it were a done deal. Before I'd had a chance to tell her I'd need to ask Ma, Deidre had spit on her palm and grabbed mine. I felt the sticky spittle slime between our palms, making the pact. I hoped whatever the secret was that it was worth it.

"Well, what is it then? What's the big secret?" I asked, wiping my hand on my skirt, not looking at Deidre.

Though nobody was anywhere near us, she whispered, "I know a way into the Hall." That got my attention, but I tried not to look excited and shrugged instead. "Don't you want to get in then?"

I wanted to say, 'No,' that I had better things to do, but I was intrigued. I did want to go into Quercus Hall. I think Deidre had sensed it on me like an animal tell. In the back of my head a little voice was crying a warning. *There'll be a price to pay. Nothing ever comes for free.* Even with the shrieking voice I found myself nodding, "Okay."

"We're gonna break in. You're gonna come with me right?" Again, the voice warned me. Deidre was regarding me as if I might refuse, at which point she'd not only call me stinking but scared as well. "Promise? Cross your heart and hope to die."

She did the relevant arm actions and I mirrored the movements. "Okay, I promise."

I could sense her squirming beside me, twisting her greasy hair between her fingers; her feet stepping from side to side in a little dance. "We'll go tomorrow after school then, meet you by the elephant tree. And I'll come home for tea at yours tonight."

She'd skipped off before I could say Ma might not like me just turning up with somebody, but the moment had gone.

In the event Ma seemed pleased that I had invited a friend

home. "We're just having eggs but you're welcome to stay," she said.

"Oh, you have a piano," Deidre noticed, and plinked a few notes. I pushed her away and sat on the stool and played a tune called, 'Greensleeves,' a piece that Ma had just taught me. The melancholy notes throbbed through the room, as I mouthed the words, *'Alas, my love you do me wrong ...'*

"Time for tea", called Ma, before I'd had a chance to finish the song.

Whilst we ate our omelettes, Ma and Deidre had a little chat about school and the day, making me wonder where the nasty Deidre had gone. She even asked about the wood mushrooms and herbs Ma had put in the meal. "Delicious, Mrs Ramson. Thank you."

The Deidre I was acquainted with re-emerged a little later when we were up in my room. She was annoying me by taking things off my shelf and looking at them. I'd said nothing even when she'd picked up my book of fairy tales. In fact, she'd treated it with respect saying, "Wow, this is old. It looks interesting."

I made no comment, knowing that if I said how wonderful it was and how special then Deidre would have suddenly wanted to borrow it and would not have taken 'No' for an answer. However, she replaced the book carefully back on the shelf and came to sit beside me on the bed. "You know the story they should have put in that book ..."

"No." I shook my head.

Deidre looked about her. Suddenly, she got up and went to the window, looking out as though she was searching for spies; "... the story about the witch and the curse on this house."

"What? Ma says that's just stupid gossip."

Deidre had turned back to face me, she was blocking the window, so grey light strobed across her face, making her insubstantial.

"No, it's definitely true. That's why they couldn't put it in a book of fairy tales."

She looked out at the wood again, fiddling with the curtain hanging at the side of the frame. I watched her fingers spider up the edge and knew she would tell me. Part of me hoped she knew the truth. The proper story about the house I lived in rather than the saccharine version my mother would repeat whenever I mentioned somebody had made a remark. I knew Ma had lived here as a child, and I knew the story had something to do with her and her family, but nobody would be completely honest with me.

"Once upon a time …" Deidre began. A little flutter, like breath blown across my neck made me gasp. Deidre heard it and swung back to observe my reaction. She repeated in a deeper, dramatic voice, as though she was stepping on a stage to perform, "Once upon a time … there was an old cottage in the forest. A family lived in the cottage. A mother and a father with their two daughters … Holly and Ivy …"

I frowned because I'd only once or twice heard Ma mention she had a sister, and even then I wasn't sure it was true. I was going to ask Deidre about it, but watching her, strutting up and down the room, I decided to keep quiet; I didn't think she'd be happy if I kept interrupting.

"… Though they didn't have a lot of money, they were a happy family. Now, in the forest lived a witch. She was a good witch, a white witch who helped people by making medicines and spells. She often visited the cottage and the two girls would help her look for herbs and the special plants of the forest which could make her potions. Everything was alright until a wicked west wind blew up from the valley."

Deidre paused again, and made a dramatic "Whoosh …" Her fetid breath reached my face and I winced, she didn't appear to notice and continued, "… and all the family fell ill. The good witch brewed teas and potions but none of them could cure the family. Finally, she was so desperate that she went to her sister, Laurel, to ask for her help. Now Laurel was a brilliant witch but she was also a bad witch who delved in black magic ..."

Deidre came over to the bed and sat on the end looking at me. Her eyes had widened and she carried on in a softer, whispering voice that chilled me as she continued.

"... Yes, very, very dark magic indeed. She came to the house and said she could make a cure, but for a price. *'Anything, we'll give you anything,'* the parents said, they were weak and feverish, *'Anything, please save us.'* Laurel answered, *'Are you sure? You'll pay my price?'*

'Yes. Yes. Just make our family well again.' The parents were so overcome with fever, they didn't have any idea what the wicked witch might demand. They took the horrible medicine the witch gave them and listened as she chanted her dark charm around the cottage and the glade. The next morning Laurel had gone, but when the mother awoke her head felt light and her temperature had gone down. She looked at her husband who was just waking but he had colour back in his cheeks. The mother raced upstairs to find her daughters sitting up in their beds and stretching, looking healthy. She went over and hugged each of them. Later they all had breakfast in the kitchen below, eggs and bread and homemade jam. They chatted and smiled. Suddenly there was a loud knocking on the door, *rap, rap, rap ...* which made them all jump." Deidre had knocked the wooden bedstead as she spoke, and gave a little smile of satisfaction as I jumped too. "The mother went to the door and standing in the doorway was Laurel. *'I've come for my payment,'* Laurel said.

'Of course, of course. Thank you so much. We were just having breakfast. Can I fetch you something?' 'No, I'll just take my payment and then I'll be gone.' 'So, what do we owe you? We haven't much, but whatever it is we'll give you gladly.' 'I want one of your daughters. The youngest I think would do,' Laurel said. *'You mean to help you?' 'No, I mean to take from here and bring up as my own. I have no children.' 'But you can't take one of our children. Holly is only three, she needs her mother.' 'You said you would give me anything. That is my fee'.* There was a

lot of arguing and then pleading and then crying, but Laurel would not change her mind. Finally, the parents grabbed their children and shouted, *'No! No! You're not having them.'* *'Alright if that's how you want it to be,'* Laurel said, *'Your debt will never be fully paid. Curses on this house. Curses on you all. This family and this place will carry sorrow forever!'* She swept her arm around the room as if scattering seeds over the ground. But then she left. *'Thank goodness, for that,'* the parents sighed, and they all sat down to finish their meal, though there was no more chatter."

Deidre grinned again; delighted I was such an attentive audience. My breath held, my mouth agape. A dribble of salvia on my tongue.

"Several weeks passed and the family grew stronger. In fact, they almost forgot about having been so ill and Laurel's visit to the cottage. But one day the good witch visited them and warned them to be careful, *'My sister is not very happy with you. I think she may try something. You must take care.'* However, when it came there was no warning. One morning Ivy woke up and looked over to her sister's bed expecting to see Holly's pretty face. Instead, there was nothing but a prickly wreath of holly on the counterpane. There was nothing the family could do. They pleaded for the good witch to intervene, but she said her powers could not overcome Laurel's dark magic and nothing could make Laurel return the child. *'What will she do with her?'* the mother asked. *'She will bring her up with the knowledge of magic. It might not be as bad as you think. I'm sure Laurel will look after the child.'*

It was of no comfort to the parents; and Ivy, the sister was distraught and wondered if she should have gone in Holly's place, being five years older. But Holly had vanished. All they could do was plant the holly sprig from the wreath in the ground. They planted it just beyond the church wall."

Suddenly Deidre jumped up, clapping her hands. "What do you think? What do you think?" she said.

I remained seated, stunned by what Deidre had recounted.

The story filtered through me like trickles of sand, making me uncomfortable. I didn't want Deidre to know that, so just said, "Well yeah … but it's only a story." The beginning of a headache was gripping me; I could feel a tight band tugging against my forehead. My vision was swimming and my palms clammy.

"Think what you like," she retorted, "I know it's true." She grabbed her coat and started for the stairs. "I'm going home now." I was pleased to see her go; I needed time to think. Perhaps ask Ma if the story was true. But an idea beamed through the fug and muddle in my head, "I'll walk with you," I said.

Dusk was falling and the air was cool as we took the track back to the village. We did not speak until we reached the green and I turned to leave her. Deidre walked away, her parting words, "Meet me after school tomorrow. By the elephant tree." It wasn't a request but an order.

I continued up towards the church, my brain seeming to lurch from side to side with each step. The sky was nearly black but the gleam from a streetlamp flickered orange light over the churchyard. I followed the path through to the far side and went through the kissing gate. Yes, it was there. A holly tree. In the dusk the shine of leaves caught the light, making the sharp points gleam like needles suspended in the still air. I placed my hand on the bark. There was a scar on the tree trunk which was again the stuff of local folklore. It sometimes bled, a sappy rust coloured liquid. The blood of a tree. Under my fingers I could feel the gash and the ridged edges on the otherwise smooth surface. I started. From deeper in the wood I heard a cough. I looked around me, a chill brushing my shoulders, sensing something was watching me. I waited and listened but now it was more a crackling sound. It was probably just a forest creature, but with the remnants of Deidre's story in my head, it made me anxious and I sprinted back home.

"What's up with you?" Ma asked when I hurried in. "What's

spooked you?"

"Is it true? Did you have a sister called Holly who was taken by a witch? Is she in the churchyard?"

"Hang on a minute," Ma said, turning towards the sink, running the tap. She put a glass of water in front of me. "Are you having one of your turns?" Ma placed a hand on my forehead. "You need to rest. Has that girl Deidre been filling your head with silly stories?"

"They're not silly though. The holly tree with the blood is growing just outside the churchyard."

Ma scraped back a chair and sat down opposite me. "Look people make up things to explain stuff. Yes, I did have a sister called Holly, and she died of a fever when she was three. My parents planted a holly tree just outside the churchyard as a memorial."

"But what about the witches, the good one and the bad one?"

The door clicked and Daddy came in. "Who's talking about witches?" He came up behind me and tickled me. "Scary, scary, ooh …"

I couldn't help but giggle.

"Time for bed," Ma said, "Up you go. I'll bring you your medicine and some hot milk."

I climbed the stairs to my room, only then realising Ma hadn't answered my question about the witch sisters. I was going to go down again but as I turned back I heard Ma and Daddy were talking quietly below.

"What was that all about?" Daddy said.

"Deidre Alderman came over for tea and was telling her the story of Holly and Laurel. Annie's been to the churchyard and found the holly tree. You know, the one planted after she'd gone?"

That interested me, Holly had simply gone, rather than died of a fever.

"I don't know, this village just loves to stir things up."

"I didn't know how much to tell Annie. Should I have told

her how Holly was taken and about the curse on the house; or would that just scare her?"

"Of course, it would scare her, and unnecessarily." A shudder resonated through the house as I heard the thump of Daddy's fist on the table. "It's you who thinks this place is cursed … which is plain stupid. Whatever went on in this house, we decided to forget it. Nothing bad has happened to you. You and this house are not cursed."

"I can't believe that, I worry about it, that something bad is going to happen, just around the next corner."

I was huddled against the post at the top of the stairs, clinging on to stop my shaking. Trying not to shout out at what I was hearing. Holly had been taken by a bad witch called Laurel. There had been a curse!

I jumped as Daddy slapped his hand on the table again. "You have to stop this. All you'll end up doing is making sure the prophecy is fulfilled. Now make Annie her milk and then fetch me my tea." My head shook with the vibration, making me dizzier. The jangle as Ma moved crockery and plates made me feel sick. I hurried to my room and by the time Ma had brought my milk up, I was in bed; my blanket tightly pulled around my shoulders.

Even with the soothing drink inside me I could not settle to sleep. Every time I closed my eyes I thought of Holly and Ivy lying in their beds and then waking up and only Ma being in the room. The space echoed with loss, the trees outside murmuring, 'she's gone, yes, she's gone.' The hushed refrain did not make sleep come any easier.

I had to drag myself to school the following morning, tiredness and a residual headache weighing on me throughout the day. I was not looking forward to my excursion with Deidre. But knew she would hound me if I didn't turn up. So, after school I made my way to the green and waited for Deidre to join me. It was a cold damp day in early March. The buds were not yet showing on the beech tree. The span of black branches was skeletal against the grey cloud cover. Deidre was late and I was considering just going home. It had been a trick after all. But then there she was, walking towards me with a jaunty sort of step, looking about her as if she was playing to the crowd. This was definitely an elaborate joke; I just didn't know what the punchline was going to be.

We didn't greet each other. Deidre shrugged a, 'come on then' motion and I followed her down towards the Hall. I could never work the house out or just what it was that gripped you as soon as you walked through the village to the point of the path where its odd roof came into view. "Come on," said Deidre, as I dawdled. "Not scared are you?" She said this with the sound of glee in her voice as if she wanted me to be freaked out. "I'm not scared," she boasted.

She walked ahead of me past the FOR SALE sign that indicated 'Mountain and De Witt Country Prestige Properties' were still trying to sell it. I felt a sense of relief as I realised the metal bars of the gates were locked with a twisted cord of chains wrapped round the centre. Deidre took no notice and pushed against the central bars. The chain shook and creaked, stretching the gates a foot apart. She bent down and wriggled through. I had no choice but to follow. Once within the gates Deidre appeared more uncertain and crept alongside the wall close to the stone so that tendrils of ivy kept brushing my hair and face when she flicked the vegetation aside. As dusk approached the clouds became heavier and the air cooled. I thought it might rain. The house kept watch as we progressed around the perimeter wall, its windows, unblinking eyes.

Suddenly, Deidre broke cover and said in a loud whisper, "Come on." She crossed a yard at the back of the Hall. Here there were steps; made of stone and greasy with algae. Again, in a theatrical whisper she said, "Down here." I couldn't see how we'd get through the door in front of us, but I hadn't noticed the small broken window to the side. "You can get through there," she told me. "You go first." My reaction was to recoil but Deidre grasped my shoulder and looked at me with a hard stare; dissent was not an option. I stood on the window ledge, the stone felt as if it was crumbling under my plimsolls. But I managed to haul myself up to the gap and thread my way through the broken pane. There was still some glass on the edges which scratched my thigh as I pushed inside. That wasn't the worst thing though. It was the complete darkness pooling below which made me gasp with terror. A shove on my bottom and hysterical laughter followed as I fell through the window. I didn't hear Deidre's final words to me, just her laughter and her feet running away. As I landed in a heap on the floor I knew she had gone.

I sat in the pitch black, my heart racing, hardly able to breathe, as the last of her laughter faded. I was filled with hatred. I screamed, not out of fear but venting my rage. Why did people continue to torment me, when I tried to keep clear of them? The scream filled every corner of the dark basement, and I imagined it seeping upwards in to the house above, because the building shivered at the disturbance. I vowed in that moment I would get my own back. I didn't know how, but I would.

Without my body blocking the window a smudge of late afternoon light gave enough illumination to look around. The space was large and dark and so black in the distance, I was unable to gauge how far it might extend. I supposed it was the basement of the Hall though I had no knowledge of the layout. The initial panic had set my heart racing, but now, as I sat and looked around, my breath slowed and I became calmer. I'd wanted to visit the house and now I was here. I thought of Daddy sneaking into Quercus Hall ... had he been in the basement? Maybe coming in through the side door ... or was he visiting some other place in the house or the grounds?

I clambered up, rubbing my scratched thigh, blood making my fingers sticky. The bleeding didn't seem too bad. The door just to the right of the window which led to the outside steps was locked and there was no key. I looked for a light switch; after all, even my shack in the woods had electricity. I wasn't disappointed. A switch near the door clicked on and a single bulb, hummed like a wasp trapped in a jar, giving a flicker of light. The sound broke what had been complete silence, dense and thick. With the glow of light, I could make out shapes squatting in the space. Objects draped with sheeting. Everything was dusty and I coughed, the sound echoing deep into the dark corners, reverberating back at me, transformed into cackles. I shuffled around peeking under dust sheets. Furniture in heavy black wood lurked beneath. There was a grandfather clock without hands. On the floor were marks that I presumed had been made by moving furniture around; they conformed into a pattern of some kind. I couldn't decipher it and didn't want to spend time investigating. Was that why Daddy had been here? Did he actually come into this dark space beneath the Hall or simply climb the wall to access the grounds? He definitely wouldn't fit through the window I'd been pushed through, so perhaps he had a key or somebody let him in. The cut on my thigh throbbed and I brushed my hand against it, feeling it sting; annoyed I'd been lured here and I wasn't going to find the reason Daddy had come here after all.

I gasped and jumped as I saw a giant spider, motionless in a network of cobweb. But on moving closer I could see it was only a dead plant spilling out of a pot. My eyes had now adjusted to the gloom and I walked further into the far shadows and discovered a door, I rattled the handle, but it did not give. I continued along the wall placing my palms against the brick. Beneath my skin I could feel flakes of paint shedding; rough, like bark below my hands. Under the glow from the bulb, a black design on the white-washed walls was revealed. The outline of a tree. The flicker of light made the marks appear to sway. Three thick trunks reached upwards, dividing into branches like clawing hands. I stared at the mural, and squinted. Within the lines, I could make out faces captured in two of the limbs. Though both faces were aged, lined and wrinkled with the contours of the strokes; one appeared to have a pursed mouth and disapproval in the dark knot of an eye, the other almost smiled and was softened by a kindlier expression. But both winked and watched me, making me shiver. In my fairy tale book were stories of creatures who lived within tree trunks, called Dryads; but they were beautiful maidens not old crones. The darkness behind me shifted, enclosing me as the light flickered and dimmed. I stepped beyond the mural and blindly continued my circuit feeling the gaze from the faces on me as I moved.

I came to a second door. This was locked as well. Beside it a large object lurked, making me step away from the wall. A huge wardrobe. It didn't have a drape over it. I was reminded of a book I had read about a magical land reached through a portal at the back of a wardrobe just like this. The door creaked as I opened it, like something tearing. Inside was a velvet of blackness. It was so dark it had the density of void. I put my hand in and jumped. My skin touched something. Fabric. Brushing my hand along, I felt the edges of garments; the space filled with them. They smelt of smoke and wax. I wasn't as brave as I had first imagined so didn't venture inside, instead I pulled one out. I could see it was a cloak as it tumbled down at my feet. The outside of the cloak was black and the inner lining was a shimmer of grey satin. I picked it up and draped it round my shoulders. The garment swamped me and I put the hood over my head, feeling the smooth coolness of satin against my cheeks. This was a cloak just like the ones worn by witches and wizards in my book, so I took a step and flicked my wrist pretending I held a wand. "Death to my enemies," I said, "Death to Deidre Alderman!" It sounded so good; I repeated it several times.

I tired of my game and took off the cloak, folding it up and putting it in the base of the wardrobe and closed the door. Why was there a cupboard full of black cloaks here? Who were they for? And was that why Daddy came here; to meet others and put a cloak on as well? I shuddered, not liking that thought at all.

I needed to find a way out. I put my hand out again and felt my way to the next wall and another door. This stood ajar, propped with a metal door stop in the shape of a tree trunk. I pushed it open further and through into a small area of corridor, relieved to come across a flight of steps. I climbed them and discovered the door at the top was unlocked. I let out a deep breath, relieved I wouldn't have to clamber out through the basement window. Even in my plimsolls, my footsteps echoed in the hall and I was aware of how much empty space surrounded me. In the main house the sense of being watched was even more acute and I hurried through to a back room. I found a window that could be opened and scrambled out into the March evening.

When I got to the glade it was quiet, I breathed a sigh of relief, no arguments tonight, but at the front door step was something which made me halt. Under the glow from the lamp were circular splashes of liquid. The light made them gleam like black shiny discs. Bending down, I put my finger on one; it was sticky, unmistakeable. Blood. My fingers were tipped with red, smearing the door as I pushed inside. My thoughts a whirl of, 'It's happened!' The terrible thing which Ma had foretold; *'One day he'll kill me …'* I pushed through the doorway. "Ma … Ma …" I cried out.

She was kneeling on the floor looking at me. Beside her, seated on a kitchen chair, was Woody with his arm outstretched and a tea towel wrapped around it. The white fabric was stained red. Ma's head leaned in close to Woody. The scene looked so intimate I hesitated, not wanting to intrude. As I went in Ma turned, her expression changing from a gentle one, to a frown as she glared at me.

"What's the matter Annie?" Ma asked, "You look like you've seen a ghost."

"I thought … I thought …" I began and couldn't finish.

"Woody cut himself."

The idea of Woody having an accident, when he was so skilled at wood work, confused me. Still, Ma was so absorbed in her task of nursing Woody that she didn't comment on my torn skirt or grubby, bloodied knees.

CHAPTER 23

I put the crate on the floor and take another document out. Archie said he'd put them in some sort of order but I guess he'd spoken as somebody who doesn't have a clue about archiving.

The pamphlet in my hand is a gig programme. In scrolled font the heading announces, 'Dryad Tour: 1978'. An image reproduced from a portrait of Lorelei adorns the cover. The painting which it replicates has caught the mood of the album perfectly. Lorelei is naked, her body moulding into the trunk of a tree. Flicking through the booklet; there are photographs of Lorelei and quotes from the songs. I recognise them all; can see them scrawled across pages of a sketch pad, words written by my mother.

'... *moving like the wind through trees, unseen but bringing truth in touch,*'
'... *like a rainbow, and coloured space between the bands, you hold them in your hands,*'
'... *black and white, colours of your heart, shadows and darkness pulling me apart.*'

I stop and look at the space around me, noticing how even in the still air the shadows move and transform from grey to charcoal and black. In my memory I can hear my mother singing and then the stronger harmony of Lorelei's voice eclipsing it.

There are several sheets of papers with lyrics in Ma's handwriting, her notes annotating the paper quite clearly.

Even if Archie had taken a brief look he must have realised that a lot of Lorelei's early songs on the Dryad album were my mother's, unless he really didn't recognise that the writing wasn't Lorelei's. I shake my head. No, he couldn't be that blind to her plagiarism.

I take another object out. This one is a greetings card, it looks homemade. It resembles the one which I'd crafted for Roderick many years ago. I wonder whether it is something that Archie might have made for his mother, but it is not at all childish. It is a Valentine's card; large and pink with tiny paper roses stuck over the front. It creaks as I open it. *'Lorelei my love'* it says, *'Forever yours'*. There is no name or initial.

The silence in the basement is broken by footsteps approaching. I hold my breath and wait.

"Hi there," Poppy says, "I've brought you coffee and I thought you'd like cake as well." She places the tray on the table beside the crate of documents.

"Are you alright down here?"

I nod. At least it's quiet. "Yes, I'm fine. Thanks for the coffee."

Poppy twists her fingers together as if she wants to say something else or is waiting for me to speak. "The cake looks lovely," I manage.

She turns to go, her footsteps clipping across the floor, but at the doorway she pauses and turns back to face me. "It's probably not my place to say," she starts, pacing towards me again. "But you know what Archie really needs to know?"

I shake my head; feel my forehead crease as I try to work out the answer to the question she's posed. "He's asked me to write Lorelei's biography. That's what I intend to do."

Poppy avoids my puzzled look, fiddling with her collar and looking down at the floor. Finally, she gives a little cough and says, "His father ... he wants to know who his father is." She doesn't wait for my response and turns away. The sound of her steps now rings with the rhythm of a bell, similar to the note of realisation resonating in my head. Of course, that's what Archie wants to know. That's what every human needs to know … has a right to know. Perhaps that is what his whole request is about. I take another piece of paper out of the box, not seeing the words. It may be harder to discover who Archie's father is, even more difficult than unravelling Lorelei's story.

I finish my tea and cake but can't settle. The knowledge of needing to find Archie's father presses on my temples, rousing a headache. Deciding I need a break, I walk the length of the basement, my footsteps echoing behind me. The key is rusting in the back door but turns to allow me passage and I climb the steps quickly.

The air feels fresher outside. But the mouldy odour of the basement clings to me. My hair and my clothes are embedded with it. Even a hot shower and scrubbing might not be enough to cleanse it. But maybe that is just the past, like a cobweb, sticky, catching remnants to it.

I get to the gates of the Hall but still feel trapped so continue down the hill to the brook at the other end of the village. The water is wide but shallow. After crossing the bridge, I find myself stopping by the Broomstone village sign. Here I sense an invisible hand preventing me from progressing further. I go back to the centre of the bridge and look down at the shallow water. It folds in light and shadow ribbons, rippling over brown and grey pebbles. Bright green tails of weed wave like the hair of magical river creatures. Further downstream, after passing behind the village, the brook meanders between fields. I imagine it winding on. Some way away, beneath weeping willows I had found Lorelei all those years before. Today with the sun shining on the water, it looks too benign to try and take a life. But this river has claimed others. Just around the bend there is a deep pool, where my father is supposed to have drowned. The bank there is steeper and edged with spiking reed beds, making it difficult to climb from if you fell in.

The memories make me feel sick as I look at the water flow

over the pebble bed, bubbling away and indifferent to what has gone before. I push myself away from the wall and take a pathway by the opposite bank which heads upwards from the brook, alongside a field and a hedge of hawthorn. I know it will eventually bring me to the back of the church.

I think back to how things changed when Lorelei moved away. Before she arrived I had always been on my own, content in my little world, not knowing any different, but once she and Archie left, part of my world went with them. I was lonely. After hiding away in the caravan, a new phase followed. I would wander aimlessly around the farm buildings as if I was looking for something but didn't know what; I'd climb up to the hayloft but quickly become bored and clamber down again. I'd walk to the river, crossing the forbidden field and stand at the water's edge hoping to see another egg shape underneath the willows. It was a good thing that we moved because at least there were new places to discover in Broomstone forest.

And I had my own room. I owned very little but what I had could now be put on a shelf. The fairy tale book. Rapunzel and Cat sat on the bed, though it was odd without Ted. Now when I looked out of the window there were trees rather than fields stretching on and on to the horizon. If I undid the rusty hinge of the window and opened it, instead of dusty farm air blowing in, a breeze laden with sappy residue would wind itself around the space, like a cat weaving itself round my legs. And the Cyclops tree observed me always. It wasn't unfriendly, with its lidless eye-ball, but just curious about somebody living in the house once again. Somebody on the same level, greeting it in the morning, when I pulled the gingham curtains open.

Daddy found a job in a garden centre and grumbled because of the distance he had to walk to get there. He'd set off before I got up for school but on a Sunday he'd be at home and Ma would cook us all breakfast. Woody would often join us and then sit in the glade working. Occasionally, they'd play music in the evenings. Mum playing the piano that stood at the edge of the room, Daddy on guitar and Woody with his drums. These were late night events though when wine had been consumed. I would already have been sent to bed, but would creep out and eavesdrop at the top of the stairs, as notes and herbal cigarette smoke floated upwards. I'd finally slip into bed soothed into dreaming that maybe things would be alright.

The only thing that was troublesome were the headaches. They could arrive at any time, blurring my vision and making me sick.

That first winter I would still drag my way to school behind Ma, shivering in a too thin coat, usually in wellies which would chaff my shins. I'd change them when I got to the school gates. I was already bedraggled by the time I arrived; freakish amidst the gaggle of sleek girls of my peer group. During the day I would listen to the drone of Miss Rowan. And do my work as best I could. At break and lunch, I would find a place in the corner of the playground and make up a song or story with myself as the heroine, hoping that if I immersed myself in my imagination then I wouldn't be seen and bothered by the other children. Usually, it worked and I would be ignored.

Ma would be there to meet me at the end of the day, standing away from the other parents and we would walk home alone.

That was the weekdays, but at the weekend I felt the release of freedom and took my imagination into the forest. There were banks where roots twisted like the legs of goblins and I imagined them coming to life in the dusk. The beech trees always had pools between their roots where fairies held their banquets. If I heard voices I would hide and watch kids cavorting in the glades. Often they'd bring cans and music and unsettle the trees and the magical creatures. Sometimes it was dog walkers who disturbed my play. And occasionally I'd meet people who were in the wood for no reason, so I didn't know if they were real people at all.

One day I saw a magpie cawing in a tree. "Good afternoon, Mr Magpie," I said, just as Ma had taught me, to protect me from the magpie's curse of 'one for sorrow.'

There was a cackle behind me and I turned to see Miss Dryden laughing at me. "Silly sapling, you can't dodge a curse with simple niceties, you have to do more than that."

"What do I have to do then?" I asked, expecting the answer to be turning in a circle three times, or clapping or singing. But Miss Dryden continued to laugh. Then she turned away and moved into the shadow of a tree and I couldn't see her even though I tried to follow her. The magpie had watched the little scene and as I moved back onto the path, it dived at me in a flash of black and white feathers. With a last chuckle it flew away. I recollected the sensation of it cutting the air and the breeze against my face, the sense of dread it left. Because when I returned to the house something terrible was happening. I had missed my father coming back from the pub. As I reached the cottage glade, shouting and screaming were emanating from within the house. I hesitated. I opened the door to see my father with his hand around Ma's throat. "Cow! Stupid cow!" he was yelling. For a moment I wondered if it was my Daddy. His face was so disfigured and red, he looked like a monster. When he saw me he let his hand drop and pushed his way out past me, into the wood. I ran to Ma who had slumped to the floor and hugged her. I put my arms around her and said, "Ma, Ma," cuddling into her. She managed to croak "Water," so I got up and filled a glass for her. "One day he'll kill me," she repeated over and over. We sat together on the floor propped up by the Welsh dresser until the afternoon faded into night.

One other occasion still makes me shiver when I think of it; the time after the debacle with Deidre. I was still trying to work out how I could get my revenge. I had picked up a stick and was beating it on the ground saying, "I hate you; I hate you," cursing Deidre who had been so mean to me and imagining it was her being beaten and not the forest floor. The frustration of not knowing what to do made me sob. That's when Miss Dryden appeared.

"What are you doing?" I stopped my flailing and sniffed, wiping my face against my sleeve. The stench of wild garlic permeated the air.

"She ... she locked me in," I snivelled, "She ... she deliberately locked me in ..."

Miss Dryden's voice creaked at me, "Who is it you hate so much, any ways?"

"Deidre Alderman," I swallowed another sob. "She left me in Quercus Hall all alone."

"Did she now?"

"I hate her, I hate her," I said with defiance, and then continued with force, "And I want her to die!"

Miss Dryden didn't tell me off for saying terrible things, all she muttered was, "Be careful what you wish for."

I slunk off home, assuming I'd been chided.

....

I have arrived at the back of the churchyard. The gate is cloaked in ivy. This area of the cemetery is shadowed by the summer foliage so beneath it the graves are permanently in shade. The dimness and damp have encouraged moss and lichen to stain the stones, some names are impossible to read and others barely visible. One monument stands out though; a glistening monolith. In one hand a cherub holds a trumpet and the other points at me with an accusing finger. There's an inscription carved into the white granite, 'Our darling daughter. Taken too soon.' Below the name inscribed is, 'Deidre Alderman.' I shudder; I will always have Deidre's death on my conscience.

CHAPTER 24

I have rarely been into the church, but today I go inside. The interior is cool and quiet, bands of stained light twist through the windows, dappling the gravestones on the floor. The smell of lilies suffuses the air, mingling with the scent of wood and dust. I sit in a pew and close my eyes. My thoughts are prayer like. Settling on my guilt and exploring it.

How it actually came to pass I don't really know, or want to know. Looking at it through the perspective of time, there are certain parts I avoid. I may have modified the story completely.

One Monday morning, I went into school much as any day. Dragging my heels, wondering if I dared to stay in the woods rather than face the torment of a school day. Through the previous week, I'd already contended with the backlash of Deidre's trick. She had told enough people for it to network through the whole school. I tried not to let it rile me. I'd ignored the giggling behind hands, the stares and sneers. I'd noticed Deidre insinuating herself into the top girl group. I knew it couldn't last long. She would never belong to that clique. Her clothes were wrong, her hair was wrong, her body language was wrong. In fact, her whole being was wrong. Still, she had bought herself a little time in their reflected glow. And I hated her all the more for it.

That Monday morning, I generated a different type of contempt. Instead of loud mouthed mockery with laughter and shoving; people were silent. They didn't get close enough to shoulder me or nudge me, they kept their distance. Grouped together in huddles I couldn't hear what they said,

I could only try and interpret their mean glances. Something was wrong; very wrong. I looked around for Deidre, I expected that she'd been stirring things again, but couldn't see her. The bell rang and I made my way to my classroom. I sat near the front hoping that I would be protected from the worst of the bullying by being within the teacher's range. Often it didn't work.

Miss Rowan came in slightly late and was flushed and out of breath, as if she had been running. I always thought of her as a neat person. She was small with pretty dainty features. Her reddish hair was cut short and always hung in a gleaming bob around her face. Something was definitely amiss, because her hair was mussed up and her make up smudged as if she'd got something caught in her eye and had difficulty removing it.

Instead of the usual noise and racket the class made before registration, everybody was sitting quietly.

"Class," said Miss Rowan; she was trembling, "As some of you may know, there's been a most terrible event. Your classmate and friend Deidre Alderman ..." Miss Rowan paused, giving me a moment to feel a chill spreading through my body. I knew what she was going to say. As if sensing my panic, Miss Rowan looked directly at me, "... Deidre had an accident at the weekend. She was taken to the hospital but she died." Tears started to roll down her cheeks and she gave a pathetic sniff. "Nobody knows exactly what happened yet." She was still looking at me, "But the police are investigating. Please be helpful if they should wish to talk with any of you." Her gaze remained on me. I sensed all the other eyes in the room turn towards me, accusing me of something. 'It wasn't me,' I wanted to shout. 'I didn't even know she'd had an accident.' But I said nothing and kept my face turned away from the condemning stares.

Sure enough the police arrived after lunch. Several girls and a couple of boys were selected, me included.

I sat in the Head's office whilst I was questioned. The officer who spoke to me was big and gangling. He moved his hands as if he couldn't quite keep them under control, and when he spoke he gesticulated so that I was worried he'd knock something over and I would be blamed for that. He had very black eyebrows, which were also expressive. Although he was physically intimidating he did have a soft pleasant voice as he asked me questions.

"You knew Deidre well, I gather."

"Not really well, but I knew her."

"I understand she played a bit of a trick on you recently. Left you locked up in Quercus Hall."

"Yes, but that was alright. People often tease and trick me."

"Well, that's as may be, but you would have been angry with Deidre, wouldn't you?"

"I suppose so but ..." Before I was able to continue he'd already started on the next question.

"Did you see her on Sunday then?"

"No."

"So where were you on Sunday?"

"I was in the forest."

"On your own?"

"Yes, I'm always on my own."

The officer shrugged, as if that was of no concern to him. I flinched worried that he was going to knock a pen holder off the Head's desk as he waved a hand.

"So, statements made that you were seen with her that day are wrong?" His eye brows met together, like two caterpillars bumping heads. I nearly giggled.

"Yes, they must be."

"So, when you were in the woods ... on your own ..." he emphasised the words, "... you didn't happen to go down to the brook and meet up with Deidre?"

"No."

"Miss Rowan told me you sometimes have funny turns, is that correct?"

"I get migraines. They're nasty headaches."

"Mmm." He scribbled something in a notebook, inky blots following the pen marks. "And did you get a migraine on Sunday?"

"No, I don't think so." I couldn't think straight. I might have. My head was thumping now, a beating by my temples that signalled a headache coming on.

"Okay then, that's it for now. But we might want to talk to you later."

I went back to the classroom, wishing I could go straight home. As I went into the room the usual talking behind hands and the mean looks had resumed. I could hear words that sounded like, 'She did it ... of course she did it ... you can see she's guilty ... cursed ... she's a murderer ... in the blood ...'

Somebody stuck their leg out as I went in and I tripped, the whispers stopped whilst everybody had a laugh at my expense.

The afternoon passed too slowly. It was alright if you were a teacher. Miss Rowan had managed to be relieved of her duties. (In fact, we had stand-in teachers until the end of term. I don't retain an inkling of what was taught, even the subject matter. My classmates found it an excuse to mess around. Soggy bits of paper were lobbed at me, landing in my hair. If I unravelled them, the crooked messages screamed, 'MURDERER,' at me.)

That day, I could only think of Deidre and what had happened to her. Had I seen her at the brook? I couldn't remember. I vaguely recalled a conversation with Miss Dryden near the church ... but might have been muddling that with another time. Who had said that they had seen me? I didn't even know what had happened, yet I had an image in my head of Deidre slipping down the bank, her face smooth and pale under the water, and her stringy brown hair weaving in and out, twisting with the movement of weeds.

When the bell went for the end of school I raced home. I was already telling the story as I opened the cottage door. "Ma, Ma! Deidre Alderman's dead." I halted. Taken aback as I entered. Facing me, seated at the table was Mrs Alderman.

Ma at the sink was signalling me, above Mrs Alderman's head, to be quiet. I dropped my bag where I stood, not knowing what to say.

"It was you, wasn't it?" Mrs Alderman said. "I was asking your mother about where you were on Sunday and she said you came back home wet and muddy."

My mind went completely blank. Mrs Alderman was blowing her nose into a crumpled tissue. Her face was blotchy, her eyes red. Why was everybody accusing me of this dreadful crime?

"I was playing in the woods on Sunday; I didn't go down to the brook."

"Well, there's people who are saying you did. They saw you."

"Who? Who's been making things up about me?"

"Don't play the innocent. I know a guilty person when I see one. You'll be found out, mark my words." Mrs Alderman got up and started towards the door.

"Lin, please …" Ma said, but didn't finish the sentence.

"Deidre always said you were an odd one," Mrs Alderman said as she pushed past me. "This place is cursed." The words echoed through the cottage; her final judgement left hammering on the beams as she went out.

My mouth was dry, a funny taste burning in my throat. I sat down at the table. "Can I have a cup of tea please?" I asked Ma. She usually made me one as soon as I came in.

"Okay. But then you'd better tell me everything … absolutely everything."

But I couldn't say anything. There really was nothing to tell.

CHAPTER 25

Once we'd moved to the forest I'd sometimes make my way to the church on Sundays. I didn't go in but I would hide beneath the yew, which bent over to form a den. I'd watch as people entered the church. Then I would listen to the singing as it suffused the churchyard. Even if it was wet I'd keep dry under the spread of branches. I'd watch rain water spill from the mouths of gargoyles which observed me from the eaves of the church building. I tried to decide which one I liked best, the dog with his lapping tongue and flopping ears, the devil with his horns and bulging eyes or the green man who stared through a garland of leaves.

Daddy would walk down to the village most Sundays for what he called his 'constitutional'. I did not know the meaning of this, but he went to the Linden Tree. He'd arrive home in the afternoon, rolling along the track, sometimes humming, sometimes having an argument with himself.

I would run through the side tracks so that I would arrive beside the house before him.

"Hey, where did you come from, Princess?" he would say, "Have you come to bestow your favours and help your old Dad get home?"

And I would run to him and hold his hand and we'd go in the house together.

Ma would make a pot of tea and there would be cake for us, and the house would be warm with the aroma of baking. I'm not certain how or when things changed, perhaps when one day Daddy slammed the paper down on the kitchen table. "There she is, the whore!"

"Ryan, try not to swear in front of Annie,"

"Whore is not a swear word. Whore is a descriptive word for a woman who's sold herself. There, read it yourself, then tell me she's not a whore."

He fumbled with the pages of newspaper so they pulled apart, some slipping to the floor. I couldn't see what Ma was looking at. "Okay, she's doing well. But you getting angry is going to make no difference."

"But they were your songs, they were our music. She's a thief as well as a whore. Look at her cavorting, prostituting herself in that ridiculous see-through negligee as if she's something spiritual. She's wanton and wicked."

I had never heard my father rant about a particular person before. Yes, he'd attacked items of furniture and kicked doors when he was angry, he'd shouted at Ma, but this vitriol from his mouth was something different.

"Have some tea and cake," Ma soothed.

I climbed up on a chair and was able to see the article that had caused so much offence.

I came face to face with a photograph of Lorelei. She positively glowed on the page. Her eyes were the first thing you looked at, black and deep as the dark pools in the wood, but then I took in the rest of her, draped in a flimsy construction of lace, which allowed me to see her nipples through fabric which clung around her body and legs.

I could not look away. **'Straight to number one'**, was the headline. And I wondered what that meant.

"Let's put that away whilst we have tea, shall we?" Ma folded up the paper.

But Daddy grabbed it from her and ripped it, tearing it straight through into several pieces. The scraps fell to the floor. After that he was calmer and sat and drank his tea. When we'd eaten our cake I thought it safe enough to ask,

"What's Lorelei done?"

Daddy gazed at me as if I had said something terrible and I thought he might slam his fist on the table again. It was obviously taking time for him to build up to what he wanted to say, because before he could reply Ma explained, "Lorelei's record is number one in the charts."

I must have looked blank because she continued, "Yes, there's a chart, a top twenty, of all the records and depending on how many get sold, somebody gets to number one. Lorelei has done that this week."

"What's a whore?"

"It's not a very nice word for a woman."

"Why's Lorelei a whore?" Neither of them answered. "Is it like a bitch?" This time my father did slap his hand down on the table. "Enough!" he shouted and then went out of the house slamming the door. I turned to Ma to repeat the question, but she was standing at the sink with her back to me washing up the tea plates.

The next few months became a time of discovery for me. I tried to follow all the articles about Lorelei in the papers, of which there were many.

When I met Daddy after his Sunday walk he sometimes didn't have a paper any more. When I asked why, he'd just say, "More whore." And leave it at that.

Without being able to mention Lorelei's name in the house, I decided to find an ally. I found it in Myrtill. I followed her like a stray, waiting until she finally took pity on me and said, "Do you want to come in then?" I nodded and followed her up the wooden staircase at the back of the little house. It led to a long low room like an attic which she later told me was her studio. "How do you like your coffee?" I had shrugged, "Wet and warm then." She made me coffee in a china cup, strong and sweet, with no milk." It tasted special. Slowly I moved through the room. It had a dusty feeling to it, as though time twisted at a different pace to anywhere else. There were a couple of easels, one with a work in progress and one blank.

On the easel the picture was of trees and bark, the hint of berries and pin-pricked flowers. But it wasn't a painting; it was made of fabric and threads. I could see lace and ribbon and loose stitching so together it gave an effect of deep wood and shadows. I put my hand up to touch it, but thought I'd better not. "It's okay," laughed Myrtill, "Touch it if you want." I decided I didn't want to. The effect of the composition was so mesmerising I wouldn't want to spoil the sensation by making my fingers realise it was just fabrics and thread that had made this wonderful creation. On the floor were baskets of remnants and cotton reels, and beside them paints. In a corner was a sewing machine.

I'd flick through the Newspapers and magazines that Myrtill had accumulated. When I showed an interest she said, "Look at this one ... it's all about Lorelei." I enjoyed reading them and soaking up all the bits of tittle tattle regarding Lorelei. I took them to be the truth. Myrtill was interested in her as well. Our discussions focussed on Lorelei's looks, her clothing, her relationships; hardly ever about her music.

No mention was made of Archie which troubled me somewhere distant and deep inside me. But I did gain knowledge of her stream of male admirers. Then after some months one name became regular. A man named Cedric Libani. He'd been a top flight rugby player but then had a severe knee injury in a tackle. He now took up column inches with celebrity style antics. In all the photographs Lorelei and Cedric made a handsome couple. Lorelei pale and ethereal, Cedric dark and exotic. When I went foraging in the forest I would create games where Lorelei and Cedric were married. I was chief bridesmaid dressed in a sparkling rose dress.

My dream did come to fruition in a way. After much speculation and gossip in all the papers, Cedric and Lorelei tied the knot, witnessed by a few glamourous celebrity friends on an Island in the Caribbean. But I was not a bridesmaid or flower girl. From the photographs in print, no mention was made of the step-children she'd taken on. Even Archie hadn't been paraded in a page-boy outfit.

Following the celebrations things in the village became more interesting. I heard rumours that the happy couple were moving back to Broomstone. I couldn't think why they would do such a thing, when their days were spent in exotic locations usually out of England. It was all very hush-hush. I couldn't help asking though.

"Ma, is Lorelei coming back to Broomstone?"

Ma appeared to start as if the question had taken her by surprise. "That's what some of the villagers say. But it could just be rumour."

Nobody I asked would give me a definite answer. Even Myrtill who was usually direct with her responses could only say, "Don't believe everything you hear." Which wasn't any help at all.

CHAPTER 26

I have only brought one dress suitable for a soiree, a satin affair with large rose prints in scarlet and pink. Putting it on I regret not bringing an alternative. Whether it is the way the light slants in through the dormer window or the angle of the glass; when I regard my reflection in mirror, I look wrong. I've lost weight, so instead of the fabric being moulded around curves, it hangs from my shoulders, exposing bones and saggy flesh. The floral pattern drains any colour from my skin so I look wan. I put more powder on my face, apply lipstick and practice smiling.

Instead of returning to the ground floor the back way, I go to the front flight of stairs with the curved bannister swirling into the hall below. For a moment I preen and imagine myself as a princess about to attend a ball. Something I contemplated in the past, when I had dreams of marrying Roderick. But my heel catches in the carpet and I nearly fall. After that I grip the rail more tightly and concentrate on my steps. Rasputin speeds past me in a blur of grey.

I follow the sound of voices to a room I've rarely visited. High-ceilinged, with original dark panelled walls. It is not a gloomy space though as multiple glass doors form an arc in the bay, with views down the garden. Some of the doors are open allowing a breeze to move the long voile drapes, bringing with it a nostalgic scent of summers past. Fairy lights wink from the terrrace beyond. A dozen or so people are circling the room, their backs towards me. They don't look up as I enter. I recognise the music instantly, "... *and all the trees in the wood sing your name ...*" The first track of Lorelei's debut album, 'Dryad,' the one which had won prizes and accolades and made her an instant celebrity. The tone is high pitched, loaded with emotion, swirling from the depths to soaring vibrato. It is unmistakeable and mesmerising.

I feel awkward, not sure of who to approach. I twist the non-existent wedding band on my finger. I stare at the back of a tall figure with broad shoulders and black hair. Could it be Roderick? My stomach swirls in a familiar way. Then the man turns, it is not him. The seasick motion stops; whether from relief or disappointment, I'm not sure. I hadn't braved asking about Roderick directly, but by some means had gleaned from Poppy that Roderick is a rare visitor, now based in Australia.

Finally, Poppy sees me hovering and comes to welcome me. She wears a mandarin type jacket which hides most of her birthmark. Then she introduces me. People peck my cheeks with air kisses, a contact of air loaded with saliva, more spit than kiss. I recognise one or two of the other guests. Myrtill is here and she hugs me. Mr and Mrs Alderman give cooler handshakes and I sense we are all thinking about their daughter, Deidre.

After introductions the guests lose interest in me and turn away. I shuffle into a corner. Sipping wine too fast.

On one wall is what must be the original artwork for the 'Dryad' album cover. The one reproduced on the gig pamphlet I'd found. It depicts a wood nymph from Greek mythology. A woman transforming into or from a tree. The woman is Lorelei. Her wide staring eyes watch me as I circle the room. The iris is sapphire, haloed with a ring of ice blue. They are similar to Archie's. In the picture Lorelei is naked. She clings to a tree but the curves of her body mould with it. Her skin and the tree have been painted the exact same hue so separating the woman from the tree is impossible. A scattering of autumn leaves clings to her hair as if she is either emerging from the wood or being absorbed by it.

"Yes, she was beautiful wasn't she?" The words startle me and my wine glass tips. I'm surprised at how quietly Cedric has moved to be at my shoulder. He is a tall, broad man. But now he holds a walking stick. He's had a limp for as long as I can remember, the reason for his retirement from professional rugby, but he never carried a stick before. He still makes me nervous. He must be in his seventies now but has a handsome angular face which Roderick inherited. "That's how I always think of her, as if she belongs to another world."

I murmur my agreement. Because he is right. I think of the day I found her lying between the willow tree roots. Believing she could have emerged from the pages of my fairy tale book. "Did Archie tell you he's asked me to write her biography?"

"Yes."

His monosyllabic response doesn't seem very promising. As he'd ignored my previous messages, I think he might forbid me to write it. What would I do then? We continue to look at the image before us. I'm wondering if I should ask his permission, but then he says, "Now that my wife and Archie are on board, I will talk to you. But I don't want dirt digging up about Lorelei. I want this to be a book of celebration about her life, her music and her talent."

I turn to look at him, but he is already limping away, his back to me, his stick tapping on the parquet. This is the man who allowed a baby to be laid out in the room next door. What kind of man does that? I dare not tell him that I will write about everything I find out; warts and all.

There is a tap on my shoulder, causing my arm to twitch. If my glass had been full my drink would have spilt. I turn with some annoyance to a face I don't recognise. "Hi I'm Danny Webbe," the intruder says, smiling. I swap my wine glass to my left hand and shake his proffered palm. "But everybody calls me Spider. My title is Detective Inspector Webbe. But soon I'll just be Spider again … I'm about to retire … won't know what to do with myself then." He grins and winks. I wonder whether I should know him, he certainly appears to know me. He continues, "Archie said I should talk with you. He said you were writing a biography on Lorelei." I say nothing and continue to look blank. "I was one of the detectives on the original case after Lorelei's incident and hospitalisation."

"Oh." I am sure there had been a lot of flak towards the whole police investigation. They had been all over the press. Almost as if they'd been responsible for Lorelei's poisoning and were covering it up.

"I was a junior at the time, and it was my first high profile case. I'll tell you now that I don't think we could have done anything more. But it still worries me that we never found out what happened to her. Whether it was self-inflicted or a crime. Originally she said she couldn't remember. At least that was her excuse. And then we stopped investigating. But she's not given us any more information. Of course, that's understandable, considering her condition."

"I can't remember the details," I tell him. "Except for a while you didn't hear of anything else and then suddenly it was gone."

"Yes, it was a bit like that."

Danny, (I'm not sure I know him well enough to think of him as Spider), has a pleasant face, sandy hair and freckles. He must be in his fifties but has the ghost of boyhood in his manner. His floral shirt in pink and mauve adds to that impression.

"So Annie, how's the research and writing going?"

I am disconcerted that he calls me by my first name; his whole manner is one of old chums meeting in a bar.

"Not very fast actually," I tell him truthfully, "But I've only just started."

"Yes, of course. Didn't we investigate your dad going missing earlier that same year?"

I'm again surprised that Danny knows so much about me, it makes my response abrupt. "Well, you said there was nothing to investigate, he was a grown man and circumstances at home made it likely he might just have left … Yes, that was the extent of it." I can't hide the bitterness in my voice. The police had definitely let me and my mother down. And there had been no mention of that in any paper.

He nods his head in agreement. A gold link chain flashes at his neck. "Unfortunately, that's all the police can do when an adult goes missing. And a boot and his wallet were found later."

"Yes and you said that proved he was dead. Concluded that he had probably drowned. His body had been washed further down river to the open sea. As his body was never found, it wasn't a satisfactory explanation for me or my mother."

"You're right. I don't think it was a satisfactory explanation ..."

I pass my glass from hand to hand. "What? Why do you say that?"

"The boot and wallet could have been planted." My mouth has opened. I stare at him. "It's just a thought that bugged me for a while. I only remembered when I got out the notes I kept when Archie told me you were researching Lorelei."

"I don't understand ..."

"There was an empty vodka bottle as well as the wallet and single boot. The bottle was tested; it had no fingerprints on it, nothing. I would expect your dad's prints to be on it, at the very least. It was as if it had been deliberately wiped. It struck me at the time as odd."

"So, what are you saying?"

"It might have been planted. And his wallet didn't have anything important in it. To me it appeared your dad might have been making it look as if he'd gone into the river. Perhaps so that he could leave to pursue a new life."

My thoughts are too confused, to ask the obvious question, if he was planning to make it look as if he'd disappeared ... why didn't he at least leave his own prints on the bottle? Because running from a hot place behind my ribcage to a throbbing pulse at my temple, an altogether more hopeful idea is forming. "So, you're saying my daddy could still be alive?" My breathing is ragged; the throb at my temple pulsing the thought ... *Daddy's alive ... Daddy's alive.* I vaguely hear Danny's response.

"I don't know. I don't know if that's what I'm saying. Just that it's something that should have been considered."

"Why didn't you say anything at the time?" My voice is too loud. Danny grips my elbow and manoeuvres me further into the corner. His answer is low, almost a whisper.

"I did. But my superiors decided nothing could be proved and it was wasting police resources."

Hope opens up in my chest, like a shockwave. Danny is agreeing with me that Daddy could be alive. I could talk to him again. He would tell me why he had gone away. He would lift me up, spin me round. The thought makes me dizzy just thinking about it.

Danny looks at me as if trying to decide whether to continue. Probably regretting he has brought the topic up.

I stumble from the room to the downstairs loo and throw up. My claret stained vomit looks like blood splatter.

Finally, the dizzy sensation stops and the merry-go-round possibility of Daddy's survival ebbs away. He is dead. He must be dead to leave me for so long. If he was alive he'd have returned years ago.

I cry, still on my knees, as I watch water turn over in the toilet pan.

I'd never said 'Goodbye' to him. Ma never spoke of him. I don't think she was glad that he had gone, but she accepted it and moved on. I know they argued and that he probably hit her more than once. But he was still my daddy, and he loved me. I think he loved me.

Gradually I calm down, my sobbing turns to hiccoughs. I get up, swill my mouth out and repair my make up as best I can. I return to the dining room, pick up my glass and go to get a refill.

Returning to stand beside the painting, Danny is hovering. I'm not sure if he is expecting me to say something. I look at the portrait of Lorelei, trying to see things, shapes or shadows

I haven't noticed before. But there isn't a pixel I haven't already scrutinised.

Danny coughs. "I've still got some notes from that time." I turn to face him.

"Yes, as it was my first case I kept notes. And there are a few scraps from when your father vanished. You could see them if you wanted … If you think it might help."

I'm trying to work out what his agenda is, but fail to discern anything. I just nod and say, "Yes, thanks. That would be useful."

"I'll drop them in at some point then or we could meet up."

Danny edges away into the central circle of people. Cedric slaps him on the back and says something which makes everybody around him smile. It looks as though Cedric doesn't hold a grudge towards Danny and the police's inept investigation of Lorelei's poisoning.

I have wandered back and stare at the portrait of Lorelei whilst my thoughts tumble round. The early stirring of migraine throbs behind my eyes.

"You like my painting then?" Another voice disturbs my contemplation. It is Myrtill.

"You painted it?"

"Yep."

"But where's your signature?" I peer at the lower right hand corner for the typical signature that Myrtill scrawls across all her artwork and I'm certain I would have recognised.

"I don't know what happened to it. Somehow any reference to my artwork got scrubbed. Not even a mention on the album sleeve."

"But didn't you say anything? Surely you'd have been owed royalties or something?"

"I tried, but at every turn there were more obstacles to go through, usually with a price tag which ultimately I couldn't afford. I decided to let it go."

She pauses, reaches up and traces one tapered finger along the curve of Lorelei's shoulder. "It might be my best work."

CHAPTER 27

It starts the same way. A coffee and cake brought down at eleven then I continue for another hour. At midday I go upstairs to find something to eat. There is nobody about except Rasputin who is hogging the cushions, so I leave for a short walk. The atmosphere is muggy. I see nobody. No one gardening or sunbathing or even wandering the street. I cross the green, sit on the bench under the beech tree; still nobody. The sign on the door to The Gallery says *'Closed'*. It's spooky. I return to the Hall and go up to my room. Looking out of the windows I can't see anyone. The view appears silent and still, as if the air has stopped. There aren't any birds flying across the expanse of sky either. The only movement is a spiral of what might be smoke circling from the centre of the island, adding to the grey cauldron of cloud.

I turn and watch my reflection in the mirror and wonder if somehow I have switched places with my reflection and am trapped in another world. I consider where they all could be. It feels wrong and uncomfortable. I go down to the landing and call out "Archie? Poppy?" But there is no response. My words hang in the dense air and I feel more adrift. I suppose they could be with Lorelei and I probably shouldn't disturb them. There is a rattle and I look down to see the cat slink from the lounge and push through the door to the basement.

In the kitchen, after a bit of searching, I find teabags and make myself a cup of tea. I sit down in the warm hollow left by Rasputin on the cushions. The garden remains silent and devoid of people. I return to the basement, trying to forget the empty house above me, and the deserted village beyond.

I pause and take my time to look at the display of stuffed birds. Some of the exotic feathers in a multitude of gleaming colours are so vivid it is impossible to believe that they have existed in the real world. They regard me with black eyes that glint. The light bulb flickers making the movement all the more real and I wonder who made them, prepared all those warm bodies and stuffed and stitched them. It seems a macabre type of hobby.

I leave the display and go into what I now consider my office. Rasputin is sitting in the box on the floor and spits at me when I approach. "Come on now, kitty, you need to budge." Instead of using my hand I kick the box and the cat flies out, tipping the box over so another pile of papers spills to the floor. "Oi, be more careful," I tell the cat. He ignores me and prowls off towards the bird cabinet, occasionally jumping up at the glass, attempting to catch the still creatures within. Picking up the spilt papers, I return them to the box, but one piece catches my eye. It is a torn out page with handwriting scrawled over it. At first glance I think it looks like my mother's hand and might be an original script for a song. But on closer inspection it is something different, more like a recipe. And, although it's difficult to decipher, after reading through it, I decide it could be a spell. The hairs on my arms lift, making my skin creep. I can't work out what the spell might be for, but there's a list of ingredients and instructions. I shiver. It makes me feel so uncomfortable I decide I'll look at it later, somewhere where the light is better. I fold it and put it into the back pocket of my trousers.

I'm organising documents into little piles. Those that look personal, those that are related to touring and gigs, and another for music notes. I intend to ask Archie if he has any in and out trays I can use to keep things in order. I've been working for some time when I hear a click sound loudly, making me look up. I take a couple of steps to see if the cat has jumped up at something, but his shadow is lurking in a corner. It must have been the door then, but that's propped open with a cast iron doorstop.

I get up to have a look. Somehow the door has closed; the stump pushed aside. It makes the space even more airless so I grab the handle expecting it to open. It holds firm. I do that silly thing where you rattle the handle from side to side, even though I know it is locked. I peer through the keyhole but that is blocked by the key. Somebody must have assumed there was nobody down here, otherwise why would they have locked the door? The light is on though, the cat in the corner. Have I been shut in here deliberately? The thought makes me anxious. My breathing starts to increase. Since being locked in here all those years ago I've become nervous of enclosed spaces.

When I try my mobile, there isn't a signal. I walk through the basement holding it out and up ahead of me, but there's nothing. I return to the door and start to rattle the door handle again, shouting, "Hello, Hello! I'm locked in. Let me out!" I continue for several minutes but nobody comes to my rescue.

At the far end of the basement the back door is bolted and locked, the rusted key absent. I study the window which I had once been pushed through. There is no way I can squeeze through even if I could reach to open it. The world outside is distorted, viewed through the grubby pane.

I must have been down here for longer than I'd planned because the light outside is beginning to dim. The basement bulb has also taken to flickering; I pray it will not give up.

In the corner Rasputin stretches and then runs to the door mewling to get out. "Can't help you," I tell him. He gives me a withering look and starts prowling the shadows. I return to the study space, considering whether just to carry on until somebody realises either I or the cat have disappeared. Surely someone must come soon? I can hear Rasputin meowing again but this time the noise sounds muffled and distant. I look for him. When I can't see him I call, "Here Kitty, Kitty," making silly noises. I don't think he's the type of cat who will respond to such gestures, but I can hear him and don't want to be accused of leading him into harm's way when we're finally released.

The noise is coming from behind the cabinet of birds. Bending down I use my mobile as a torch and look underneath. I expect to get a claw in my face but instead feel the draught of a gap beyond. A dank smell accompanies the breeze. Standing up again I notice the cabinet has been pulled away from the wall and the black line of an open door is visible. I recall there was another door down here, by the huge wardrobe which had contained the cloaks. I manage to shift the cabinet a bit further out and discover a passageway behind it. Keeping my phone light on, I can see roughly hewn steps heading down steeply. I really do not want to be here but think it might be a way out. I descend further, and keep going. One foot in front of the other, into the smudge of light cast by the phone. I pause and take a few deep breaths. The passageway is becoming danker and I guess that if it does lead anywhere it will come out at the island. In front of me Rasputin has stopped meowing and is sitting in the middle of the passage. In the glow of phone light his eyes gleam amber, but he doesn't appear as surly as he has previously. I am surprised he hasn't gone further along but then see the passage is completely blocked by a fall of stones and earth. There is just the smell of stagnant water coming through a space between the ceiling and the rubble. Then Rasputin disappears. He meows loudly. He has managed to slip between a gap to the side. Holding the phone up into the space, another tunnel is revealed, at an angle to the first. Carefully, I push past the edge of rubble and walk along. This passage is drier and leads upwards. After several minutes I reach a flight of steps. Rasputin is sitting on the top with a triumphant grin on his face. "Okay, you're a clever cat … now we've just got to get out." I pass him and try to push up on the stone above me, but nothing happens. I put my shoulder to it. It won't shift. Suddenly the toll of bells resounds from the walls, making the air vibrate. They sound close by. "We're somewhere in or near the church, then," I say to the cat. "But we can't get out here." I turn back, not very happy to be heading back under the village to the bowels of the building. Rasputin slips by me and leads the way up the steps, past the cabinet and back into the basement. We creep out and Rasputin flies up the stairs. I stop, bewildered. The door is now wide open, propped with the tree stump ornament, as if it had been there all the time.

In the study space I'm greeted by the sight of papers from the crate spread over the floor. My neatly sorted piles are messed all over the table top. Had I not seen Rasputin in the tunnel, I'd probably have blamed him. But this isn't accidental. Somebody is trying to disrupt me. I collect the papers together in one pile and shove them into the box. I'll have to start again. Something is missing though. The Valentine's card. I flick through the pile but it is definitely gone. Why would someone have taken that? Perhaps other things have been removed as well. Things I have yet to sort. I put my hand to my pocket and feel the rustle of paper. If somebody didn't want me uncovering things, I am glad I've slipped the spell away.

I switch the lights off and make my way back upstairs. In the reception area Rasputin is playing with something, with the mean expression cats have when they've caught a creature. Even if it's only a spider I think I should rescue it. However, on closer inspection it is a tiny rose, one of those from the card.

I can hear voices coming from the kitchen and lounge but am not ready to face anybody yet. I leave Rasputin with his toy and go up to my room. On the landing there is another dusty paper rose. I follow the landing around trying to work out which room the thief might inhabit, but the trail goes no further. In my room I wash my face and hands and change my shirt, trying to get rid of the stagnant air that clings to me. Then I go downstairs to the den. Archie and Poppy are chatting. Cedric is sitting in an armchair which looks too small for him, reading a paper.

"Are you making progress?" Archie asks.

For a moment I consider saying that I'd been shut in, but decide against it, so instead say, "I was doing well, until Rasputin jumped on the table and tipped up the documents I'd put in order."

Rasputin is winding in and out of Poppy's legs and looks at me, narrowing his eyes. If I was nearer I think I would hear him hiss.

Archie is still looking expectantly at me, so I continue. "But there's some interesting stuff and I'll carry on tomorrow."

"Mum wants to see you," Archie says. Cedric shifts in his seat and rattles the paper.

"Oh, when?"

"Well now ... When you're done come and have some tea with us."

I nod, realising there is to be no discussion.

....

My first impression is a still from a black and white movie. The room is dim. There is a four poster bed in the centre of the room. The wood of the headboard is dark, carved into leaves and branches like a willow, so for a moment I see her as I did when I found her. Her white hair is spread wing-like across pillows. The bedding is grey, made of satin fabric, giving an impression of water. Her face is pale and smooth as stone. She does not appear to have aged.

It does not look or smell like a hospital room. In fact, there is no odour at all.

I think she beckons me with a crooked finger. Her hands, in contrast to her face, look ancient.

"Annie ..." she whispers and the word flutters from her lips. She points at a jug and I pour a glass of water for her. Then hold it for her to sip.

"I'm looking through your box of mementos. Archie says

you want a memoir written." I'm not sure what to expect, how much speech she is capable of, but she replies.

"Your father ... you want to find out about your father."

"Well yes. I suppose so. But Archie said you wanted me to write your biography." I frown at her. How can she know that since I returned to Broomstone, it is Daddy's disappearance which is overwhelming me?

"Yes, you must write it. You will find out about your father too." She is gripping my hand with icy fingers. They are so cold they sting my skin.

"What about Archie's father?" I ask remembering Poppy's words.

Lorelei is silent, a tiny dark dimple blemishing her brow like a question mark. Then she chuckles, a cry like a magpie call, so harsh it prickles my skin. "No. Not Archie's father. No. No. No father," she says, and chuckles again.

The sound carries around the room with a menace of madness. I want to leave, bring this odd conversation to a close. "Is there anything particular you want me to write, anything I won't know?"

"Annie ... you know everything ... you don't think so ... but you do."

I smile at her, this half-alive sort of woman. I am again reminded of when I found her and she needed saving.

"I'm tired," she tells me and closes her eyes.

"I'll go then." I try to move my hand away but her fingers are like roots clinging to me. I have to twist my wrist to release it and her hand falls away. I see something caught in her fingers. It is a tiny paper rose. How the hell did she get that? I've been told she's bed bound; it couldn't have been her who trashed my study.

As I reach the door I think I hear a whisper behind me, "... I did love him."

....

"We're just having sandwiches tonight," Poppy says when I

return to the den. She puts down a huge platter in the middle of the table, piled high. "Help yourself."

I take a couple, pour myself a cup of tea and sit on the edge of the bank of scattered cushions. Looking out, down the expanse of lawn, makes me remember how everyone had vanished in the afternoon and the spiral of smoke above the island.

I speak without thinking. "Where was everybody this afternoon? It was like the whole village population vanished." I put my teacup on a side table so I can eat my sandwiches. Rasputin comes, circles the table stand and jumps up beside me.

Cedric looks up from his paper. I'm not certain but I sense them looking at each other, asking the unspoken question, 'What shall we tell her?'

Finally, Archie says, "Well this is a big house and grounds. We're not always in earshot. And we may have been with Mum. We try and spend time with her in the afternoon."

There's another pause. Cedric turns to me and asks, "Found anything useful?" I tell him not really. "I saw Spider talking to you. He said he'd got some records from that time."

"Yes, I gather he's Detective Inspector now. I'm glad he's got time to spare for me."

"Well, he's a good man ... completely green when he was investigating Lorelei's poisoning of course. Between him and the other chap who was waiting for early retirement, they made a complete pig's ear out of it. Yes, Spider's completely changed, well ... matured I suppose over time. Plays a good round of golf too. We occasionally get out on the course."

So that's why they were so chummy. "You don't think it was an accidental overdose then? You think somebody did it deliberately?"

"What else? She certainly wasn't trying to take her own life,"

"Not an accident then but an attempted murder?" I mumble, through a mouthful of sandwich.

"I think the latter, but the police wouldn't take it any further. She wasn't stupid; she knew what she was doing."

"But has she said anything now? Has she remembered anything more?" The image of a row of little green bottles fills my head, and I'm scared that a migraine is developing. The cream cheese and salmon sandwich forms a sticky stopper in my mouth. I'm too hot. The evening is dimming and the air outside looks thick and heavy. I glance around to see if there is a window to open but besides some hooks in the top panels, there doesn't seem to be anything.

"You can't believe anything Lorelei says now. She's damaged." Cedric looks so sad; I think he might be about to cry.

I make my excuses and leave.

As soon as I close the door I hear conversation start up again, and the gruff voice of Cedric saying, "Are you sure you want all this dragged up again? I'm really not comfortable with it at all."

"It's what Mum wanted."

"You have no idea what you might discover. Things that you really don't want to know."

"I'm sorry you feel that way about it, Cedric. And you know Mum was very clear she wanted her biography written."

"You say that, but she doesn't know what she wants. She's barely coherent."

I hear a chair shift and I move up to the landing. Cedric lumbers out but doesn't come towards the stairs. Instead, he goes to the corner of the lobby and unlatches the door that leads down to the basement.

CHAPTER 28

Upstairs it is even hotter. Completely airless in the attic room. I open the window but there is no hint of breeze. It's like being in an oven; the heat burning below me and steam rising above.

When I sit down the paper in my pocket rustles and I pull it out to look more closely.

The page is what I'd describe as parchment. It has the texture of blotting paper and the letters written in black ink have been absorbed so the lines are not clear. It has been folded and unfolded many times and is torn in places. The ink spiders across the page in a looping style. The words are difficult to read, and the actual letters that I can make out are smeared. It will be a challenge to decipher.

I put the paper on the window ledge and smooth it down with my palms; it is gritty under my touch. The first line is underlined. I think it says *Elixir for ... 'something' ... love.*

The next lines are almost illegible, but could be a list of ingredients. *'San'* or *'Song'* possibly and, *'of both'.*

Further down the word *'mix'* is clear but the paper has a feathery rip, distorting the marks following. There's another *'x'* which I suspect indicates *'wax'* but any indication of what type of wax is smudged beyond recognition.

Following on are instructions. The word *'moon'* distinct and then letters '... *c o r p u'.*

My eyes are straining; I blink several times. Looking again I realise there is a symbol in one corner which resembles a tree. Leaves depicted in sharp arrows indicate holly. The opposite edge is torn off and all that's left is a sprig of dots which could be a star or flower.

It's too dark in here to see any more, so reluctantly I fold the paper away and put it under my pillow. I have a sense that this piece of paper is important. Somebody might think it worth stealing. Who, I have not fathomed, but it is a compelling sensation prickling the back of my neck with forewarning.

As the darkness outside deepens the temperature drops a little and I find it's easier to breathe.

I slip between the sheets, the paper rustling beneath my head. I dwell on the meaning of the spell. From my understanding of magic gleaned from fairy tales, I am sure it is a love potion. But instead of a light romantic concoction, the whole thing exudes the weight of dark magic. I shudder beneath the sheets as a handful of raindrops strike the glass above me. In the distance the shift and judder of thunder rolls, then lightening forks, blinding me for a moment.

The storm crashes on making the air smell sulphurous, but finally subdues with a lighter patter of raindrops on the roof and windows. A cool breeze stirs the room, carrying with it rain filled air which I sense on my skin. It is like bathing in dew. I take a deep breath and close my eyes thinking I will be able to sleep. However, sleep does not come, only memories. Within their clouded forms, I try and construct Daddy's face, straining to glimpse the last time I'd seen him, remember the lines and features that comprised him. Hear the last words he spoke to me.

CHAPTER 29

After finally drifting off in the early hours, I wake late the following morning. By the time I am dressed and downstairs Archie, Poppy and Cedric are not around. I make a slice of toast for breakfast and decide what to do. The spell is still on my mind and I consider how I can find out more.

As the writing looks like Ma's I consider going to see her. But she might know nothing about it and I'd have wasted a whole morning driving to Stonewick. It has to be somebody more local. Perhaps Myrtill would know something?

I head towards the gallery. The postcard stand is outside, the '*Open*' sign hanging on the door. The jangle of trinkets announces my arrival as I enter.

"Hello, my dear Annie," Myrtill's voice calls from somewhere at the back of the shop. I can't see her and look around, expecting to discover a mirror or some device above the door which would indicate who had come in. I'm unsuccessful. "How can I help you?" she asks, appearing behind the desk, as if she knows I have a question for her.

"I've found something that I can't work out. Thought you might have an idea."

"Probably best if you come through then," she says, again making me think she knows why I am there.

She turns the sign on the door to '*Closed*' and I follow her to the back, into her lounge. I sit on a sofa and spread the paper on the coffee table. "Whoa!" she says, putting her hands out as if to stop me. "I think we're going to need strong coffee with this."

When she returns with our drinks, I ask, "What's the

problem?" She puts the mug beside me. "Why did you react like that?"

She pokes the very edge of the paper as if is soiling the table top. "This is a magic spell."

"I gathered that much but ..."

"No, you don't understand. It's a dark magic spell. A dangerous spell. You really don't want to be around this."

"I just want to find out what it means. What it's for?"

Myrtill pinches a corner of the paper and squints at the writing.

"Elixir for everlasting love. That doesn't mean a simple silly love potion, this means a spell for love that won't simply exist in this life time ... but for time eternal. And look at what they have to find and do!" Myrtill regards me through narrowed eyes. She must glean that I don't have a clue. "Potentially poisonous herbs picked at specific times of the day and night. Then blood and sex basically ... Repeated during different phases of the moon, concluding at the full moon. The blending of both physical bodies and souls." She shudders dropping the paper back onto the table as if it disgusts her.

I have a distinct memory of being in my father's wood shed, the night before he'd disappeared. The stench of sweat, and what I later realised was the odour of sex. The sight of Lorelei running away from the glade, blood on her hands. My father and Lorelei. Was that possible? Making a lover's bond so strong it couldn't be undone.

"Watch out!" Myrtill grabs my hand to stop my coffee from spilling. I take a sip, glad of the warm bitterness. "What is it?"

I don't see the point in lying to Myrtill. "I remembered something." I tell her about seeing Lorelei running from the house and having to wait in the woodshed and what I'd seen and smelt in there. "How would I know if it was a spell for them?"

"Well, you see the symbols in the corners? Here and here." She points at the corners but doesn't touch the paper. "One is a holly tree, the other like the flower of wild garlic. These would usually symbolise the couple who the spell was for."

"And could that be Lorelei and my father?"

"Possibly."

Myrtill gets up quickly and moves back to the kitchen area. From her abrupt response and movement, I consider that her answer should have been 'Probably.' I think of my mother believing that Lorelei was her sister Holly. And another name for wild garlic is Ramsons, nearly my surname. In one way it made sense. In another it did not.

"But after Lorelei left the band and Broomstone, Daddy hated her."

Myrtill answers from the kitchen area. "Sometimes these strong emotions can't simply be defined in black and white."

"Like your beauty crone collage,"

"Ha ... you remember that? Yes, pretty much."

Another thought pops up, a premature baby of about six months. My sister?

The sound of a tap turning and water splashing comes from the kitchen area. "The night I talked about, I'd been to the Hall and saw a group of people in cloaks going towards the lake. Was there something going on ... to do with witchcraft? Is that a thing in Broomstone?"

Myrtill does not reply immediately, I'm not sure she's heard me. From the noises, she is rinsing cups or plates. I'm about to repeat my question when she says, "Only in a typical small village way. There's a group of us who practice the Wiccan ways. Using herbs and plants to ward off evil, make healing spells, even mild love or fertility potions. It's been happening for generations."

I had worked this out anyway, years ago. After all, magic surrounded the house I lived in. Yet there is a distinct difference between dark magic and white healing magic.

"And was Miss Dryden involved?"

"What do you mean, was? She still is."

"She's still alive then? But she was so old."

Myrtill's laugh carries through the room. "When you're a young girl, everybody seems old. And those that are older appear ancient."

"So, she still lives in Broomstone then?"

"Well, in the forest."

Myrtill returns to sit on the sofa. She's rubbing her hands together as if coming to a decision. "Look, we meet when there's a full moon. You could come with me."

"I could?"

"I don't see why not. But there are some rules you'd have to follow."

"Okay. That's not a problem. Where do we meet?"

"Look, come here on Wednesday evening, about half nine and we'll go together."

When I get back to the Hall there's a letter on the reception desk. My name is printed in neat black capitals. It's an invitation to meet Danny Webbe for lunch at the golf club outside Stonewick tomorrow.

CHAPTER 30

Though Jay had occasionally played golf with his mates, I have never been to a golf club. I park my rusting mini on the far side of the carpark, away from a gleaming Jag and BMWs. My boots crunch on the gravel as I walk up the path between manicured lawns and flower beds. The building had been a stately home and retains the impression of grandeur. However, when I go inside, the fittings are shabby in a dated maroon and navy colour scheme. There are boards and signs advertising various events which add to the air of untidiness. I detect the faint smell of sweat.

"Hi. Can I help you?"

A woman has come through a door. She is wearing a polo shirt with the club logo on it and a name badge which indicates her name is Sara. "Yes, I've been invited to lunch with Danny Webbe."

"Oh, Spider. It's Annie, isn't it?" I nod, "Yes, he's expecting you in the dining room. Just follow the stairs upwards, turn right, the dining room's at the end of the corridor." She makes a note of something in a log book, presumably that I'm in the building, and hands me a guest name badge. Interesting that she called him Spider, perhaps everybody *does* call him Spider.

I follow the instructions, up the maroon carpeted staircase to a landing where a window gives a view towards a driving range, before stepping into a corridor leading me to the back of the building. The dining room is large with a mahogany and brass bar in one corner and seating spread out to take advantage of the view beyond bay windows.

From here you look down onto the 18th green and see

people finishing their rounds, shaking hands. The rain in the night has made everything damp and the vegetation appears greener.

The Detective Inspector, who I try to think of as Spider, waves a hand at me and I go and join him. "Lovely day for it," he nods to the green below and I smile. "Do you play?" he asks.

"No." I don't tell him that getting sweaty for the best part of a day, hitting a tiny ball a long way to put it into a small hole, is not my idea of time well spent. Spider must recognise my reluctance though. "Not your cup of tea?" and he smiles, this time accompanied with a wink. I laugh and shrug.

Once we have drinks, (I've opted for sparkling water as I think Spider might be concerned about drinking and driving), he opens a briefcase, and removes three black books from it. One is a diary, the others notebooks.

"Where do you want to start?" Spider asks. "Lorelei or your dad?"

I take a deep breath and say, "Daddy." I'm going to have to face it at some point, so why not now, in this big room with lots of people around and a friendly face in front of me.

Spider opens the least worn notebook. "There might not be much I can tell you, but as you know he went missing on the night of Saturday the twelfth of February.

"Yes."

"Well, that was the last time he was seen at least. But your mother didn't report him missing until late on the Tuesday evening."

I'm not sure of the point he's making, but immediately come to Ma's defence. "Well, my parents didn't have a phone line and it was difficult to get to Stonewick without transport … and if she'd been there too soon you'd just have told her to go away. Which is pretty much what you did anyway."

"Sorry." Spider holds his hands up in mock apology. "I suppose so. Anyway …" He ruffles a few more pages over, "… we did tell her to ask friends when they'd last seen him, maybe do a search around the woods and places he might go.

And then your mum came by with Tom Hart, two days later."

"Woody," I interrupt.

"Yes, that's the guy, and they made a formal missing person statement. We came and did some interviews in Broomstone. I was really excited; going to the village where one of the big pop stars lived was a big deal for me."

I can see Spider's excitement. His eyes have widened, there is a flush on his face and he keeps fiddling with the edges of the notebook. "We did some searching of the local area, which is when we discovered the boot and bottle near the river. I always thought that was odd, because your mum and Woody had searched and presumably others had too, and yet not one of them thought to go down to the banks of the river behind the pub. That was another reason I thought the things could have been planted." I nod, agreeing that it did seem strange. Spider continues, "I was even allowed to interview Lorelei myself. I guess I was so star struck that I probably didn't make a very good job of it."

Spider pauses and sips his drink.

"What did she say?"

He looks at his notes. "Said she'd seen him on Friday as he'd been working in the Hall gardens. He'd have gone up to the house for his break and lunch, but she didn't recall seeing him then."

"What did you think of her?"

"Lorelei? I thought she was wonderful. She had an aura that was dazzling. Well, you've met her. Perhaps you understand what I mean?"

"Yes, she could be mesmerising." I don't say she could also be mean and cross and deceptive. But I do say, "Her story can't be completely true."

"What do you mean?"

"I mean that Lorelei must have seen Daddy after Friday because I saw her running from my house on the Saturday evening."

Spider makes a little come on gesture with his fingers, as if he knows there's more, "Tell me everything."

"I saw Lorelei that evening. I was sneaking back home and I saw Lorelei running down the path from my house. She was wearing a black cloak and I'm sure she had blood on her hands."

"But she might not have been to see your father?"

"No, but where else could she have been, other than the cottage?" I'm disappointed in Spider, but guess it's usual for Lorelei to be without guilt, to always be the innocent.

"And why wasn't this mentioned at the time?"

"I was twelve. Nobody bothered to ask me anything."

"Are you suggesting Lorelei had something to do with your father's disappearance, that maybe she killed him?"

"I think she might have been involved in some way. But killing him? I don't think so. But there was something strange going on because I found another similar cloak in my father's shed. I thought they must have been involved in something together."

"It's a pity you didn't tell us this at the time."

"Nobody asked me!" Spider regards me as though I'm being unreasonable. "There was a bag as well."

"Go on."

"A backpack with a jumper, some shoes; my dad's I think. I always thought it was just a spare set of clothing he kept in the woodshed, but now … well he might have been going to run away."

"And the backpack was gone after you last saw him?"

"No, that's the thing … I don't think it was. And there's something else … I think the bag had toiletries in. Daddy wouldn't have put those in there unless he was planning to go away … as if he kept a bag packed so he could leave at any time." My voice dwindles away. The words echo in my head having spoken things I never realised were there. Am I suggesting Daddy, who I thought loved me, could plan to disappear at any moment? With or without Lorelei?

Spider is staring at me; I feel as though we could be having this conversation in an interview room at the police station. With me under suspicion.

"There is something else …" he says. From the notebook he pulls a slip of paper and hands it to me. "I'd forgotten about this as well."

I scan the paper. It's a photocopy of a witness document, and states that somebody reported seeing a man they think was Ryan Ramson in Bristol. I look at the date. "This is December 1983. That's months after Daddy disappeared."

"Yes. That's probably why nothing was followed up. The case was firmly closed then."

"So, another suggestion that Daddy could still be alive?"

Spider says, "That's the problem. It's so long ago; nothing can be proved or disproved. Really we need your father either to turn up alive or his body to be discovered."

I have no reply to that.

"The police can't do anything now, though. Maybe you need to put something out there on social media. Somebody somewhere might know something, or if your dad is out there he might see it." His fingers tap against the notebook cover. "The other thing I think we failed to have a look at was *'the goings on'* in the village. Something that was never spoken about when we investigated but obviously surrounded the whole event. Again, people just wouldn't speak to us."

"How do you mean, 'goings on'?"

"Well, there's always been rumours of a coven operating out of Broomstone; witchcraft and the like."

My mouth is dry. Perhaps I should tell him about my invitation from Myrtill. But decide not to. There is something else I should mention. I take a sip of my water and say, "You know that my parents had a row that night? When I got back they were shouting the place down, I couldn't go in straight away. That's why I waited in the wood shed."

"Your mother did say they had an argument. That he'd stayed away for a couple of nights before after a big row. It was given as the most likely reason as to why he'd gone. In the end it was deemed there was really no reason for the police to get involved."

"But you didn't talk to me. He would never have gone without saying goodbye to me. Would he?" The question hangs in the air as it has done for so many years. Because perhaps he had done that after all. Even if he had left his escape backpack. Maybe he'd just had enough of Ma and the endless arguments and walked out. Maybe he'd had enough of me.

"What do you think can have happened then, if he didn't just leave? Where did he go?" Spider asks.

"I accepted that he'd drowned. That's what everyone told me had happened. He'd been in the pub most of the evening, got drunk as usual, came home, argued with Ma and then gone down to the river to think about things and accidentally slipped."

But Spider is suggesting that was not what had occurred. So, if my father hadn't run off and hadn't fallen in the river, then Spider was right to ask, 'where was he?' My brain can't cope with the answer to that; it's like contemplating infinity ... just endless questions echoing on and on, with the answers getting darker and darker as they go. The fizzy water is making my stomach unsettled and the bubbles make me belch. I catch sight of the TV screen behind Spider, showing a golf tournament. A figure I don't recognise hits a ball to land inches from the hole. The green, the flowers and the outfit are all too bright. I blink several times and try to bring my focus back to Spider.

"What about Lorelei?"

He takes a moment to consider what has made me change the topic but then says, "Okay then, let's move on."

Spider opens another notebook and squints at his writing. Recognising the edge of a test result document, I ask, "There were blood tests after the incident then?"

Spider looks up briefly and frowns at me. He picks the document up. "Of course. And they showed high levels of ...

Tyramine and Viscumin." I shake my head; the long chemical names mean nothing. "Apparently those are poisonous substances found in mistletoe." I shift in my chair and think of little bottles of green tonic in the cottage kitchen. Spider puts his hands on the table and looks directly at me as if he's about to accuse me of poisoning her. He says, "You know Lorelei was pregnant don't you?"

I nod, but don't mention she was pregnant with my sister.

"It's likely that whatever she took was used to induce an abortion."

"What ... that can't be right." I was certain Lorelei wanted that child.

"It's too late now, but there ..." He stops abruptly, closing the notebook, obviously deciding against saying more.

"Go on," I encourage.

"Well, I shouldn't really say but I think there was something about the foetus which was unusual."

"In what way?"

"Perhaps a deformity. I really don't know more."

"But you could find out?"

"Possibly, but I'd be getting onto shaky ground."

I don't press for him to promise to search further; I think he will follow it up anyway. I wonder whether I have the nerve to ask Cedric about it. It seems even stranger that he should want the baby laid out if that was the case. "If it was deformed, do you think that was the reason she was trying to get rid of it?"

"My guess, is that she had three step children and one of her own anyway. Perhaps she couldn't cope with being a mother to more children. I don't know. I don't have children myself."

"No, thinking back, she probably wasn't the most natural mother. But terminating her pregnancy ... I don't think she'd do that." My stomach, more likely my own womb, aches as I say it; the loss of my own baby ten years ago drags at me. I might have vocalised the internal groan of pain, because

Spider frowns at me. I continue, "I'm not sure I can make that assumption though. I really didn't know her very well. But did anybody have a reason to harm her?"

"There are a lot of people who would become envious of somebody so successful. Perhaps if the pregnancy was starting to show, somebody would want to stop that."

There's a battle going on in my head. My brain won't accept the idea that Ma would try to harm Lorelei or her baby, even if she'd thought it was my father's.

"What about Cedric ... if he thought the baby wasn't his?"

"He was devastated, and look at how supportive he's been since."

"He might just be a good actor. And he might feel guilty."

Spider flicks another page over. "No, when he was questioned there was nothing to suggest he'd had anything to do with it."

"What about Miss Dryden then. Do you think she gave her the medicine?"

"Is that the old lady? The one everybody called a witch?"

I nod.

"We think it likely but we never got the chance to interview her. We could never pin down an actual address, just that she lived somewhere in the woods. I presumed she was Romany, and moved around selling her wares. When it was deemed an accidental overdose nobody thought it worthwhile chasing up."

I watch the bubbles in my sparkling water rise and pop and I sigh. Spider says with a new firmness in his voice, "It was a difficult case. In fact, getting anybody to say anything was impossible. It was as if there was some massive secret that the police weren't privy to as we were outsiders. The responses were always, 'I didn't know her, or I didn't know her well.' We had a number of conflicting statements about who she was last seen with and it was impossible to work out conclusively where she got the poison from. Let me read you this. It's from when I interviewed your mother." He opened the diary to a page marked with a pink post-it note.

"'Mrs Ramson said she didn't really speak to Lorelei. When Lorelei moved back to Broomstone she did bring Archie to be looked after quite often.' I've put a note here that your mother was paid to look after the child."

A sequence of those days when Archie was dropped off at weekends or after school float through my mind. Rosa sometimes hung around, though they never wanted to play the games that I liked. But just occasionally Roderick would come too and I cherished those days. I shudder at the thought of my diary from then, filled with hopeless poems of unrequited love.

Through this haze of memory, Spider continues to tell me what my mother had said.

"'Often it wasn't Lorelei who brought Archie to the cottage, more likely I would collect him from school or the girls would bring him,' She went on to say that, 'I didn't visit the Hall during that time, in fact I was only invited to the party because of my daughter Annie.'"

Spider is looking at me, expecting me to respond.

"That might have been true," I say. "I don't think my mother ever went to see Lorelei. But she was excited about being invited to the party ... I think ... but that might just have been me."

I thought of something else though. My father worked at the Hall for at least seven months from when Lorelei returned to Broomstone in the summer of 1982. He'd tidied everything up in the Libani gardens, mowed the lawns. I had not seen him as happy working for a long time. It was only a short walk from home and it seemed the Libanis treated him well. Even though he had professed to hate Lorelei when she left, he said nothing negative her about her during those days. I'm wondering whether to say anything, but Spider seeing me hesitate says, "Go on then, what is it? You've obviously remembered something." So, I tell him.

"And you think he had a relationship with Lorelei?"

"No, of course not. Only that they were on friendlier terms again."

"Could it be they were involved, maybe planning to run away together when your father disappeared? Perhaps he was going to wait for her. Could the baby have been his?"

"How the hell should I know?" Other diners turn to look at me. I hadn't meant to shout. I lower my voice to a whisper. "Nobody ever told me anything. Daddy hated her … I think …" But an image of Daddy's smiling face appears, returning from work at the Hall. His jaunty steps back home from the pub on Sundays. And Lorelei saying she was carrying my sister. There was another memory that flickered into my head, like a roll of old movie film. A view of Daddy, glimpsed from a bus, sitting on a bench beside Lorelei. I'd been returning from secondary school, scrunched up on the top deck. Minding my own business. The bus had to make a detour due to roadworks on the bypass, so we were circuiting the Hall grounds. To me it was just a blur of a man and a woman sitting closely together, but then the kids at the front of the bus started to snigger and sing, "… *Annie's Dad, Sitting in a tree, K - I - S - S - I - N - G …*" Then they made ugly noises and gestures, turning to look at me. I stared out of the window, trying to ignore them, trying not to think about what I'd seen.

On the 18th green a foursome shake hands; from this distance they could be saying anything.

I finish my drink, then turn the glass so that the ice cubes move making patterns of light. This conversation really hasn't been helpful. More questions than answers. It has also generated a familiar longing inside me, one I have not learnt to ignore. My own lost baby.

"Look, I'll see if I can find out more about the baby. As it was six months, I think there might have been a post mortem." Spider says. We finish our drinks in silence and then I say, "Goodbye," and murmur a reluctant thank you under my breath.

As I get back to the car I feel aimless. So, I just drive.

The thought that Lorelei might deliberately terminate her pregnancy grips me. I think of my baby, my baby who should be ten years old. A cramp spasms across my stomach making me grimace. I had met and married Jay in my thirties. For me certainly, and for Jay probably, there was a sense of desperation about our marriage. To be a couple before it was too late. We'd tried for a baby at the beginning and nothing happened, then just when I was going to give up, the test came back positive. I thought I would burst with happiness. It didn't last. No wonder Jay had left me. For a time, I had lost interest in everything.

As if to torment me, fate takes me past a school and a playground. There are children everywhere, boys and girls, toddlers and infants in prams. I think of Archie as a baby. Archie was the first thing I had ever truly loved.

His eyes were big and blue and full of wonder. His skin was pinky and pale reminding me of when a shoot unfurls from earth, with the translucence of something precious and new. His tiny fingers clutched mine when I put my hand near his. When I made a funny face at him he would reflect back what I did. In fact, his eyes were always on me, following each move I made, as though he was learning how to be a human. I was somebody special to him. I sniff and wipe tears from my eyes.

I have driven past the turn off to Broomstone, then find myself pulling into a parking space outside my flat. I nearly turn round, but think I may as well go in and have a drink.

I shouldn't have done. As I go into the building, I can tell there's somebody waiting outside my door. I hesitate wondering whether to continue but it is too late. A voice calls, "Hey, Annie love. Is that you?" The greeting makes me move forward and as I clamber up the steps I see first trainers, then the blue of jeans and gradually Jay, my ex, comes fully into view. He is smiling at me. "There you are. I wondered where you'd got to." He is the same age as me, but manages to exude youth. His blonde hair is tousled and he gives me a crooked smile which always has the stupid effect of making my knees weak and my stomach flip.

"Been busy," I state simply, trying to push past him.

"Aren't you going to invite me in for a drink then?"

I want to say 'No' but the word seems to stick to my tongue like a feather. I can't spit it out. Jay stands up pressing himself against me as I fumble the keys in the lock. His breath is on my neck and I can smell his familiar smell and sense the warmth of his familiar body beneath his clothing.

Finally, I manage to find the will power to say, "What do you want? I've got things to do."

I turn the key and Jay pushes through behind me as I open the door. I am unable to stop him.

"Jay …" I begin, wanting to tell him to go. Knowing what has happened on previous occasions when he'd left me and then insinuated himself back into my life, my bed.

"Just thought I'd say hello. Nothing wrong with being friendly is there?"

The dank smell of the flat hits me. Why had I bothered coming in? I'm wishing I hadn't.

"Here I've got a bottle of wine. Shall we order take out?"

And before I have a chance to say 'No,' he's got his mobile out and is ordering my favourite Chinese dishes and asking them to deliver.

I give in and pull two glasses and some cutlery from the cupboards. Jay twists off the cap and pours the wine. It's dry and smooth against my tongue. I take another swig.

"So, what are you up to?" Jay asks.

"It's just an article about Broomstone village … where I used to live."

"More weird things going on there?"

"What do you mean more weird things?"

"Well, it was always known to be a strange place. Didn't that famous pop star live there?"

"Yes …" for some reason I always find it difficult to be evasive with Jay; he has a way of looking at me that makes me tell him things. He does it now, a tilt of his head and a smile that turns up in one corner, "... that's who I'm supposed to be writing about."

"Well, good for you. Hope they're paying you well."

A ring of the bell and Jay goes and pays for the meal, which is unusual. Maybe he has changed?

We scoop food onto our plates and pour more wine, and when we've finished the bottle he's brought, I open another.

As he tells me, "I'm doing well. Enjoying life. Had lots of time to meet up with my mates," I feel a habitual loneliness wrap around me. I have nobody. The people in Broomstone are not really friends and Ma is becoming more distant as time goes on. Especially since I've started going back to Broomstone.

"Hey, you," Jay is round my side of the table, enclosing me in his arms. I haven't realised I'm crying. I sniff into the fabric of his shirt. It is warm and comfortable. Safe. "Don't cry. It's alright," he soothes, "I'm here now." He is rubbing my back, stroking my hair.

The Chinese meal feels heavy in my stomach, the wine making me soporific, so when Jay pulls me up and walks me to my bed; starts to undress me, I don't resist. I sink onto the cold mattress and let him make love to me.

I wake hours later, my eyes gritty with smudged makeup, my throat dry and my body soiled. Coming to, I hear Jay snoring, his arm thrown out, his splayed legs pushing me to the edge of the bed. Now I'm sober I wonder why I'd believed him when he'd said how happy he was ... he wouldn't have turned up here if that was the case. It is too late to undo last night. I frown at Jay, spreading out in my bed as if he owns it, owns me. Against the pillow his hair looks greasy and I notice it is starting to thin at the temples. In the dim dawn light, his skin is sallow as well and his face more lined. I feel repulsed. Not just with Jay, but with myself, for letting him into my life again.

I get up and shower and dress quietly. I grab a few extra items of clothing and I'm just going to tip toe away. But then

I backtrack and grab a piece of junk mail. On it I write, 'Leave me alone Jay. I don't want to see you again.' I underline the sentence twice, hoping he'll get the message. And as I press the nib of pen into the paper I tell myself I must not let him manipulate me again.

CHAPTER 31

I escape my flat and exchange it for the claustrophobia of Broomstone. Today I am actually glad at the swap; at least Broomstone doesn't have Jay in it, muddling my thoughts.

It is still only half light as I drive into the village. Mist is lifting off the brook, smoke-like wisps curling over the water; it shrouds everything so that the hill of Broomstone rises out like a veiled island. The lump of badger is still by the roadside but is now decaying into a black mound. It could be anything. Morphed into something unrecognisable.

At the Hall everything is silent. I hope nobody will be about to see me sneak in. But I sense the house judging me, watching me as I turn the key in the lock. As I enter, Rasputin is sitting on the reception desk washing himself. He looks up from the business of licking his paw and jumps down, meowing round my feet. I tiptoe across the hallway, stepping side-to-side in an uneasy dance, so as not to trip over as he winds in and out of my legs. He follows me down to the basement. The air seems different this morning, but I put that down to the early hour and my state of guilt.

Rasputin takes up a position in front of the bird cabinet and I sit behind my desk and start sorting again.

I must have been at work for about half an hour, when I hear a noise. A dull thudding sound from the other side of the basement. I wonder what Rasputin is doing and go to look. Rasputin is asleep on the floor, curled in front of the cabinet. The knocking has stopped so I remain still, listening again, holding my breath. Perhaps the noise has come from outside or upstairs. Then it starts again. Definitely emanating from the other end of the basement. Stepping quietly over the stone floor, I make my way to the door at the side. The noise stops and then continues from right behind it. The door had been locked before but now I try it again, turning the handle as slowly as possible, it lets out a whine of resistance. And opens. The first thing that hits me is the smell. I have to put my hand across my nose; even then I gag. It is a mixture of blood and disinfectant.

"Keep the bloody cat out!" Cedric shouts at me, as Rasputin glides in through my legs. I grab him and throw him back into the basement. He manages to scratch me as he falls and then races up the stairs, mewling.

Cedric is sitting at a table surrounded by feathers, and is holding what looks like a piece of bloody cloth. "What the hell are you doing here?" he demands.

"I was working and I heard a noise."

"Well, this is where I do my taxidermy. Nobody is allowed here, nobody. Especially that bloody cat. Do you know what he'd do if he got in here?"

I imagine it would look in a similar state. "I'm sorry, but nobody told me you had a room down here."

"Hmmm." Cedric's response is grumpy and tired. The skin beneath his eyes is bagged with grey. He had evidently got down here before me. Maybe he'd been here the entire night. The whole room is monochrome, as if it's a shrine to the magpie. Cedric in the middle is dressed in a cream kaftan which gleams against his dark skin, the walls are white-washed and the furnishings are ebony. Even the blood on the bird's feathers has congealed to black.

"I was just going to get myself some coffee," I say, hoping to appease him. "Would you like some?"

"Okay. But make sure that bloody cat is kept away from here."

When I return with coffee, Cedric appears less annoyed. He actually invites me in and says he'll show me what he's doing. I hesitate because the stench in the room is so foul.

Misunderstanding my reluctance, he says, "Don't worry, it's not as gory as you might think."

I hold my coffee mug close to my nose, inhaling the aroma, which helps mask the other smell. I step forward. Cedric proceeds to take me through the process of removing the innards from a bird, then washing it out, filling its body and adding back features. I look at his hands; they seem too big for such delicate work. "I know," he comments, "You're thinking it's a strange sort of hobby for a bloke like me."

"Yes."

"I like doing magpies best. It makes me feel close to her." And I know he is thinking about Lorelei.

On a high shelf along the wall is a row of already stuffed magpies. There are six. I mutter to myself, "… six for gold, seven for a secret never to be told …" and watch as Cedric picks up the bird he is working on.

"No," he says, hearing my words and shaking his head. "That's the modern version. The original is: one for sorrow, two for mirth, three for a funeral, four for birth, five for heaven, six for hell, seven for the devil, his own self." Cedric continues to manipulate the magpie's skin. "This will be the seventh, and I think I should stop there. Seven is enough magpies."

The birds watch me. I'm aware of being scrutinised by their gleaming bead eyes. My reflection trapped behind those twelve shining surfaces. The version of the rhyme that Cedric has recited is horrible. A feathery touch chills my neck, with the thought that when the seventh is placed on the shelf, it will represent the devil. I shudder and turn away.

"Where does that door lead?" I ask, noticing an arched doorway at the back of the room.

"Oh, just further under the house. There are a number of passageways that have never been explored. The old stories say they lead from the Hall to the lake, to the church and to some of the cottages in the village."

I step back, reluctant to take the coffee mug he hands me.

174

There are streaks of bloody matter on the handle. "Thanks for that," he says, and I know I am being dismissed.

I take the mugs back upstairs. Archie is in the kitchen, "Everything okay?" he asks.

I smile and say, "Yes," hoping he won't ask me where I'd been last night, and considering how much I'll tell him. But he doesn't say more. "I think I'll go out for a while," I say, feeling the need to justify my movements.

I don't want to go back to the confines of the basement. I can smell the odour of the taxidermy room; it stings the back of my throat. I make my way back to the Broomstone Forest path and start to walk to where my home had once been.

It is cooler today, the waft of wild garlic strong. I pass a brush of hazel bushes, the bank below them a mass of roots. They remind me of an illustration from my fairy tale book; goblins squeezed below ground whilst they sleep. Their slender sepia tinted limbs bent. Above me in the taller trees, balls of mistletoe are growing. Now I know what Lorelei was poisoned with I'm wondering how you would reach the berries. I miss my footing, jarring my ankle, startled by a rustling sound coming from the undergrowth. A skinny leg appearing.

"Going to see the witchy house again?" the boy I met before asks. "Lots of history there ... lots of his ... ss ... tory." He exaggerates the word and it sounds like a long hiss.

I shudder. When I continue to walk forward, trying to ignore him, he stands in my way. "I knows things ... I knows things ..." I try to step around him but as I move to the left he blocks my way. I sense that if I move right he will too and we'll end up doing a kind of dance.

"Let me by, please."

He grins, the look of a boy, but with deep lines on his face.

"I knows things 'bout your mum."

I bristle against his annoying, teasing voice. "I'm sure you do. Now please move out of my way."

"I knows things about your mum ... I knows things about

your mum and the woodman."

I should just continue on, pushing him aside if necessary, but stupidly I say, "You mean Woody?"

"Yes, Woody and your mum are very cosy in his caravan. Very cosy indeed."

"They're friends," I say, "Friends for a long time."

"More than friends ... lots more than friends. Ham's seen them ... being friends." He gives a guffaw that makes me and the surrounding trees shiver.

"You're Ham then, are you?"

"Yes that's me, that's me. Ham in the woods ... Ham in the woods ..."

As he dances round, singing his name, I manage to advance a few steps. He notices and swiftly moves back in front of me. "Where are you going, so where you going?"

Hearing Ham's information, I consider whether I should go and see Woody or return to the Hall and drive to see Ma. I don't want to tell Ham he's stirred something up, which is obviously his intention. And then I remember that Myrtill said Miss Dryden was still alive. If anybody knows of her whereabouts, this boy who says he lives in the forest is likely to know.

"Well, I'm trying to find somebody. You might be able to help?"

"Maybe I will, maybe I won't."

"Miss Dryden."

"My grandmama. You can't find her."

"I'd like to try though." He peers at me, as if he is trying to calculate something.

"Okay, see that door?" He indicates, not a door but a tree trunk. Around its base is an archway of ivy making it look as if there is an entrance. "Knock on that three times, close your eyes and turn around three times and wish for Miss Dryden to come to the door."

The boy is hunching over, his arms tight around his body, and is hopping from foot to foot. I look dubious. "Go on," he says, "Three knocks, three turns and a wish."

I step forward and knock on the tree trunk three times as instructed. I can hear Ham shuffling behind me and hesitate. "Go on," he commands. "Close your eyes, and turn round, turn round, turn round ..."

I stumble round in a circle three times and then open my eyes to an empty space. I feel stupid.

Suddenly the boy jumps out at me from behind the tree laughing. "You did it, you did it." He skips about with obvious glee that I have fallen for his trick. He is jigging round, doubled up with laughter.

I wait until he's calmed down and then say, "Okay, you've had your joke. Now will you tell me where I can find your grandmother?"

He stares at me. Narrowing his eyes, calculating again. I am too hot for game playing. "Well, are you going to tell me, or are you just going to wind me up?"

"Can't find her," he says, and I start to walk away. "She'll know though, come find you if she wants to talk." His words follow me as I stride away from the main path and deeper into the wood.

Under the cover of the trees, I take a deep breath, filling my lungs with the familiar scent of garlic and nettle sap. I pick up a wider track and know it leads out towards the edge of the forest where Woody has his caravan. I have some questions for him.

He is sitting on the steps of the van, whittling a piece of wood. He doesn't seem to notice me approach so I wait for a time, just watching him; the easy movement of his hands, turning an old branch into something beautiful.

After a while he puts down his knife and picks up his tobacco pouch. I watch his nimble fingers roll a paper around golden threads of tobacco and then light the cigarette. It reminds me of when I was a child, watching him going through exactly the same process. He hasn't changed in all the time I have known him. Still that same tanned skin, his skinny frame, his hair a bit long.

"Come out then," he calls. "I know you're standing there. What do you want?"

I'm not sure if he knows it is me spying on him, or is expecting somebody else, as he seems surprised when I step out of the shadows. "Well, Annie. What are you doing in this neck of the woods, spying on your old mate?"

"I wasn't spying," I say sounding stupid. "I was just watching you. Like I always did."

"Okay, if you say so. Do you want a brew then?" he asks.

I nod and go over to the van. I hear him muttering to himself as he boils the kettle. I don't go inside but wait until he brings two enamel mugs of tea outside. He sits back down on the step and rolls another cigarette. I sit on the ground just as I had when I was a girl, listening to him telling stories or watching him work on his wood.

"I met a boy in the woods. Calls himself Ham. Said things about you and Ma."

Woody doesn't look at me, just blows smoke rings and watches as they dissipate. "You don't want to believe what he tells you. He just likes to annoy folk."

"Well, it wouldn't matter really, anyway. You and Ma? You're free to do what you want."

"Exactly. So why do I think you're accusing me of something?"

"I'm not." I'm not sure what I am doing. It is their business but it feels like it should be mine.

"Me and your ma are close, of course we are … lots of history. Look …" Now he does raise his eyes to mine. "You know what your dad was like, how he treated her. Long ago I told her to leave him, move away and live with me. But she wouldn't of course. Then your dad disappeared and I was there for her. More recently we've talked about moving in together, but I can't live in a town and she can't live in the forest. Now, does that make you more satisfied?"

I look away and pick up a twig, breaking off bits and

throwing them on the ground. He is telling me they are having an affair now, but just how long has that been going on for? Is he saying it started before Daddy disappeared or afterwards.

"No, I thought not," Woody said.

"But were you and Ma having an affair before Daddy went missing?"

"Annie you need to grow up, realise your dad was not some sort of king with the world pitted against him."

I pick up another twig; he hasn't answered my question. "That's not what I think, but it's just being back here and looking at Lorelei's life. Nothing really makes sense. Except she did steal Ma's songs and that's what propelled her to stardom."

"That again? Annie, your mother put that behind her a long time ago. So should you."

He grinds his cigarette stub under his boot and takes out his tobacco pouch. He starts rolling another immediately. "Your mother really isn't happy about you delving into Lorelei's past." He pauses to lick the cigarette paper. "Perhaps you should quit now, before you find out something you really don't want to know."

"See you then," I say, annoyed with Woody. So many people I've spoken to are warning me off. Being no help at all. I stand up and walk away. As I make my way back towards Quercus Hall, I feel there is something else I should have asked. I need to uncover the things Woody isn't telling me.

CHAPTER 32 - IVY

After Annie had left, Woody called into the van. "It's safe now, she's gone." Ivy stood up from where she'd been crouching on the caravan floor. "Thank goodness, I was getting cramp." Ivy squeezed past Woody on the steps and sat on a log stump. "Do you think she knew I was here?"

"No. If she'd realised that she'd have said something. Maybe I should have told her anyway?"

"No, I'm not ready for that. And why was she asking about when we'd started seeing each other?"

"She's just curious, that's all. It doesn't mean anything. I think it's time you were honest with her. She's not a kid anymore." Seeing the look of panic on Ivy's face, Woody added, "Not about then but about now. I alluded to that anyhow."

"You were right to tell her I wasn't comfortable with her digging round. I wish she'd just leave it."

CHAPTER 33

As I approach the Hall I feel dispirited. I know I should do a bit more work. I go down and start to sort through the box again. However, I do more staring into space than investigating anything in the box. I'm anxious about meeting with Myrtill later; just what am I walking into? I'm glad to hear Poppy's footsteps and her call. "You need a break. Come and have supper, I've cooked a casserole."

After supper I make my excuses and leave them playing cards. In my room I dress in black jeans and a black sweater; it seems an appropriate outfit for an undercover operation. Time drags. At a quarter past nine I creep down the back staircase and make my way across the green to Myrtill's. The dusk is closing in, stealing the colour from objects. The front door of 'The Gallery,' has a closed sign up, so I go round the back. I climb the flight of steps at the rear, thinking how long it has been since I'd last done so. The stairs are worn; the hand rail wobbles and the treads creak. It signals my approach because suddenly Myrtill appears at the top door and beckons me forward. "Come in, and we'll get ready." I follow her into her studio room. It doesn't look any different and the smell is just as I remember. The magpie skull sits on the window ledge, its lacy structure now embellished with embroidery of cobweb.

"It might be a good idea to have a drink before we go. Calm your nerves." I'm going to say I'm not nervous but that is a lie, and Myrtill will know. I try to see what work is in progress on the easel but it is covered with a sheet. Myrtill seeing the direction of my glance, says, "Not ready for viewing yet.

Maybe next week."

She hands me a small thick glass filled with a yellow liquid. "Straight down," she advises and tips her head back and drinks her own glassful. I follow, expecting the concoction to be medicinal, but it is sweet and clear and cool in my mouth and then as it reaches my stomach starts to warm, making me tingle.

"Good, isn't it? My special brew." Myrtill laughs. She grabs the bottle and pours us each another. "Right. We head down just as dark is falling, but first we need to get ready."

She goes out and opens a wardrobe which stands on the landing at the top of the stairs from the shop. It is huge allowing very little space along the corridor. It might easily be the one I'd seen in the basement of Quercus Hall all those years ago.

When Myrtill comes back she's carrying two black cloaks. Each has a hood lined with grey satin. "This should fit," she says, throwing one to me. I slip it on feeling the lining cool against my skin. "It's important that your face isn't seen. You must pull your hood as far forward as you can, and keep your hands under the sleeves." I do as she asks, feeling like a child playing dressing up in grandma's clothes.

"There will be movement and singing. The moves are straightforward, like this ..." She shows me a simple routine. "Now you." I copy her actions as she repeats them. "Got it?"

"Got it," I assure her.

"There will also be some chanting but, whatever you do, don't speak. You must just watch."

"Okay."

"You must be clear on this. No speaking, absolute silence."

I nod, "Got it." I don't ask what would happen if I'm found out. I really don't want to know.

"Ready?"

"Yes."

"Silence from now on then." I sign a zip across my mouth and follow as Myrtill lights a candle and places it in a lantern hooked onto a metal pole. Any lightness in the sky has gone but the full moon is out and it and the candle light our way. We cross the green, the moon playing hide and seek behind the canopy of leaves fluttering on the beech tree.

Nearer Quercus Hall I make out other figures joining us. Some of them carry lanterns; others are just dark shapes floating into view. The moonlight glints off the weird windows and roof tiles of the building. I shiver and try to concentrate on Myrtill. I don't want to be separated from her. There are about fifteen of us. We walk alongside the wall and cross the yard, and then down the outside steps to the basement, the very path I had taken when Deidre had tricked me. We enter through the side door. My small study area is silent and dark; I cannot imagine myself sitting there earlier or the conversation I'd had with Cedric when we enter his taxidermy room. Even the foul odour has dissipated. The magpies hop and blink in the candlelight. The seventh winks at me from the end of the row. We have to crouch low to climb through the arched door in the corner of the studio. The ground slopes downwards and I smell the dank stench of damp earth. The candles wisp smoke tails and I try not to choke in the enclosed space. After walking for maybe quarter of a mile the ground starts to rise up again and the air becomes clearer. The group gathers at the top of the final steps and we exit into moonlight. I try to work out the height and shape of the figures around me, trying to discern who my companions are. But it is impossible. I'm not sure if I am still following Myrtill.

There is a breeze as we progress further into the trees on the island, the air moving against us. My cloak shifts around me so I feel that I'm not in control of my movement. I am being manoeuvred and pushed onward.

Nobody speaks but there are noises and rustling. Not from the trees but whispering overhead and around us, as if incantations are being spoken by somebody unseen. With every step I take, I am more and more certain that the group know exactly who I am. Rather than being the spy, I am the one being spied on, every movement, every breath; being monitored by an unknown force.

Finally, we reach the central area where the stone pit is. The leader of this bizarre company moves forward and puts a flame to the centre. It leaps up and dances, greedy for the twigs and leaves that are thrown onto it. The figure is small and hunched, the fingers clawed. It must be Miss Dryden. Smoky scent and dense perfume of wild garlic fills the glade. Then a hum starts. At first it sounds just like the trees, but I realise my companions are making the tune. The atmosphere vibrates, like fingertips pressing my skin at random. The thrill starts to invade my body making me twitch. A ball of air rises in my throat and I almost shout out at the weird sensation, but stop in time. I know I must not speak. I clench my teeth, managing to remain silent.

My head is dizzy as the pungent herbs burn. The edges of vision blurring with the typical aura before a migraine. The heat of the fire burnishes my skin. The group are now stepping and I follow them as we circle the glade. I copy the hand actions as well, as Myrtill had showed me; lifting my right arm and then left, swinging my arms forward up over my head, then back down, and turning around. I am part of the dance; free and happy. I feel a little drunk. I want to laugh. Then suddenly everybody stops. I nearly collide with the figure I think is Myrtill.

Someone is moving around the circle, sharing something out. All the party are extending a hand. I do the same and a scrap that looks like bark is placed on my palm. Myrtill hadn't mentioned this but I just copy the others, lifting my hand to my mouth and eating the morsel. It tastes earthy, like truffle.

The central figure shouts and the others chant a response. Things are being thrown into the fire; feathers like arrows glint silver in the moonlight. 'Shush... shush... shush...' a sound stirs from the flames and suddenly magpies fly upwards from the pit, with their chuckling call and wing beats striking the air. I count them silently, 'one, two, three, four, five, six, seven ...' and I think of the shelf in Cedric's work shop now empty. As each bird flies upwards, the company murmur the magpie rhyme. Their words hushed, so I hear '... sorrow ... mirth ... funeral ...birth ...heaven ... hell ...' The final audible word, '... Devil,' resonates for longer as the beat of wings recedes.

"Go and do our bidding," the group chant.

Another shout from the leader, another response, something else thrown into the pit. This time a cloud of grey dust, so I think it is embers from the fire. But the flakes transform into moths. Bluish white under the moonlight and I'm reminded of the insects I've seen pinned behind glass, outside my room. There is more murmuring, as if wishes are being made, then the louder chorus of, "Go and do our bidding ..." as the cloud of moths fades.

Again, a shout, this time louder, bounds around the glade, making the surroundings reverberate with a noise like thunder. As it dwindles, hissing rises from the pit. My vision is blurred, my head aching and heavy, so I'm not sure what I'm seeing. But it looks like a snake. Diamond scales gleam like molten tar as it slithers away into the undergrowth. I shudder, my burnished skin suddenly cold as if I've been dropped in ice water. I can't stop shaking. The group's words of "Go and do our bidding ..." chorus after the creature and linger, echoing around us, drumming into my mind.

The fire is still giving off heat, but I remain chilled. I can't make sense of what I'm seeing. Myrtill had suggested, 'healing spells,' and 'warding off evil,' but nothing about this feels light or wholesome. My skin is sweaty and slick, the taste in my mouth like bile. The swimming in my head intensifies as if I am being dragged into a nightmare. This is more than a conjuring trick. Not just pulling objects from a hat but creating them. If birds and moths and snakes can come to life ... what else has been conceived here?

I stare at the pit, the fire glow stinging my eyes and for

a moment I don't see people around me, but trees, as if I am being enclosed in a copse. Amongst them cedar, alder, linden, rowan and willow. Within them faces I know from Broomstone ... Cedric, Deidre's parents, the pub landlord, Miss Rowan and Myrtill. Their faces are shadowed but they're laughing at me. I look at my hands to check that I am still human. My fingers are cold and gleam a ghostly grey. But flesh and blood.

The fire is dwindling. Its smoking remains twirl and entwine like an old tree trunk. The hum has altered in tone and is a lull in my head, my eyes gritty from the wood smoke. I blink but my vision does not clear. Something else is emerging from the smoke. Blinking again does not make the creature go away. I gasp, taking a step backwards, immediately realising I should not make a sound. Regaining my balance, I glance around but the others all seem to be concentrating on the fire pit and not on me. The embers spark and crackle and from it a full figure now emerges. A grey lady rising from the ashes. Lorelei. She smiles at me, beckoning with a stretched out palm. "*Come to me Annie,*" she whispers, "*Come to me.*" I am like iron, unable to resist the magnetic pull. I lift my right foot to take a step forward, to obey her command. Then my elbow jerks as a restraining grip clasps my arm. "No!" a hushed voice says urgently. It doesn't sound like Myrtill. But it jolts me out of my stupor and when I look again the smoke has all but vanished and coiled away, leaving the pit grey and cold.

I follow again, my steps unsteady, as the company moves away, heading for the return trip through the tunnel. Stumbling several times, I negotiate the rough tunnel floor towards the basement. In Cedric's room the top shelf is in darkness. The carried lamplight appears dimmed, just tawny smudges not reaching into corners. I can't tell if the magpies are still there. My body is numb, my steps making a thud, thud as I walk over the stone tiles. I try to remember what I'd seen. The image of Lorelei in the smoke lingers, like a veil across my mind, making my thoughts muddled. As we cross the green, the others melt away to their homes and I am left with just Myrtill beside me.

Myrtill does not speak until we're back inside. We enter at the front and walk to the room behind the shop, our bodies brushing the objects hanging there, leaving a tinkling trail. Myrtill lights candles in wall sconces from the lantern she carries. Halos of light hang around us in amber puddles which do not fully extinguish the darkness.

Myrtill slips off her cloak but I haven't moved. She comes over and stands in front of me and draws the hood away from my face. Placing her hands on my cheeks, she says, "You're freezing, Annie. Sit down and I'll make you a drink."

I do as she instructs, unable to speak. I sit on the couch and wait.

Soon Myrtill is sitting beside me, offering a cup of hot liquid. The fragrance of herbal tisane infiltrates my nostrils. "You said ... you said ..." I sniff the brew again. "How can those things be created, the magpies, the moths, the snake?"

"They're just illusions. Sometimes they're part of a spell. Sometimes they're just for show."

"But can anything be created?"

"Of course." Myrtill's response is so matter of fact, I feel stupid. I sip my drink and finally say, "I saw her."

"What do you mean? You saw who?"

"Lorelei. I saw her in the smoke from the pit."

"No. The smoke is just smoke. Don't you understand, everybody sees something different in that smoke. It might be an answer to a question they've asked or the conclusion to a spell they've made. But it's different for everybody."

"She wanted me to follow her."

"Annie, calm down." Myrtill places her hand on my shoulder.

"She couldn't have been there could she?" Was Lorelei well enough to walk outside? From what I'd seen of her I didn't think so. But what other explanation is there.

"No, she's bedbound, or at least wheel chair bound. You probably saw Lorelei because you're telling her story. She's in your mind."

"It felt different than that though. As if she was reaching out for me, as if she wanted me to follow her somewhere dark."

"Try not to let it upset you," Myrtill pats my arm. "It's like a bad dream, it will fade with time."

I take another sip of my drink, keeping my hands cupped around the mug, allowing the warmth to seep into them. I try to believe what Myrtill's told me. What had happened on the island was just my imagination. However, my insides though warmed by the drink do not seem to be thawing, I am left with a sensation of doom.

"It's time you went home now, Annie," Myrtill says, "You'll feel better after a night's sleep." I get up, and take off the cloak. "Can you carry the cloaks up the back stairs and put them in the wardrobe? Then you can go out through the back of the house."

I do as she asks, my steps heavy on the narrow flight going up towards Myrtill's studio. A flickering candle chequers light at the top of the stairs. Beside the wardrobe I stop and open the door. There is very little room and I have to squeeze myself between the door and the chasm of the wardrobe to reach for hangers. The door blocks light making me use touch rather than sight. As I put the second cloak away my arm brushes against something. Something soft and smooth as fur. Intrigued by the sensation; I take it out. A badger pelt slips from its hanger and lies at my feet. It makes my stomach lurch with a shock of recognition. I shut the wardrobe door, letting candle light flicker again. It highlights the striping of the fur, making it undulate as if it might get up and amble away to its sett. That badger skin ... so familiar. Another thought besides Lorelei enters my head, 'Why was the badger stole here in a wardrobe in Myrtill's home?'

I lift it into my arms, remembering the look of it when

Lorelei had brought the creature home, dangling from her arms.

I descend the stairs again, calling Myrtill's name as I go.

"What is it?" she asks, sounding annoyed at the disturbance. Myrtill is extinguishing the lights. A lone candle burns giving only the slightest respite to darkness.

"I wanted to know why you've got this?"

"Got what?" She sighs as she stamps over to me to inspect the fur. She lifts it up and then lets it drop.

"That old thing? That's just something that's been up there for ages. I probably used it in a painting."

"But it was Lorelei's. My mother made it for her. It was a precious thing to her."

"Hell's teeth, Annie! Why can't you leave things alone? Why do you have to go snooping around?"

"I wasn't snooping, it was just there. Are you going to tell me why?"

A clock strikes one, chiming through the house, the whole building trembles and the candle flickers making patterns of light through the dark.

"Do we have to do this now?" She looks at me and answers her own question. "I guess so. But you're not going to like it."

"Just tell me."

"It was a gift from Lorelei."

"A gift? Bit of a special gift."

"It was a lover's gift."

Her answer leaves me speechless; so many questions flood my head at once. I manage to stutter, "… but … but you hated her. She cheated you with the Dryad portrait."

"Haven't you learnt yet? Hate and love are similar emotions. Ridge and furrow, black and white, wax and wane; they can't be separated. As for the portrait, I forgave her … in a way." She pauses, "Anyway it didn't matter, that had occurred a long time before. Our affair happened when she came back. It was always meant to be. You can't fight that type of destiny."

"I don't understand." My brain wasn't functioning, a pulse throbbing at my temple. Were people so complicated? I preferred the simplicity of fairy tales; Good vs Evil. How could love and hate be similar? I had loved Jay and now I hated him. I hated him but had slept with him again so recently. Perhaps Myrtill was right. I must look foolish standing in this room with a badger stole draped across my arms. Myrtill is squinting at me. Dark shadows make the planes of her face hard, reflections of flame flare in her eyes. She looks angry.

"We had a love affair. Lorelei was the most beautiful being I have ever laid eyes on. She was my muse. Perhaps she was sometimes cruel but at the time I was only concentrating on her looks. I was doing another portrait, and she seduced me, I suppose. It was a brief affair but wonderful." Myrtill sighs and it fades to a groan as if she can sense the warmth of Lorelei's embrace and then the missing of it.

"But she was married, lived with her husband and step children and child."

"And? ... And? When did those things stop people having affairs?"

Myrtill laughs and turns away from me as if she's had enough of the conversation, as if she is dismissing me. I wish I'd gone because exasperation compels her to make one final comment, sharp and nasty. "And there were others in the village ... at one time or another. I suspect she slept with most of the people here. Anyone she wanted. Never stopped her and your *daddy*, did it?"

I can feel spittle engulf my mouth. For a moment I can't speak. I don't want my father's adultery confirmed like this.

"My father? You're sure?"

"Yes, your father, Annie. He was nuts about her. You've seen the spell. That was their spell; the holly tree in one corner for Lorelei, the wild garlic, ramson flower in the other for your father. I explained the nature of that spell to you. They were possibly going to run away together. Your father would have thought they were, even if Lorelei wasn't going to follow it through." She pauses and takes a breath. "In fact, your father and Lorelei were made for each other; both just looked out for themselves, cheated and lied to everybody." She stops, takes another deep breath so I wonder how long her rant is going to last. "Now go! Leave me alone, and if you've any sense, you'll leave the whole mess be. Goodnight!"

With that she turns and is gone. I stand dumbly for a moment but then find the strength to move. I climb the back stairs again past the wardrobe and into Myrtill's studio. Finding the badger fur still in my hands, I drape it across Myrtill's stool. In this upper room without curtains, the moon is bright. The white cloth over the easel shines and I lift it up. Icy eyes in the painting below stare at me, just like the spirit I had seen earlier. In this portrait a beautiful woman rises from a column of smoke spiralling upwards to reveal a hooded face, pale beneath the black of the covering.

Silver lines the garment making the image of Lorelei glow in the dim light. It is as if this moment had been preordained. I had seen Lorelei in the smoke and now here she is, not beckoning but mocking. I raise my hand to strike her but a moment of sense prevails and I let the cover drop. I clamber down the stairs outside, tripping on the last step and grazing my knee as I fall. I hobble back to the Hall. In the early hours of the morning all is still. I take the back flight of stairs and creep up to my room having already made my decision. I have to see Ma. Ask her for the truth for once. I grab my car keys and handbag and head out again, as silently as I had come in. Rasputin appears and watches accusingly as I cross the reception and close the front door.

CHAPTER 34

I leave the village in silence. Even the thrub of the tyres is hushed. I head for Stonewick and Ma's flat. The glow of street lamps is brighter as I reach the outskirts of the town. I can't find a parking space, so I leave the car blocking the entrance. I punch in the code Ma's given me and head upstairs to the third floor. I do not have the spare door key with me so knock; quietly at first. When there is no reply I rap loudly and call through the letter box. "Ma let me in, it's me."

There is no response, so I look through the gap. Nothing. No movement, I cannot hear breathing or snoring. I don't think she's here. "Ma! Ma!" I call again.

"What do you think you're doing?" A voice hisses from along the corridor. A door has opened and a man doing up the belt of a dressing gown is scowling at me. "Are you trying to wake the whole building? 'Cos you've succeeded."

"Sorry, sorry. I need to see my mother, but I don't think she's here."

"Well, we've guessed that you're trying to see your mother, luv. And aren't you a bit long in the tooth to be calling for Mummy in the middle of the night?" I shrug, and apologise again. "And I haven't seen Ivy for a couple of days. Comes and goes that one. And don't ask me where she is, I can't answer that either."

"Thanks," I mutter, "Sorry to have disturbed you."

The door slams loudly as the neighbour returns to his rest.

I'm annoyed. Where can Ma have got to? A suspicion gnaws at me. There is part of her life which she keeps hidden from me. Probably involving Woody. It's too late to go there straight away. My flat is not far, so I decide to go there though I'm in no mood for sleeping.

As I open the door, the smell of left over Chinese reminds me of my previous visit. There is also a sentence written under the note I'd left Jay. *'I'll be back – you know you want me.'* A row of kisses follows. I pick up the paper, scrunch it into a ball and throw it across the room. After tidying and washing up, dawn light is filtering through the window. It might be early but Woody was generally up with the dawn. I'll demand he tells me what he knows about my father's affair with Lorelei. Another thought trickles in, like grains of sand under clothing, making me uneasy. I might find Ma there.

....

I leave the car in a layby beside Broomstone bridge, trying to ignore the rotting black remains of the badger, where a buzz of flies feast. I follow the footpath along the field edge, the dew wetting the fabric of my trousers. As I reach Woody's home, the early light exposes all the rust and wear on the van. I wonder how Woody can live in such a dump. But then I listen to the bird song and look at the view across the fields and the colours of the forest. It's peaceful. I take a deep breath of morning air, it soothes me. *'Do it ... Do it ... Do it ...'* A great tit's piping call, encourages me from within the wood.

I knock on the caravan door, I didn't think Woody the type who sleeps late, but he takes his time getting to the door and grumbling, "Who is it?"

"It's Annie."

He opens the door ajar, and I see his eyes thick with sleep. "What the fuck, Annie. It's barely five o'clock. What are you doing here?"

I smell the fug of sleep emanating from the enclosed space of the van and another perfume I recognise; patchouli. A voice says, "What's going on Woody? Is everything alright?"

Shit! So, Ma is here. Well, this has certainly been a night of revelations. First confirmation of Daddy's affair and now Ma and Woody co-habiting.

Woody turns back and says into the caravan's interior, "It's Annie."

"Annie?" the voice asks, "What's she doing here?"

"I have no idea." Woody turns back to me and asks again, "What do you want?"

In the dim morning light with the wood all round, chuntering like old ladies having a gossip, I ask myself, 'Why have I decided to come here?' My head and pulse are beating out of time. There is some shuffling behind the half open door and then Ma peers out behind Woody's shoulder, squinting out at me, "Annie, what is it? Has there been an accident?"

"No, No, nothing like that … It's just I needed to speak to you … But it's not really important."

"Give me a chance to get dressed and we'll talk."

As she goes back inside I can hear Woody muttering, "If it's not important why is she here at this goddamn hour?"

The door shuts on me and I hang around feeling displaced in the cool morning air. What on earth am I doing here? The bird mocks me with it's, 'Do it … Do it … Do it,' cry, a magpie chuckles from deeper in the wood.

Finally, the door opens and Ma wafts outside in a long purple smock, her feet in sandals. She is holding two enamel mugs and holds one out to me. I take the tea, grateful to have been included in the brew.

Ma sits on one log and I sit on another looking at her. Every movement she makes is graceful. The light through the trees captures her in a halo of light and I think how beautiful she still is. Not the ethereal loveliness of Lorelei but beauty nonetheless. I feel soiled and dull sitting opposite her.

"Annie, what is all this about?"

"I don't know really. Myrtill said something about Lorelei and I needed to talk to you about it."

She inhales deeply, her shoulders rising in a shrug, "Well, what did she say?"

I take a breath, considering how to begin. This isn't where

or how I'd expected to talk to Ma about this. I choke on a sip of tea, stutter. "That Daddy had an affair with Lorelei."

Ma says nothing for a few moments and I again listen to the wood creaking and chuntering, birds calling. "Yes, he did."

I'm surprised at her candour. "I thought he hated her?"

"He did, when she left the band and went away. He thought she'd betrayed us. But when she came back she was different, and I suppose she seduced him. Your father was a pretty weak man Annie, you know that."

"Do you think he planned to run away with her?"

"Maybe. But your dad was always full of grand schemes that never quite came off. What's more likely is that they may have planned it, but he got cold feet, had too much to drink and fell in the river. Now that she's so ill, we're never going to know the full story."

"So, you don't think he could be alive somewhere?"

Ma shakes her head so bands of daylight dance across her face, making it impossible to interpret her expression. "Annie, he's dead. Gone. I know it's difficult, but this happened so long ago you should have moved on by now."

"He was my daddy," I sob. "I never got to say goodbye."

Ma gets up and comes to me. Leaning down she hugs me. I stay wrapped in her purple patchouli warmth and cry.

"Breakfast's up!" Woody's words break through the glade, together with the smell of fried mushrooms. We sit and eat them with refreshed mugs of tea.

I feel the dried pull of tears across my cheeks but don't wipe them away. We don't talk whilst we eat, just listen to natural tunes within the forest. Then, I hear another sound, a more human crack and creak, and occasional chuckle, as if somebody is sitting high above us watching. I look up from time to time but see nothing. I wonder if the strange boy is there. Woody notices and says, "Just Ham. He watches us ... it's his thing."

"He spies on us you mean," Ma says,

"He's harmless," Woody insists.

I'm not so sure. He obviously sees things which he discloses only to make things difficult.

"If you're there Ham, come and join us for breakfast!" Woody shouts into the branches above. The glade becomes silent for a moment, even the birds and trees pausing in their business. "Ha, scaredy cat!" Woody shouts, and then more quietly he says to us, "He'd come down if it was just me."

As the food fills my stomach and I relax a bit, another thought comes to me. Something I want to ask Woody about the night my father had last been seen.

I don't look at him as I ask, but mop some juice from the mushrooms on my plate with a piece of bread. "Woody, did you see my father on that last evening? The Saturday evening." There is a quick glance between him and Ma.

"No. Why do you ask?"

"Because you were at our cottage early the next morning."

He puts his plate down, picks up his tea, brings it to his mouth but doesn't drink. "Well, I often came round early on Sundays. That was where I did most of my work. Your Ma would make me a brew before I started." He looks annoyed, plonking his mug down so it topples over on the ground. Tea spilling between roots and leaves like a miniature flood. "Is that the end of the interrogation, or just the beginning?"

"Sorry," a rivulet of tea reaches my shoe, "but I'm trying to get things straight in my head. I thought I heard things that night, people moving things around."

"Wasn't that the night of the storm though, Annie," Ma interrupts. "There was a lot of noise just from the thunder and lightning. And your dad and me argued as well. Worse than usual." She puts her hand to her neck as if reminded of the bruises he had left.

"Yes, I expect you're right. I just want ..." I gulp down a sob, "I just want some answers." I want to tell her I'd stayed in the shed whilst the storm raged and they argued. By the time I went into the house the storm had died down and their argument too. But no words come, just more sobs, out of rhythm with my breathing, making it difficult to speak.

"There might not be any answers, Annie. I'm sorry to say."

Woody's words are harsher, "Annie this isn't a fairy tale. Your dad isn't going to suddenly trot back home on a white horse. Not everybody gets to live happily ever after. This is real life. It's bloody hard."

I look at Woody's caravan, flakes of rust peeling away like autumn leaves. The wear on the mugs and plates is similar; even Woody's hands are rough workman's hands. I don't ask anymore and finish my meal. I leave them and walk down the field and forest edge, back to my car.

CHAPTER 35 - IVY

Woody boiled more water. He and Ivy washed the plates up in a bowl.

"Why are you crying, lovely?" Woody asked, putting his arm around her.

"I can't live with the guilt anymore," she mumbled.

"It's over. Like you said to Annie. He's dead, gone. It all happened a long time ago. Too long to be upsetting yourself again."

"... But Annie?"

"She'll be done with her story soon enough. Get bored and move on." He kissed her cheek. "You go and sit down, I'll finish this." And he moved her aside to continue the washing.

From the branches above Ham sat watching. Listening to the conversation, storing it all up. He hoarded remarks like a squirrel. Tucked words away. Ready for when they would be most useful. The time might almost be here.

CHAPTER 36

I wait for a while on the bridge. Looking over at the water rippling below and think of Lorelei being washed up much further down the valley; and how this all started.

Early morning light washes over the water reminding me of stained glass, lighter strands separated by darker bands. From the edge of the road, I pick up a stick and throw it from one side of the bridge into the water. I cross over, looking down to watch as it's steered by the current to the middle channel. It bobs against splaying weeds which grab at it but moves steadily on. I wonder where it will end up. And before I have realised what I'm doing, I'm on a muddy pathway beside the river and am stumbling along the bank trying to keep up with the twig as it moves along. Willows act like curtains draping over the water's edge and the vegetation is overgrown. Grass seeds brush against me. Nettles sting my hand. But I keep sight of the twig as I reach the pool below the village.

Another overgrown track branches to the left up the hill to the back of The Linden Tree. Here is the place where my father must have fallen. It is not difficult to see how it could happen. Though initially the bank is not steep; there is a level patch and then a bed of reeds sweeping into the river. It would be easy to mistake the reeds for firm ground if it was dark and your faculties were impaired. The area just beyond is a deeper dark circle of water, smoother than the current rushing by on the far side. A tree overhangs from that point making the water below black, its roots stretched out across the bank like the bars of a gate. Long ago, children used to learn to swim in this pool, but even in Broomstone that tradition was banned before I moved here. For a moment the stick I threw in circles round the deep part of the pool and I wonder if it will get caught in an eddy and stay there, but then it is released and I follow, watching it as I walk further along the path.

As the river widens it becomes faster, there are more channels fanning over hidden obstacles. The stick turns and twists through them as if it knows where it is going. Then it moves to the far side of the river, close to the bank and disappears behind trails of willow. It is only then I recognise where I am; far from the boundary of Broomstone and into the flood plains below. Where the trees hang and the stick has lodged is the place where I found Lorelei. Do floating bodies behave the same way as sticks, I wonder?

I stand just listening to the sounds of early morning ... the birdsong, the rhythm of the water, a vehicle in the distance. And I see myself as a five year old in red Wellingtons standing at the edge of the river. It makes me shiver to think of all that has happened since then.

My return journey to the bridge is slower, measured. I stop at the deep pool and imagine my father missing his footing and consider the sounds he might have made as he fell. On an impulse I take the track up towards the back of the pub, my ankles pushing through the moist grasses and nettles growing over the path.

I can hear movement and a clang like the sound a cowbell might make. The path is steep and I am panting as I reach the rear of the building. In the yard a man is rolling beer barrels. He takes a moment to catch his breath leaning back and stretching. That's when he sees me. He wasn't expecting to meet anybody and jumps but quickly gains his balance. "Mornin' ... Nice enough for an early walk."

"Yes," I reply.

He's probably in his sixties with salt and pepper hair. The sleeves of a tartan shirt are rolled up to his elbows revealing muscular arms. The buttons also pull tightly across a rounded stomach. He continues to smile at me.

"Aren't you Annie Ramson?" I nod at him. "Back for long then?"

"Archie Libani has asked me to write about his mother, about Lorelei ... her life ... her music ... you know."

"Yes, it's quite the gossip of the moment." He puts his hands on his hips, seeming pleased to have an excuse for a break. "I knew your dad well. Used to be drinking in here all the time. Well until he got involved with Lorelei."

A cool breeze blows against my neck as if somebody has whispered, 'I told you so'.

"So, they did have an affair?"

"Sorry love, that was oafish of me, I thought you knew."

"Don't worry; it's not a complete shock."

The affair must have been local knowledge as well. I shouldn't be surprised; everything in a small village is everybody's business. It struck me that Ma didn't have a choice but to hear the gossip even if she tried to ignore it.

I turn to go. "Bye then."

"Bye. Pop in for a drink sometime; let us know how you're getting on. I might be able to help you with some info for your book ..." I turn back again and wait, intrigued by what he might have to tell me. He pauses scratching his head as if thinking, "... though Lorelei never came to the pub when she became 'Lady of the Manor' ..." His voice takes on a high posh tone, "... Beneath her then. But before when you were all living in the vans, and Lorelei was living with that Tom Hart chap ... Woody ..." I must have made a grimace, because his voice trails off to a halt. "What have I said now? You didn't know about them then?"

I shake my head, unable to speak. I want to say Woody had never lived with Lorelei; he'd lived with other girls in his caravan. I'd seen him kissing Lorelei but I had never considered them a couple. Obviously that's not the impression they gave when they were away from the barn site, sitting in the pub. I shouldn't be shocked; Myrtill had said something along the lines of Lorelei having had affairs with the whole village. I feel anger at Woody more than anything. He should have mentioned it to me.

"I'll see you around then ..." I realise I don't know his name; "... Trevor," he finishes for me.

I start to take the track back towards the river. "Oi! Do you think you should go down by the river there? That's where they say your dad drowned." I stop again. Trevor was trying to be helpful I suppose.

"Yes, I realised that was the place when I was walking. Do you think he did drown?"

"Ryan could hold his drink ... that's all I'll say. He wasn't stupid about drink ... maybe stupid about that woman ... besotted like. I think it more likely that they were going to run away together."

There is a shout somewhere from inside the pub, and Trevor turns and says, "That's my Mrs wondering what on earth I'm doing chatting rather than stocking up. But like I said, pop by sometime and I'll tell you anything I know about Lorelei." He spits on the ground. "Sorry," he apologises, "but I couldn't stand the woman. Though I wouldn't wish ... well you know ... on her. Don't know why everybody made such a fuss about her wailing." He answers his own observation, "A pretty face, and a perfect figure, dressed in practically nothing, titivates a lot of people apparently."

Another holler comes from inside the pub, "Trevor!"

I return to my car deep in thought, hardly seeing the river beside me. Not thinking of Daddy falling into the pool, nor Deidre's face, warped by a wash of water. Before I get to the bridge a sudden stench of wild garlic encloses me, making me cough. I look around to see where the flowers are growing, but there don't appear to be any nearby. A shadow crosses my path and when I look up Miss Dryden is standing in front of me. A sensation like a wave breaking, chills my skin, making me tremble. I'd wanted to see her. Here she is.

"Come to see where your friend died?" she asks, looking at

the water. I can't see her face just a dark reflection on the river surface. It ripples and distorts making her appear to move, though she is motionless in front of me.

"What do you mean?"

"The Alder tree child. Deidre ... the girl you wanted dead."

"I didn't want her to die."

"Oh, yes ... you told me so. You said, '... *I want her to die ...*' Yes, that's what you said ... and that is much the same thing as killing her."

"I didn't kill her."

"But you made a curse. Once you make it you can't go back."

"I was a kid. I'd been hurt. I didn't mean it. It was just words."

"A curse is a curse when it's spoken with truth in the heart."

"No ... No!" I am shouting, shaking my head, trying to work out what happened to Deidre. "I didn't kill her. Did you? Did *you* kill her?" Still, she won't look at me.

She points to the river bank at the knotted roots of willow and then bends down to caress them. Her fingers are as dark and furrowed as the wood. "The trees heard your curse. They killed her for you. Deidre caught her foot, slipped over and fell into the water."

The river surface is made up of blue green fragments, rippling like a glassy mosaic from darker to light. In it I imagine a mirage of Deidre stumbling on the willow root and falling down. The sensation of flickering light and moving shapes is the aura I get before a migraine. I put my hands to my head. Tears are running down my face. I'd wanted to see Miss Dryden, ask her something, but my thoughts are fuzzy and I can't think what the questions were. The shadow on the water is suddenly gone, and all that is left is the winding river with its ever changing light and the willows trailing their branches over the surface, like fingers teasing it.

CHAPTER 37

I return to the Hall and creep in, my steps quiet on the tiles, as though guilty of a misdemeanour. I feel as if I am being watched, and when I turn and look at the stairs I realise I'm right. At the top stand Rosa, eyeing me with identical cat-like eyes and secretive smiles on their faces. They are wearing black and white striped shirts, the lines are diagonal but in the opposite direction, so together they make a triangle of fabric. They are still so identical I would never be able to distinguish one from the other. They regularly appear in papers and magazine articles on style. I think they have a design studio in London. People seem to like their eccentricity. They glide down the stairs, holding hands and peer at me. "Look who we have here, Rosa ..." And the other says, "... Little Annie."

But in my head I know she wants to say 'Stinking Annie,' and I realise what a state I must be in after my excursion last night and my early morning pursuits. I scratch the nettle rash on my hands.

"So, Archie tells us you're writing about Lorelei?"

"Yes, her biography."

"Well, good luck with that." They smirk and giggle as they move past me.

"Will you help me?" I call to their zebra striped backs, my echoing voice sounding desperate.

Without turning, one of them says, "Don't think we've much to say about our step-mother, have we Rosa?" And the other agrees, "No, Rosa ... Nothing good anyway." And with more laughter they disappear towards the kitchen.

Something about the way they move reminds me of the figures from last night. They must have been on the island, identical shadows, holding hands as they moved around the fire pit.

I return to my room, ready to shower, perhaps even to rest; but when I open the door a note has been shoved under it.

Hi Annie,

Got some information. Meet me at the golf club for coffee. 10am.
Spider.

He's left a contact number to ring if I can't make it, but it is only eight thirty so at least I'll be able to shower and change. My stomach rumbles as I dress. Breakfast with Woody and Ma seems an age ago. I decide to grab a bite to eat as well. I'm not sure I want to meet up with Rosa again, but carefully put on make-up and do my hair, so I'll look neat and tidy if they should be there. When I get to the kitchen, it is only Poppy. She insists on warming croissants for me.

"Nice that Rosa are home," I say making small talk.

"Is it?" Poppy replies, continuing to mix something in a bowl. "And I wish people wouldn't call them Rosa as if they were one person. It's just a silly affectation. They are two, Rosalinde and Rosamunde." She speaks firmly, the pressure increasing on the wooden spoon against the bowl side.

I want to reply, but can't think of anything. Poppy hadn't been here at the start, when that's what everybody called them. She doesn't sound as if she's pleased to see them.

"I'm going to meet Spider again … at the golf club."

"Oh, right," Poppy says, not looking up from the bowl. I get up; brushing croissant crumbs off me, and thank her for my breakfast. She doesn't acknowledge my departure.

CHAPTER 38

I'm signed in at the golf club desk and labelled as a 'Visitor.'

Spider is waiting for me at the same table. There are already golfers shaking hands on the 18th green. They must have started their rounds early.

Spider stands up as I walk over. "Hi Annie, can I order you coffee ... a cake?"

"Just coffee. Black please."

Spider nods at a waiter and we sit down. On the table is a folder and from it Spider pulls out a large brown envelope.

"This is what I wanted you to look at." He slides some typed documents out and hands them to me. For a moment I'm not sure what I am looking at. But then I get it. The heading announces it's from the department of pathology.

There are several lines of introduction and then pages of boxes filled with observations about various aspects of Lorelei's still born baby. I imagine that tiny body lying on a table, being dissected piece by piece. Each organ being weighed and examined. Worse is the image that follows. A baby being remodelled, so that it could be laid out according to Cedric's wishes. A flash of his big blood stained hands around a magpie carcass makes me gag.

If Spider notices my unease he doesn't comment. "I think you'll find what you want on page 6."

I shake my head trying to clear away those unsettling thoughts and turn to page 6. Near the bottom is a box stating, 'Conclusion.'

24 weeks old. Foetal deformity. Probable cause teratogenic drug.

Beside this is a handwritten note in black pen, a scrawl of letters I can barely decipher.

Unusual appearance, histology shows plant matter, limbs deformed. Like a tree??

I look up at Spider frowning. "What on earth does that mean?"

"Well, a teratogen is a drug which causes deformity often of the limb buds. That's what I've found out. Thalidomide was the most well-known. But I'm not sure what the other note is about ... only that there was something very odd about the baby."

"But plant matter ... like a tree ... it makes it sound as if Lorelei was growing a sapling rather than a human."

"I can't explain it. I'm just showing it to you. It's what you wanted."

I am speechless. I look out to the golf course, observing the trees along fairways. I remember somebody once telling me about a lady with dementia who had eaten a cherry stone and was sure she had a cherry tree growing inside her. This was different though; this was not some imagined anomaly; this was real. Written in black and white.

"Do you think she knew? Is that why she needed to get rid of it?"

"Your guess is as good as mine," said Spider.

I sip my coffee. It is cold.

"So, is there more? Was it followed up?"

"Not so far as I know. And of course, the family wanted to have the body back for burial."

"But something unusual like this ... surely it would have been?"

"From what I understand, the word on the street is that the pathologist was on the booze most of the time, always scribbling odd little notes on reports."

"So, this could just be nonsense then?" I flick the pages in my hands in frustration. It isn't real after all. It is just some random note, made by a man with a drinking problem.

"Sorry, but that is a possibility."

I say, "Goodbye," and leave. Frustration engulfs me as I rev the engine. I am no further ahead in discovering anything. The past is like a book dropped in water, the words smudged, the pages sticking together, the cover distorted.

CHAPTER 39

I slam the door as I get out of the car in front of Quercus Hall. I push inside, ready to return to my room and contemplate my next move. I wonder whether there is any point in staying.

Rasputin is blocking my way, sitting on the bottom stair and glaring at me. He slinks away to a door ajar at the other end of the hall, the drawing room. Before I have even moved up onto the first tread, I hear a duet call of, "Annie. Come here!" with the accompaniment of sniggers.

It is Rosa demanding attention. The drawing room is a large room on the north side of the Hall and cooler than the lounge near the kitchen. This is where I had once spied on Roderick. I look out of the window imagining somebody peering in. The perspective is different when standing inside this ornate room. The décor has been updated to more modern hues, but there are still the ancient portraits in oils, and gilt ornaments and table lamps. I am dizzy as if I have been pulled through a time warp.

"Annie …" Rosa choruses from their position either side of the fireplace. They are sitting in the fireside chairs, each with a leg hooked over one arm. With their black and white outfits flecked with gold, and ringleted hair, they remind me of Staffordshire china dogs.

I pause, waiting for them to say something horrible. "Come a bit closer Annie, so that we can see you better." I take a step, as if playing a game of grandmother's footsteps. "Annie, don't be so stand offish, we've got something that might help you."

The Rosa on the left bends forward and pulls something from out of a handbag. It is an oblong of grey, a book perhaps?

Still, I am reluctant to go nearer. I'm waiting for the joke to be revealed.

"Don't trust us ... do you, Stinking Annie?"

"Not really ..."

"Well, a lot of water has passed under the bridge, one might say. We're adults now. Friends." I don't see how one thing necessarily follows from the other but I nod and try a smile, which feels false on my face.

Rosa reaches out her arm, proffering the grey object. "It's a booklet, with some writing ... stories maybe. We think it belongs to Lorelei."

I have to move forward to reach. The touch of it makes me recoil because it has the feel of decaying skin. I expect it to fall apart in my fingers. But it holds together. As I accept it, I try to decipher the script and lettering across the front.

"Well, a 'Thank you Rosa' might be nice." Two voices chime into my contemplations.

"Thank you ... Sorry ... It might be really helpful." I am certain Rosa would never help me without a hidden agenda.

"That's Stinking Annie," a muffle of laughter, "always lost in some story."

"Where did you get it, if it's Lorelei's?"

"You think we stole it?" That's exactly what I'm thinking. "Actually, we took it from the bureau in her room. Lorelei doesn't need it, not now she's ga-ga, does she?"

I am still waiting for a punch line, because a first glimpse of the cover reveals Halloweenish illustrations. This must be a joke after all. But they say no more. They get up and as they pass, one of them drops a small key onto a mahogany table, glossy enough to reflect it. Rosa says, "There are other things in the bureau." They both wink and move to the door as if we are part of a sequence dance. Rasputin pads after them with a final turn of his head and meow.

I sit on the sofa. A tap of Virginia creeper leaves flutters against the window panes and I think of Roderick sitting here all those years ago, me observing him from outside. I've never actually been in this room. The dark family portraits look at me with stern eyes. I presume Lorelei and Cedric must have bought the paintings when they moved here. After all the Libani family has no aristocratic past. I ignore the strangers' stares and look more closely at the book.

It is not an attractive item. Besides the feel of it; it has a mouldy smell as though it has been locked away and forgotten for a long time. The paper is thick and the pages sticky as I turn them. More disturbing are the illustrations. They crawl across the cover. Black ink portrays various animals; toads and snakes and rats. These are not in themselves horrible creatures but they have been given expressions which make me associate them with the darkest of fairy tales. Not like the beautiful illustrations from my story book but foul caricatures which wink and hiss at me.

The title page indicates that this is exactly what it is: *Little Book of Cautionary Tales and Curses*

I shiver as I turn the next dusty page.

'... *Once upon a time there was a witch. Like most witches she was a dual. A mix of good and evil. Two personas blended into one. This witch could not bear children, and as she so desperately wanted a child, she needed to steal one.*

... Once upon a time a family lived in a forest, a mother, a father and two beautiful daughters, Holly and Ivy. They were a happy family and deserved to be so, until they broke a promise ...

... Once upon a time, there was a tree in the forest. It was the most beautiful tree there ever was. But within the wood, beneath a skin of bark, lived the spirit of a woman. She had been taken from her home when she was an infant because of a witch's curse. Every morning a handsome young man came walking in the forest. The tree tried to stretch out her branches to touch him but though he might accidentally brush her leaves, he never paused. As time went on she became more and more sad, and was desperate to escape her binding ...

... Once upon a time a man lived with his wife and daughter in a house in a wood. They did not know the wife had an unpaid curse.

But he was not a good man, and the wife and child did not realise this until it was too late.

... Once upon a time, there lived a girl in the village. She told stories and played tricks because she was so lonely. One day she played a joke on another, not realising the girl had hidden powers. And so she was drowned as a punishment.'

As I read the start of each story, they appear recognisable, a chronicle of past events in Broomstone. I feel smothered by the familiarity of the tales and the stuffiness of the room, made worse by the stench from the book. My head is aching. The tapping of leaves outside crescendos and I get up to check nobody is spying on me. When I turn back the faces in the portraits are frowning at me, following my movements, making me uncomfortable.

I can't carry on with this at present; I'll have to do it later. Perhaps outside or in the kitchen, when ordinary things are happening, like Poppy baking or Cedric reading the paper.

I put the key, left by Rosa, in my pocket and then retreat upstairs to my room.

I place the booklet in the chest of drawers. I turn the key over in my palm. It feels heavy for such a small item, as if it is pulling me as a magnet might. I find myself in the corridor, heading down the stairs towards Lorelei's room. I listen at the door, but there are no voices, no disturbance. I creak the door ajar. She appears to be sleeping.

The light is hazy, filtering through gauze curtains at the windows. Looking around I see the ancient bureau against the wall opposite Lorelei's bed. Its walnut wood gleams like tortoiseshell. The key draws me forward and I tiptoe over to it. Lorelei stirs in her sleep and I stop mid-step. But she settles, her eye lids fluttering, deep in a dream. I move more slowly until I'm in front of the bureau. The key slides into the keyhole and turns smoothly, a smudge of oil by the lock. A few dried paper roses, scatter on the desk top as I pull it down. So, the Valentine's Card ended up here. Papers and documents are neatly stored in pigeonholes along the back. I don't know where to start, so I take one from the far right hand side.

I hear Lorelei stir again and turn quickly, as still as if I'm playing musical statues. I wait until her breathing becomes steady before examining the paper in my hands. It is thick and folded, ancient and brittle. Damp rings mark its cream surface. I realise it is a map before I've fully opened it. I spread it on the desk top as best I can, careful not to rip the creases where it has been folded. Though stained, it is clearly a hand drawn plan of Broomstone. The black ink lines are old, but the illustrations of the island, church, Linden Tree and Quercus Hall are all recognisable. There are lines crisscrossing between buildings and the island as well, which must be passageways. There are many of them. A small square on the island is marked as 'Laurel's stone.' That must have been the slab we found there so long ago. Following this, or a map like it. The one Roderick had taken when we'd gone to the island together.

I remove another lighter document. It is a long sheet of ivory paper with red typing around it. A birth certificate. It is in the name of Holly Carpin. My mother's maiden name was Carpin. She said her sister was Holly. It follows that this is my aunt's birth certificate. I turn slowly, to look at Lorelei in her bed, wondering if this is the registration of her birth. I jump, dropping the paper. She is staring at me. Her ice-cold eyes gleaming. "What are you doing going through my private things?"

The sound of her voice, though quiet, makes me quiver as if she can hear my thoughts. They grind like rusted cogs turning. I should apologise but I find myself saying, "You are my aunt then? You are Holly?"

She sighs and shakes her head. "You need a date of birth to exist, that's all. I took her birth certificate. You always did have too much imagination. Believing all the stories you heard. Naming me Lorelei … though I do like it as a name … better than boring Holly or Ivy."

Lorelei starts to cough and points to the water on her

bedside table. I go to her and hand her the glass.

"I thought you wanted me to write your biography, research your life?"

She sips and then continues. "I did. But we decided there are some things we preferred to keep private."

She hands me the glass to set down. I'm not sure why she says 'we'. I presume she means Cedric. I know he's not really happy, my being here. "Why didn't you just say that then?"

"It's not that simple," she tells me.

"So, was it Cedric who locked me in the basement, muddled things up, took things away?"

"Maybe," she says.

"And how did you make sure I found the tunnel, left the room?"

"Rasputin is a very able cat. Does what he's told."

I have no answer to that. Her face is impassive. I don't think she's joking. Perhaps she is more disturbed than I've realised. Finally, I blurt out, "You haven't told me though. Are you Holly?"

"If you want to believe that … it's entirely up to you." She gives a chuckle before closing her eyes and sinking her head back against the pillows. I want to shake her, get her to tell me the truth, but of course I can't. Instead, I return to the bureau. Lock it and leave the key beside it.

I go back to my room. The horrible booklet has leaked its smell and I unlatch the window, trying to encourage air to circulate. My head is thumping and I feel restless. Though the heat is building again, I notice the topmost branches of the trees on the island are swaying. I take it as a sign that it might be cooler there. I decide to follow my instinct.

CHAPTER 40

The track down to the lake is familiar, though now the lawns are looking brown and dusty with prolonged heat. Weeds remain unaffected and continue to shoot out spiky pods and creepers which scratch and catch me as I walk. It's downhill towards the lake and the air thickens. I stop to catch my breath. I wonder if the old boat will still be here. If so it is probably no more than splintered boards. As I approach the water I see a new jetty has been constructed and beside it there is the bronzed hull of a rowing boat. The oars have bands of brass and turquoise loops. I am glad I'm wearing trainers. They grip whilst the boat shifts as I settle in my seat. It takes a few moments to set the oars into the rowlocks and plunge them into the water. They creak as the boat moves forward. By the time I have got into a rhythm with even strokes, I am near the island. There is another fresh, pine planked jetty. I pull up alongside and climb up onto it. Fixing the boat firmly, I walk onto the beach.

The track leading into the island interior is marked out. The overhanging branches have been cut back, it is almost inviting. But as soon as I pass through the entrance, gloom envelops me; the trees dark and silent surround me. A couple of lime trees are at the height of their ripeness, dangling with flower droplets and giving off such a sticky sweet odour that it makes me feel heady. Nothing is recognisable. It is damp, with pools of black mud stretching beyond the path. The sweet air gives way to a smell of decay, mingled with the bitter stench of elder. I shiver even though it is hot; the pressure in my head increasing. From my room I had seen trees moving but within the wood they are still. The trees don't speak here, they keep their secrets. The heat and heaviness of the air make me soporific and I stumble. I try to concentrate, making sure my steps stay on the path.

As I reach the central glade, I disturb a magpie which is beating a snail against a stone. It flaps off with a 'Chuck, Churr,' and a turn of its head toward me, upset that I have interrupted its brutality. I had been here only last night, yet it seems so long ago, as if the time between then and now has been twisted. I'm confused and disorientated because I can't find the fire pit, though I am certain this is the place. There is still an odour of burning herbs in the air which catches my throat. I walk a circle around the perimeter of the glade, looking down.

I gasp in shock when I next glance up, because Miss Dryden is watching me, hunched over in her grey cloak. She may have been here all the time and I might have mistaken her for a tree.

"Well, girl. Not such a sapling now. Lots of lies, lots of sorrow. And now back here. No need to ask why."

I am shaken to see Miss Dryden appear so suddenly but the questions I wanted to ask have fled again.

"Where's the pit that was here?" I manage to say.

"Just over there."

I walk a little way and there it is, obvious now, grey ash in the centre. In the dim light, the trifurcate hawthorn bends, more twisted and distorted than I recall. Wizened branches hanging over, like a miser's crooked arms protecting treasure.

"And you'll want to see the grave as well."

I hadn't thought about that, but now Miss Dryden is leading me to the edge of the clearing where a new bank of holly obscures the ground. "In there." She nods, and I hesitate because it is dark under the cover of the glossy leaves. She is watching me intently so I do as she says. Inside is a slab of tombstone, brushed and clear of plants. The writing on it is clear. *'For a loved child … Briar-Rose … A child of the wood.'*

At the head of the stone, a rose has been planted, the stem thick and twisted; the thorns as large as eagle talons. It straggles upwards, seeking the speck of light distant above it. The roses' blooms are over and as I move, brushing the foliage, it sheds petals which fall onto the stone like splashes of blood. If Lorelei is my aunt, then this child would be my cousin. If Briar-Rose was Daddy's baby, then she would have been my half-sister. Briefly the stab of loss for any dead child intensifies. We have a deeper connection. The thought hurts like another wound within my aching head.

"Is there another grave here?" I ask, thinking this stone is so similar to the one we had found so long ago. "It said, 'Here lies ...' or something like that."

"You mean Laurel's Stone?"

"Yes, that's what I mean." That's what had been marked on the map I'd found earlier.

"It actually says, 'Here Lies Laurel'."

"Was Laurel your sister? Is it her grave?"

"She's not dead."

"Then why ... why does she have a gravestone ... and where is she?"

"I've told you she's my sister. My twin. More than a twin sister."

"You mean you're identical?"

"Something like that ... but not as simple. Magic never is."

I'm having difficulty interpreting whatever it is that Miss Dryden is telling me. Is the Laurel from the fairy tale her identical twin? And have I ever mistaken one for the other? The woman I met by the river, did seem different from the Miss Dryden in front of me. More twisted and dark. The skin scattered with raised freckles and blotches. This woman, though as wrinkled and ancient looking, has the complexion of weathered stone. "I'm writing about Lorelei's life and her music. Trying to find something out about her family. Can you help?"

"Maybe," she blinks at me, the rest of her face motionless,

giving nothing away.

"Do you know what happened? What she took to make her ill, made her lose the baby?"

She tilts her already bent head towards me. I imagine her weighing up how much to tell me. "She was having a child that couldn't be born."

My cheeks burn with indignation. "All children have a right to be born, even if they might have a disease or deformity." My words tremble and there are tears in my eyes. I've never experienced the miracle of carrying a baby to full term.

"No, this was a child of the forest, a daughter sired by forest divinities. It could not have lived. I had to give her something, so that she would lose the child."

I shake my head. The headache rolling round like ball bearings. "No. You shouldn't have done that."

"The baby would not have been of this world. A forest child."

My mind recalls the autopsy report. *'Plant matter.'* It is too strange to contemplate, but I say, "So would it have been like a tree?"

"Something like that. Not of this world. A true dryad."

I swallow in disbelief. The report Spider had showed me did make some kind of sense after all.

"And Lorelei, is she a dryad as well?"

"No, not a true dryad, she was born a human child. She was taken as the price for a spell."

"So, she was Holly? She was my mother's sister?"

Miss Dryden nods and makes a grunt of assent. Whilst my head spins with the idea that Lorelei was actually my aunt. If things had been different I'd have had an Aunt Holly. Archie and Briar-Rose would be my cousins.

"Lorelei, as you called her, broke free of her bindings and as always there was a price to pay."

"What price?"

"The curse on your family."

So, the fairy tale about my mother's family in the house in the wood might be true. And then my Grandparents died in a freak accident. And Ma miscarried a child and I did too. Daddy's disappearance and failures in my life ... I've often felt cursed. It takes me a moment to process what Miss Dryden is saying but then manage, "But you maimed her as well as aborting the baby?"

"That was never my intent. The potion was to terminate the child. Not even a human baby, but the embryo sac of a dryad. Roots, not a human being."

I am shaking my head, tears starting to fall, hot against my cheeks, at the thought of that strange, deformed foetus. Could it ever be right to abort a child?

"But Cedric laid the child out before it was buried."

"Yes, Lorelei thought it best if everybody saw that the child was normal. Just it's face visible. It's limbs hidden under a gown."

"And the medicine?"

"I think Lorelei may have taken too much by mistake ... Or it could have been ..." She trails off, "... something or somebody else. My sister, perhaps?"

The air around me is sticking in my throat. I am breathless, as if I might faint.

"I don't understand," I choke out, my foggy brain unable to grasp what I am being told.

"Let's sit down," Miss Dryden says, and pulls me into the centre of the glade where there is a thread of light and a ridge of ground where I can sit. My legs are unsteady and crumple below me.

"You know your mother's story don't you?"

"Only parts of it. I know she lived in the house in the wood and her sister was taken. Some sort of curse ... but that was just a fairy tale wasn't it?"

"All stories are based on the truth, even fairy tales. Your mother's story was no different. She was born and raised in the cottage in the wood and the whole family fell to a dark

ALL THE TREES IN THE WOOD

sickness, something I had no remedy for."

"So, you asked your sister, Laurel?"

"'Sister' is not the correct term, but yes. Laurel is a very dark witch indeed, with powerful magic. I have always been the opposite, what is called a white witch. I have used my knowledge of herbs and lore to help people."

"And you couldn't help my mother's family?"

"No, there was something about the sickness; it was not an ordinary illness. Anyway, there was nothing else I could do except plead with Laurel to help. I should have known she would want more for her help than an ordinary family could give."

"So, she took Holly?"

"Yes, I'm afraid she did." Miss Dryden's words are soft and sad; she does not look at me but at the ground.

"And there is more, isn't there?"

"I believe Laurel considers the curse has never been paid in full. I think your grandparents died because of her. I think your mother still carries a curse. Perhaps that's why your father died."

"Daddy is dead then?"

"You know he is." Miss Dryden reaches out a hand and pats mine. Her fingers are like Lorelei's, long and twig like; blemished. A pulse bounds at my temple, like blood punching against my skin.

"And me ... Am I cursed?" I whisper the words, feeling the air press me down further. My vision darkens and I have to hold my head in my hands to stop the sensation of compression.

"Yes, you as well."

I see her walking away, my vision distorted with migraine aura. Her image perplexes me. I am reminded of the portrait that Myrtill had made of the hag and the beauty, because just for a moment I think Miss Dryden has a similar appearance: — a harsh outline of a hag juxtaposed with the beautiful form of a woman. A woman with silver white hair, a black stripe running through it. My head aches as I try to interpret what I have seen. The raucous cry of a magpie chuck-churring in the trees nearby finally makes me fold over; nauseous and confused. Weeping and sobbing. The trees surrounding the glade amplify the sound. An odour winds itself around me, as if I am breathing in the stench of wild garlic. The air heavy and sour as it fills my throat, my lungs. I choke, try to breathe but instead feel suffocated.

My eye-lids flicker shut as I drift into unconsciousness. Above me is a quiver of movement and I am jolted. My legs have been gripped by a claw like vice, as if the hawthorn tree has reached down and grabbed my ankles. Then I'm dragged across the ground. I can smell grass and ash under my cheek. I hear the grate of a stone being moved. I'm shoved. And fall into a well of darkness. I land in soft earth. How long I lie there I don't know, but I come too, my body bruised, my head pounding, stars circling my vision.

I croak, "Help!" The echo does not return instantly and I realise I am not in an enclosed tomb, but in a tunnel. I get to my hands and knees and manage to crawl along in darkness until eventually I collapse.

.....

I awake lying on the bed in my room. My head is thumping as if a tribe with drums is marching around it. I am very hot, a slick of sweat across my chest. But on my forehead is a touch of ice cold. Somebody is sitting beside me.

"You have a fever, Annie," she says. In this room Lorelei looks grey as if she hardly exists. My mouth is dry but I manage to spill out words, "… You can walk then?"

"Yes, only sometimes … sometimes I am strong enough." Her touch against my skin is calming, the banging in my head lessening. "There's a drink for you. It will make you feel better."

Though I don't hear the door open or close; Lorelei has gone before I sit up and take the glass from the bedside table. It looks like water but when I sip it, is sweet and soothing. The book of cautionary tales is on the table as well. I thought I'd put it back in the drawer.

Looking out of the window, I can just glimpse the slight movement of the tree tops; a soft and gentle sway, and I imagine the green gem of island below. Have I been gripped by a fever, fallen asleep and had a nightmare? The room smells musty and I realise it emanates from the book.

After resting for a while, I get up and go downstairs taking the glass Lorelei's given me.

"Hi Annie," Poppy greets me as I enter the kitchen.

"Where shall I put this?" I ask, handing her the glass.

"Oh, I'll pop it in the dishwasher." She takes it from me and holds it for a moment looking puzzled. She strokes her finger over the engraving on the glass. It's only as she holds it to the light, I see the image sparkling as she turns it. An etching of a tree entwined with a woman's form. "The dryad crystal. Not for the dishwasher," she says, more to herself than me. "Where did you get this?"

"Lorelei gave me a glass of water."

Poppy gives a small shake of her head, as if I am a child making something up. She places the glass on the side. "I don't think so." She doesn't wait for me to explain. "Are you feeling better now? I went up to check on Lorelei when she rang her bell. She said you'd had a funny turn."

"How did Lorelei know that? She is bed bound isn't she?"

Poppy frowns at me. "You still look peaky. Sit down and I'll fetch you something to eat. There's soup and bread and cheese."

I sit, grateful for the offer and Poppy starts to lay the table. As she spreads a cloth over it she says, "Yes, Lorelei's very limited in her movement." She starts to place cheeses, rolls and a bowl of grapes in front of me. "Lorelei said that you'd gone to her room. Apparently you were speaking about a book of fairy stories but not making any sense. She rang for me and I found you in a shivering heap by her door. She wouldn't have been able to help you, she's not strong enough. Don't you remember? I helped you up to your room."

I shake my head and start to help myself to the small banquet. "No, I don't remember any of that?"

"Do you know what brought the fit on? Is it something that's happened before? I hope this task Archie has requested isn't too much for you?"

"No, I'm fine," I lie, concerned that my 'fever' has now become a 'fit.' "I've always been prone to migraines; I usually realise when one's coming on though. I must just have had a horrible dream and spooked myself a bit." I give a false laugh.

"I saw that old book by your bedside. I wouldn't be surprised if you caught something from that. It looked so mouldy."

I agree, but not in the way she means. I think perhaps some infection has seeped out of the pages with the words.

"Where on earth did you find that horrible thing, in Lorelei's box?"

"No. I ..." I don't want to tell her that Rosa took it from Lorelei and gave it to me. So I lie. "Yes. I found it in the box." I am going to continue; tell Poppy I think I've been to the island and crawled through a tunnel to return to the Hall. But she is busy heating soup, the ladle clattering against the pan, making my ears ring. I'm not sure she'll understand; I don't understand it myself.

"Well, take it easy for a while. Let me know if you need a doctor. And you can stay as long as you like. In fact, it's nice to have somebody normal around." Poppy smiles at me as she clears my plate.

It's consoling to be considered normal and I smile as I head back to my room. The air is clearer. The window is open and there is finally more breeze making it feel fresh. As I replace the book into the cabinet a magpie watches me from outside the window. As the drawer clicks shut it flies away with a chuckling cry.

CHAPTER 41

After spending another day in the basement room, looking through and sorting pieces of paper, putting them into some sort of date order; I decide to reward myself with a drink at the Linden Tree and a chat with Trevor. However, as I cross the green I find myself heading towards the churchyard. I go through the front gate, past the yew tree den I had once hidden in, and to the gate at the far side of the church. Here the air is cooler and still, almost stagnant. I look around at the paving slabs and wall, seeking out something that could be the entrance to a tunnel. But all the stones are worn and covered with moss and lichen. Nothing looks likely. Perhaps the entrance is inside the church?

Just beyond the wall is the holly tree, the leaves green and glossy, a crop of berries reddening the branches. It is the trunk I want to examine. It rises from the ground, grey and smooth until half way up, then creases into a dark tear. I touch the scarring and recoil, because now the gash truly looks like a wound on human skin, with a dribble of rusty liquid seeping from the edges, sticky on my fingers. Could a person be trapped within a tree? I tell myself, this is just a tree with a syndrome, one of those diseases that happens to other trees. Yet, the question remains: — is this tree grown from the sapling left by a witch when she had taken a child? I think I'm going to faint and grab the wall to keep from falling.

I stumble from the churchyard to the pub, taking a moment outside to blow my nose and smooth my hair down.

There are a few people taking a break from their work I presume; a painter dressed in splattered overalls, a woman in a suit and a couple of others who look as if they spend most of their time there. Trevor is behind the bar and nods a greeting as I sit on a barstool. I was going to have a soft drink but when I open my mouth I order a large glass of red wine.

"How's it going then, Annie?"

I take a swig of wine and I wonder if Trevor notices the trembling of my hand.

"Could be better. Lorelei's story is more complicated than I expected and I think I've got distracted with my dad's disappearance."

"Well, that's only to be expected. The mystery of his disappearance was never really solved, was it? Must be difficult for a child to live with that."

I agree. Since returning to Broomstone I feel as if I have reverted to my childhood self, anxious and disturbed by everything I don't know. My head constantly on the brink of migraine. My brain jumbled between a real world and fairy tale one.

Trevor moves away to serve somebody else. Daddy probably sat right here, sitting on a stool like this. One fateful evening getting more and more plastered, then stumbling out of the pub down to the river. Why would he have done that? It doesn't make sense. And why did he pack a bag and not take it, if he was going away?

Trevor comes back to me. "You know, I hate to say this, but I think your dad must be dead otherwise he'd have come back. Wouldn't he? I don't think he was the type to leave his little girl. He talked about you with such pride. Would he really have made a life somewhere else? After all, you were here."

I blush at the idea of Daddy talking about me. I take another swig of wine, surprised there's only a drop left. "That's what I've been thinking too. Once I thought he might have left me alone, particularly after the argument he had with Ma, but now I'm certain he wouldn't just have left. He would have come back to me at some point when he'd calmed down. A month, two months ... a year, two years ... but he would have returned." My eyes are moist, as I think of Daddy. The merest chance that he didn't love me enough to return, tears ready to spill. I sniff and Trevor retreats to the other end of the bar whilst I retrieve a tissue from my handbag and blow my nose.

I push my empty glass across the bar, and nod towards Trevor. He comes back and refills it. I take a couple of sips, the liquid smooth on my lips. The wine helps the flow of my thoughts. "Did the police ask you when my dad was last here drinking?"

"Yes, but I can't remember what I said now. Such a long time ago." Trevor scratches his head. "But your dad was acting strangely all that month. He usually drank on a Saturday. Would stay all night, get a couple in before last orders. Then he stopped staying until closing time ... didn't drink as much as usual. He seemed excited about something as well. I asked him several times, 'Is it a woman then?' and he always just laughed. I asked him what he was up to and he said something like, 'Changing my life mate.'"

"Which could mean he was planning to go away?"

"I suppose so. I did tell the police all this ... I expect that's the conclusion they came to."

I don't tell Trevor I'd heard Daddy arguing with Ma on that Saturday night in February. I try and work out a story line. Daddy had been in the pub but left early, probably not as inebriated as I'd assumed. He went home, possibly met with Lorelei ... maybe he'd been seeing her regularly and that's why he'd been excited ... then had a massive row with Ma. Only to be expected if he'd gone into the house smelling of Lorelei. He'd left ... but without his backpack. I turn the residue of wine in my glass. It makes shapes similar to those created by tea leaf dregs; I wish I could interpret them. My skin prickles as I have the uncomfortable sensation that somewhere in my brain I know something. A something I don't want to face.

"Penny for them?" Trevor asks.

I really want to discuss my thoughts with somebody, but

Trevor isn't the right person. I'm not sure who is. I smile, shake my head, "Just a refill please." He takes my glass and fills it with the red liquid which will help settle my thoughts. I spend the rest of the evening there, so it's late when I stumble back towards the Hall. As I step outside the pub it starts to rain, great globs that strike me with the ice cold sensation of fingertips. I jog, trying to avoid the downpour, but end up by the beech tree. I linger, reading the plaque on the bench, *'For Lorelei'* ... *'All the trees in the wood sing your name'*. I'm drenched by the time I reach the front door. My head's hazy with wine, the tiles of the reception floor spin as I enter. As I go up the stairs Rasputin comes rushing down from the uppermost floor, sweeping past me with a brush of fur. The door to my room is ajar and I suspect the cat has been lurking in there. I also suspect he has been searching through my things ... but a cat couldn't do that, could it?

Looking around, nothing appears very different, except the top drawer of the cabinet is not quite closed, the one which had the book of tales in it. I slide the drawer open, expecting the book to have vanished, but there it is lurking in the shadows. The illustrations on the cover appear to beckon, willing me to pick it up and read it. But I resist. I shut the drawer firmly, wishing I had a key to turn in the miniature lock, so the book is trapped inside.

I shower and change for bed. There's an uncomfortable idea I am trying to ignore. But it won't stay away, seeping into my mind like more wine. My father had drunk at The Linden Tree on the Saturday evening, he hadn't been drunk and he definitely didn't head down to the river, because he came back to the cottage and was in there arguing with my mother late on the Saturday night.

The rain has softened to a *pit pat pit pat* against the window. My head is spinning when I lie down so I can't sleep, half glimpsing an idea which seems just out of reach. I close my eyes again. From somewhere far away I hear shouting, an argument. As the water drips, my dream takes me back to the shed beside the cottage in the wood, where I had waited all those years ago for my parents' argument to abate. I can see myself creeping back into the house in the early hours of the morning. It was silent inside the house and I had tiptoed upstairs and slipped into bed as quietly as I could.

I'm not certain if I am awake or sleeping because I can hear the noises of lovemaking somewhere in the distance. I try to work out who it could be. A flash of lightening jolts me. Purple sparks blotching my vision in the blackness of the room. A similar jarring strikes my brain as I realise that, on that night, my father might already have gone by the time I heard noises in the morning. It might have been my mother and Woody making love, rather than Ma and Daddy. Perhaps it was Ma who had told him to leave, that she'd had enough, wanted to be with Woody. Perhaps that's what the argument had been about.

The crash of thunder and flashes of lightning continue, making the building shake, and I sit up and switch the bedside lamp on. My head is dizzy and my mouth dry, but not due to the effects of wine. I fetch a glass of water. Standing at the window, I'm unable to see anything from the lit room until another fork flashes through the sky above the island. For a second the island is clearly visible. With it the fog in my brain also shifts.

If Daddy had left during that night, he did so without taking his packed bag. He must have met with Lorelei after returning from the Linden Tree. If that had happened, he'd gone into the house after their tryst. He was probably sober, just inebriated from the adrenalin rush of having been with Lorelei and perhaps with ideas of running away with her. Maybe Ma had actually found them together and Lorelei had fled. Then they'd argued. Daddy wouldn't have returned to the pub; it would have been closed. If he had wandered down to the river, where had he got a bottle of vodka from?

As lightning fissures the sky, illuminating the grounds of the Hall, I finally allow myself to acknowledge the answer.

Perhaps Lorelei had been right when she said I knew everything.

My father had not left on the Sunday morning. He had never left the cottage that Saturday night … meaning he had been stopped. If he had not left, there were only two people who knew what had happened to him. I watch from the window for a long time waiting to see the island light up again, but the storm has passed.

I don't try to sleep. I am too restless. I sit on the bed and watch my reflection rock and sob in the mirror. Have I just connected several strands of story and made a lie of them, or is my answer the truth. If so, what should I do next? Who should I talk to?

It will have to be Spider.

I check my mobile but there is no signal here. It's very early but I dress and then pad downstairs and walk across the green to the far end of the village, hoping to find a spot where I might get a signal. My steps leave footprints on the dewy grass, a tell-tale trail of what I am about to do.

One bar of signal is indicated on the screen and I punch Spider's contact number. It rings on and I expect he is still asleep. But then a sleepy voice says, "Hi Annie. It's early. What's the problem?"

"I've thought of something. Something I need to share. It's important."

"I guess it must be to phone at this hour. Let me get dressed and we'll meet. The golf club opens at seven. I'll see you there."

CHAPTER 42

Though I'll arrive too early I fetch my car and head straight for the golf club. I sit in the carpark watching the beginnings of the golfing day. Admin and ground staff are arriving and the noise of machinery and deliveries whirring and clanging is making the thrum of hangover worse.

At five past seven I recognise Spider's car pulling in near me and I climb out to greet him. "Well, people will start talking," he says, raising his eyebrows and then winking. I manage a smile in return and say, "Good Morning. Thanks for meeting me."

"Let's head inside and get you some coffee. Looks like you need it."

"I didn't sleep."

"Must be bad, whatever it is. Come on then."

Spider leads the way, signs me in and then takes the stairs two at a time, leaving me dawdling in his wake. Considering the hour I had woken him, Spider seems remarkably cheery. When I tell him this, he says, "Goes with the territory of being a cop. Unsocial hours … a policeman's lot."

We order coffee and sit overlooking the course. Early starters are already heading to the first tee, swishing their clubs to warm up. As I ponder the benefits of standing on a tee at just past seven a.m., Spider asks, "So what's so important to get me out of bed on a Saturday morning?"

"I've been thinking about the night my father disappeared. I've been putting the bits of information together. Last night I realised something."

I pause; sip my coffee, glad of its heat and bitterness on my tongue.

"Go on then,"

"Where shall I start?"

"Wherever you want."

"I'll begin earlier in the evening, when I was watching Roderick at the Hall." I fill Spider in about my episode of stalking, feeling myself blush as I confess. I also mention seeing the group make their way towards the lake.

I continue, with the sight of Lorelei, tripping on the path, her black cloak and bloodied fingers. "It had started to rain then, so I hurried back home. That's when I heard the raised voices of Ma and Daddy. I sheltered in the wood shed but found a couple of things. One was a cloak similar to the one I'd seen on Lorelei, the other was a backpack with my father's things."

"Which is why you thought he might have been planning to run away?"

"Could be ... but there's something else. I think my father and Lorelei had sex in the shed that night. I think it might have been part of a spell." My face is prickling with embarrassment. "It could also be why Lorelei had blood on her hands. From what I can gather it was quite a dark magical spell."

"Wow, not my area of expertise." He laughs, "And then?"

"Well, finally, about one o'clock I think, I managed to creep into the house. It was quiet. The storm had passed. But during the night I heard things, banging and bumping and then love making ..."

"You think your ma and dad made up?"

"That's the thing, it wasn't unusual for that to happen, but I realise now it might not have been my parents. It could just as easily have been Ma and another man."

"Another man?" Spider frowns at me and pulls back in his chair, as if I am losing the plot. "Nobody else mentioned there was another man there."

"Woody ... Tom Hart, you know? He was there early in the

morning."

Spider nods, "So where was your father when this was going on? Had he left by then? You said before that he didn't take the backpack?"

"Well, that's the thing; I don't see how my father could have left without me knowing. Trevor the landlord said he'd left the pub early. He must have come back to the cottage to meet Lorelei. So, he can't have gone down to the river drunk and fallen in then. The next day I couldn't get into the shed, but I looked through the window, and I'm pretty sure the backpack was still there."

"What are you suggesting?"

I take another swig of coffee to lubricate my mouth, so that the words I have to say will come out. Even so I stutter. "I think perhaps my father never left. For some reason he couldn't leave, perhaps he had been hurt. I think Woody might have come over to help Ma ..." my words are coming out in sobs. "I think he might have helped to hide the body."

"Wow," Spider says again, but there is no laughter this time. He pushes himself right away from the table and tips the chair to a precarious balance. "That's a very serious conclusion to draw from what you've told me. Being 'pretty sure' and 'maybe' might not be enough if you're accusing somebody of murder."

The word is like a gun going off, loud and ricocheting in the empty dining room. I'm not just accusing 'somebody' of murder. I'm accusing Ma and Woody. I collapse forward onto the table, snivelling into my arms.

After a moment, I feel Spider patting my back and saying, "Come on now Annie, you've done the right thing telling me. We can work out what to do for the best." He presses a paper napkin into my fist and gradually I sit up, wiping my face on the rough material.

By the time I regain some composure, Spider has returned to his seat opposite me and a fresh pot of coffee is on the table. Spider pours me another cup. "Now Annie, don't take this the wrong way, but do you think you need to see a doctor?"

"Why ...?" I begin, I haven't hurt myself. But then I realise he isn't concerned about me physically.

"I gather that you sometimes have fits."

"Who told you that? I get migraines but they just make me sleepy." Spider remains silent. "You don't believe me." It is a statement. It is all I can manage but my emotions are tumbling inside me. If he doesn't believe me, nobody will.

I turn my head and glimpse my reflection in the window glass; even the blurred figure looks smeared and dishevelled. If I'd seen that image from the seat of a train, I would be certain the woman depicted was cracking up. Was I imagining things? Was it just my mind desperately searching for answers and jumbling things up?

Spider is rocking on his chair again, his fingertips pressed together. "Annie, it's not that I don't believe you ... though it does seem rather far-fetched ... it's that we have to be sure. I have to be sure what's going on before I take this further."

My tears have gone now, I'm angry. "Look, I know I'm in a state about this. I might have been over-emotional when I spoke just now, but let me tell you this ... my mental health has never been so good, my thoughts never so clear. I've finally put together some kind of explanation for my father's disappearance and I'll go and speak to my mother, with or without you!"

I'm about to stand up and walk out but realise I don't have enough energy, so I take a swig of coffee, the liquid slopping into the saucer when I put it down.

Spider rocks forward on his chair, the legs creaking onto the floor. He holds his palms up towards me. "Okay, okay. It's not that I don't believe you but we have to take things carefully. What I want is for you to make a statement, something official. Then we'll go from there."

I follow Spider downstairs, and allow him to drive me to the police station in Stonewick. We say nothing on the short journey. In a small room with no ornamentation, just peeling magnolia paintwork and an odd smell, I write a page and a half of script, exactly as I had told Spider. I am watched by a young police officer, who eyes me as if I'm a criminal who might attack her at any moment.

The statement is copied and signed and then taken somewhere. I'm worried it might just be locked away, never to be seen again. But Spider returns and asks if I'm ready to go. I want to tell him 'No. I want to stop. That I want everything to go away.'

"I need a break," I say, and go into the police station wash rooms to freshen up. My eyes won't focus in the mirror above the sink, but my reflection looks back at me with red rimmed devil eyes. I can tell my skin is blotchy and puffy as if I'm transmuting to something else. I splash tepid water onto my face and pat it dry with rough paper towels. A wild woman still stares back at me when I've finished. In a daze I manage to find my way out of the building and back into Spider's car.

After we've been travelling for a few minutes I notice we're not heading to Broomstone or back to the golf club. I ask, "Where are we going?"

"To see your mother."

"Oh." There is nothing more to add.

Spider drives in silence. When we reach mother's block of flats he says, "I'll do the talking, right?"

I nod, and press the code to let us into the building. Our steps echo as we climb the stairs, they have never seemed so loud, as if our visit is being announced to the world. A headline accompanies the thought; 'Girl accuses mother of murder, thirty-five years ago.'

When Spider says, "Ready?" I jump. He rings the bell.

I wonder whether Ma is here as there is no movement or sound. But Spider rings the bell again and I detect shuffling from inside. Then the chain is being dragged aside and Ma's face is smiling and saying, "Hello, to what do I owe ..." But before she completes the sentence, on seeing our faces, she frowns. "Come in."

She looks the same as usual, a lime green smock with handkerchief hem line which brushes against her bare feet. But as she leads us to the lounge, her graceful confident stride has left her, she appears hunched and hesitant. I guess she knows exactly why we're here. I'm thankful Spider will lead the conversation.

"Mrs Ramson ..." He is going to keep this formal, "... some information has come to light about your husband's disappearance in 1983. I'd like to ask you some questions. At this stage this is not a formal interview and you don't have to say anything."

Ma considers for a moment and then says, "Could you get me a glass of water, Annie?"

I go to the kitchen area, whilst I hear her offer Spider a seat and tell him she will help if she can. I flick the kettle, hoping there is some coffee powder lurking somewhere. No coffee but a lone Darjeeling teabag, which will have to do.

I return to the lounge with a glass of water for Ma and a mug of black tea for me.

Spider has one of his notebooks open on his knees. I sit in the corner of the room, looking out of the window onto the car park, listening to the conversation in the background.

Spider consults his notes and asks, "Can you remember the last evening you saw your husband? I believe it was Saturday the twelfth of February."

"I'll do my best," Ma replies. "It was a pretty foul day from what I remember, cloudy and cold earlier in the day. Later there was a storm. Anyway, Ryan went to work at the Hall in the morning, but I didn't see him again till much later that night, when he rolled in drunk and shouting his head off."

"And how did the argument start?"

Ma shrugs. "Like most of our arguments ... he started yelling at me. About how hopeless I was, how stupid et cetera, how he wanted to leave ..."

"And he said he was going to leave?"

"Yes, but he said that all the time."

"He didn't give a specific reason for leaving, like another woman for example?"

"Oh, I presume you're talking about Lorelei?"

"So, they were having an affair?"

"Yes, if you could call it that. I think she had affairs with all the men in Broomstone at some time. Ryan of course thought he was the ultimate, the one who would save her."

I frown and ask, "Save her from what?" Surely somebody like Lorelei had everything she could possibly want and need.

Spider coughs, irritated by my interruption.

"From boredom, I should think. All I know is, he was besotted with her. There had been other affairs in the past and he did tend to go mooning about like a love sick teenager."

I find it difficult to listen to this. My idea of Daddy, and my parents' marriage, had been so flawed.

"So did Ryan say he was leaving that night?" Spider continues.

"Yes, he said he was going to collect his bag and go."

"But Annie said that she didn't see or hear him go. She had sheltered in the wood shed where his backpack was. And he didn't take it with him."

Ma shrugs again, looking down at her toes. "You must be mistaken."

"Who were you with later then? I heard you."

Ma stops concentrating on her feet and looks at me, "Annie, he calmed down a bit before he left. He grabbed a few things and went in the early hours of the morning. Remember that storm? You might not have heard the door opening and shutting with the thunder crashing."

Watching her, I don't see my mother. Her face is different, the lies she is telling make her a stranger.

"The storm was long over by early morning. So, who were you making love with then? Was that before or after he had gone?"

Ma looks back down quickly. She doesn't want to let me see the panic in her face, how will she explain that?"

"You're mistaken Annie. You always did imagine so much … make things up. And your headaches confused you."

Her response doesn't surprise me. I shake my head, realising we're back to the old response, '… it's just silly Annie, imagining things.'

Spider appears unable to speak. I think his mouth opens to ask something and then closes again. I stand up and face my mother.

"You know what I think happened? I think you argued and I think you'd had enough. You hit him. He was hurt. You managed to move him out of the way, so I didn't see him when I came in. You came and checked that I was asleep in my bed, and then went to get Woody. Was Daddy dead when you got back? You and Woody got rid of Daddy somehow and then, feeling pleased with yourselves, went back to the warmth of Daddy's bed. No wonder you seemed so happy the next morning!"

Ma stands up and pushes past me. "Are you going to let her speak to me like this?" she demands of Spider. "Making things up, accusing me of harming her father?"

The notebook slides off Spider's knees as he stands up as well. "Why don't we all calm down?" is his feeble response. "We don't know what happened. That's what we're trying to work out. Sit down Annie."

I do as I'm told. Returning to my corner and looking out at the same car park, with the same cars. Ma almost falls back into her chair. Her skin is white and she is trembling. "I can't speak anymore," she says. "You'll have to go."

Spider indicates that we should do what we've been asked. "We're leaving now, but I might have to return for more formal questioning later. You might want to consider a lawyer."

"What for? I haven't done anything wrong."

And as I pass by her to get to the door all she says is, "Annie, Annie, what have you done?" Shaking her head and repeating it until I am on the stairs and out of ear shot.

I get into Spider's car again, thinking he'll take me back to the golf club to get my car. Probably, glad to be finished with this drama. After all it is a long time ago and nothing can be proved. However, we go in the direction of Broomstone and then take a narrow road to the other side of the forest.

"Where are we going now?"

"First rule of detection Annie. We talk to the other party and see if there are discrepancies between the two stories." We pull off the lane and stop part way up a farm track. "We'll have to walk from here."

We haven't gone far before I see Woody's van at the edge of the field. The rain in the night gives everything a gloss as in an oil painting. The field is golden, fringed with tall grasses and the glow of scarlet poppies. It looks idyllic. It seems a shame I'm about to disturb that.

Spider raps on the door of the van. "What is it?" Woody's voice shouts out. As he opens the door he says, "You again Annie, and Spider isn't it?"

"I'd like to ask you some questions about the disappearance of Annie's father. We've had some more information and I'm doing some follow up interviews."

"Why me? I have nothing to do with any of this."

"Well, you were there the following morning. The morning after Daddy left," I retort from behind Spider. Spider puts a hand on my arm and shakes his head.

Woody stomps down the steps and pulls the logs around so we can sit. Woodlice crawl from underneath, disturbed from their darkness. Woody does not offer us refreshment. "Come on then, give it to me. What 'more information' have you got?" He makes a little beckoning gesture with his fingers.

"What time did you get to the Ramsons' house on the morning of Sunday the thirteenth of February?"

"How should I remember that? It was years ago. Nobody knew anything was up then, that Ryan had walked away and left Ivy and Annie. I often visited Ivy, especially on Sunday mornings when I knew it was likely that Ryan had returned from the pub drunk and had let his fists do a bit of talking when he got home."

Spider continues to ask him the details of the Saturday evening. I switch off and watch as sunlight shines across the field beyond the edge of the woods and observe the breeze making the grass ripple like fabric, turning it from brown to gold and back again, like alchemy. Nearby a wood pigeon coos and other birds chirrup. The trees murmur as the wind lifts and falls. It should be lovely sitting here listening to Woody talk. His deep voice reminds me of when he'd told me stories as a child; the rhythm of his voice accompanied by the chip of his chisel as he whittled a piece of wood. As I listen now, he sounds so reasonable I have to remind myself that he is making up a story. What he's remembering is not true. But as Spider finishes asking Woody his questions, I realise I might be wrong. It might be me. Perhaps I am making things up, imaging things, just like Ma had said.

"If you're done I've got things to be getting on with," Woody says, getting up from his seat. He watches as we stand up and turn to go. "And you're not welcome back here. Understand?" He steps back into the van and slams the door, making the whole place rock. The forest appears to jar as well, as if the noise has created a domino effect so the whole wood is shaken. As we move away, a shape drops in front of us, and I wonder if something has been dislodged by the commotion. But the dark form morphs into a man. Well, a man or boy, I still haven't been able to discern Ham's age. He emerges from between the trees and bushes, his clothing a dirty green T-shirt, his trousers grey, camouflaging him. "Been to see the woodman, have you? I knows things … I knows things about what he did. I can take you there."

Spider is looking spooked by the sudden appearance of Ham. I make the introductions. "Spider, this is Ham, who lives in the woods here."

"I knows things … I knows things …" Ham does his dance, with Spider and me caught in the circle of his movement. He repeats his chant.

"Stop this now!" Spider says suddenly, stepping out of Ham's way. "If you've something constructive to say, then say it. Otherwise, we'll be on our way."

Ham leans towards me, then whispers words, which I don't want to hear. "I know where he's buried …"

I stand motionless, feeling the fetid breath of Ham's words hot on my face. The wood pauses, the birds fall silent.

"Who?" It is a stupid question. I'm pleased when Spider breaks the silence.

"Are you saying you know where Ryan Ramson is buried?"

Ham sniggers and ignores him. He faces me again. "Your daddy … I know where your daddy is buried."

"You're lying …" I choke.

"Is this true?" Spider asks, coming towards me and Ham. "Is there information you've been hiding all this time?"

"I'll show you, Missus … Not him …" He jerks his head in Spider's direction.

"You have to show him as well. He's a policeman, he needs to know."

"You. Only you." He points a gnarled finger at me. The nail is pointed, black and soiled.

"You'd better go with him," Spider says, "I'll wait here for you." But as I turn to follow Ham, Spider winks and indicates he'll track us.

CHAPTER 43

Ham takes a trail I can't recall. It is hardly a path, just a mud line between thick bushes of elder and hazel. Brambles wind around them and every now and again I am scratched. Occasionally, I hear a curse from further back as Spider follows. He wouldn't make a spy.

Finally, we reach an opening. In the centre is a gnarled hawthorn tree, raised on a mound of its own root system, knotted below the trunk then splaying out like tentacles. I once knew the wood so well, but I am sure I have never been here. The small space is encircled by dense foliage, it makes me want to open a door and encourage a draught to refresh the cloying air. I am hot and sticky, my hair teased by brambles and soiled by cobweb. I am having difficulty breathing. So dizzy I can't concentrate. The figure of Ham keeps moving in and out of focus, as though he might only partially exist. I wonder whether I have fainted somewhere and this is not really happening. Am I having another fit?

"Here he is … here he lies …" Ham says, patting a mossy section of ground between two roots.

"How do you know that?"

A magpie with its coarse call lands in the branches of the tree. 'One for sorrow.' Always just one magpie.

"Grandma Dryden told me … She sees everything … knows everything."

That I could believe. "We don't even know that my father's dead."

"Ham knows, Grandma knows."

"And what do you expect me to do? I can't do anything."

"Have to dig … have to dig," teases Ham, chuckling.

I look around as an expletive resonates around the space. "Fuck!" Spider says as he falls forward tripping over a bramble.

"Not him, not him," Ham hisses, and starts jigging and flapping at the base of the tree.

Spider ignores the behaviour and asks him, "So you believe Mr Ramson is buried here?"

Ham turns away from him and skulks behind the tree trunk.

I reply for him. "He says his grandma, Miss Dryden, told him my dad is buried here."

"And you believe him?" Spider asks with heavy scepticism.

"I don't know … I don't know anything." My head hurts and I put my hands to my temples and squeeze my eyes shut, trying to still my thoughts.

"I think I've got to call it in. I'll look stupid if it's a hoax. And I'll charge that Ham guy with wasting police time if it is. Hear that?" Spider calls, looking about for Ham, but he has gone, melted away into the bushes. Spider has got his phone out before I can tell him there's no point. "Fuck. No signal," he says, shaking his head. "I'll have to go out of the wood, maybe back to the car. You'll have to stay here."

My mouth is dry as I tell him, "I can't stay here. I don't know where I am. You won't find me again." I can't work out how to explain that I think this glade might be in another dimension.

"Don't be daft, of course I'll find you. The forest isn't that big."

"Please don't leave me," I plead.

"Look I'll leave a trail, unravel the wool from my jumper …"

I am nodding, relieved, until I see the smirk on his face and realise he is wearing his trademark floral shirt under his jacket. He obviously sees my dismay at his joke.

"Look, seriously, I promise I will find you again. As I go back to the car I'll put a mark by a tree or a path. Really you mustn't worry. I'll be as quick as I can." He pats my shoulder before he leaves and then is hidden from sight as the bushes devour him.

I sit at the edge of the glade and start to cry. How the hell have I ended up sitting alone in the middle of Broomstone forest? I start to hear little noises; scratches and tweeting. I try to ignore them. About me the trees and bushes murmur. That is of some comfort. Then the magpie returns cackling and chuckling at my predicament. "Go away!" I shout at it, but it just hops higher in the tree, pushing its neck out as if entertained by my dismay.

In the end I curl up into a foetal position, close my eyes and try to shut out everything. A tiny hope generates beneath my squeezed eyelids. Perhaps this is a dream or a migraine illusion. Perhaps I'll awaken in my bed. It is a brief spark and I shiver as it fades.

I don't know how long I doze but suddenly I hear the sound of boots thumping the earth and human voices.

"Said I'd find you alright, didn't I?" Spider says, approaching me with an outstretched hand to help me up. I grab it thankfully, but notice his dishevelled appearance and the look of relief in his eyes. He'd been worried that he wasn't going to find me after all. Two officers stand behind him with a holdall. I presume it contains equipment.

"Did he say exactly where the body is buried?" Spider asks.

"Well, I think he said here." I point to the place Ham had indicated. I don't put my hand on it as he had done.

"Okay, Fisher, you start. Get digging."

Fisher removes his jacket and rolls his sleeves up, then gets a spade out of the holdall. He sticks the blade near the base of the tree and a sod of earth flies out. Within about half an hour with both officers digging in tandem, there is a sizeable hole under the tree.

The officer called Carlton is taking a break, standing up stretching his back. "Anything there?" asks Spider, going over and looking in the hole. "Nothing yet, Sir."

"Let's give it another half hour, then we'll call it a day."

Fisher starts to dig again, this time with a trowel as roots are obscuring the plot.

I'm getting agitated. It seems that this is just as a ruse by Ham, who is obviously a disturbed young man.

But suddenly Fisher says, "Sir," Spider strides to his side "There's something here, I think."

I want to see, but can't as the three men are obscuring the hole. Spider bends down and is using the trowel to prod something.

"Okay, tape it off. I'm calling it in as a potential crime scene."

"What is it, what is it?" I ask, jumping up from where I'd seated myself.

"Looks like a foot." I make to push past him but he puts a hand on my shoulder. "No, Annie. You don't want to go there."

Fisher and Carlton are making themselves busy with official striped police tape. "I think it's time you went home Annie. Leave us to deal with things here." When I nod he asks, "Do you think you can find your own way back to Broomstone?"

"Yes, but my car's still at the golf club."

He shakes his head and frowns. "I think you'll appreciate I'm going to be here for a while. We'll deal with your car tomorrow."

Bindweed and ivy fall in a curtain behind me, and brambles tangle as if the glade is being sealed off. When the narrow trail meets a wider path I collect some twigs to create a marker point and make a mental note of the hazel bush and pine which conceal the entrance. As I step further away the foliage becomes familiar as if trees and bushes have moved around to create the paths I remember. I suddenly find myself on a wider track which I recognise. After another ten minutes I come to the boundary fence and keeping to that I end up at the glade where my house used to stand. I don't pause, but hurry towards the village. It is just over a week since I met with Archie and then moved into the Hall. I have made little progress with Lorelei's biography, but have found out too much about Daddy's disappearance. I shiver, even though the afternoon is warm. What am I going to do? I don't want to stay here, but I haven't even got my car, so I can't leave anyway.

The Hall is quiet, but in the kitchen I find Poppy in the middle of preparing vegetables. "Hi there," she says brightly. "Will you be eating with us later? I'm doing a roast."

"Thanks, but I really wanted to go home and grab a few bits. The thing is my car's at the golf club. Can I use the phone to call a cab?"

"Well yes, but don't do that. Give me a minute and I'll give you a lift."

After a few more chops, Poppy sweeps carrots into a pan of water. Then she wipes her hands, removes her apron and says, smiling at me, "There, all ready."

She grabs her handbag and car keys and I follow her outside.

It takes longer to get to the golf club with Poppy driving at a sedate pace and stopping at every give way sign. It is so irritating I nearly tell her she doesn't have to come to a complete stop, but then think that would be churlish; after all she is giving me a lift. I'm glad when we arrive. I thank her and wave her off.

I allow myself a moment to enjoy the normality of my mini and then head to my flat. As I climb the stairs up to my front door, the smell of cooking from the nearby kebab shop is making it stink, and I wonder why I had been so desperate to return. At least Jay is not lurking by the door.

The air smells stale as I let myself in. It still has that taint of soiled bedding and I go and rip the sheets off the bed and put them in the laundry bag. Maybe I'll go down to the launderette later.

I sit at the window watching the sky. It is too blue and calm, the clouds white and fluffy making shapes. They fold and unfold, transforming from one creature to another, a rabbit to a dragon, a fish to a monster. The troubled beating of my heart, hard against my ribcage gradually settles. But it is a long time before I'm able to move. I need to do something to stop my thoughts returning to the morning's events.

I make myself a cup of tea and get my laptop out. Sitting by the window again I look out at the view towards Broomstone and try to plan the chapters of Lorelei's biography. In most situations a life story would begin with her childhood, maybe her parents, her family and a social setting. It is odd to start without beginning at what they call the formative years. She doesn't even have a date of birth unless I'm going to use Holly's. It suddenly seems too hard. Lorelei might have been right when she suggested I wanted to find out what happened to my father rather than write her biography.

I'm making no progress when my mobile buzzes. Spider has sent a text message: *Found remains of body, consistent with burial in 1983. Can't say more at moment. Meet tomorrow, 10am usual place?*

It is some moments before I have stopped shaking enough to punch the keys to respond, '*Yes.*'

Then I collapse on my unmade bed, too shocked to cry, but with the sensation of panic building up inside me. Eventually the pressure is too much; I open my mouth and scream.

It starts quietly but builds up to a siren-like wailing. Nobody comes.

By the time I've calmed down it is dusk, the flat grey and gloomy, the air pressing in on me. I can't connect the green glade and the hawthorn tree with the burial site of my father. And for years ... years and years ... he has been lying there.

I manage to drag myself to the bathroom, but after a wee and quick wash I don't have the energy to do anything more. I slink back to bed fully clothed, lie down and close my eyes. I don't sleep but doze, waking with shock every hour, with the realisation Daddy is really dead.

CHAPTER 44

The morning light finally creeps in and transforms the interior of the flat to a different shade of grey. I manage to shower, remove and reapply make up, change my clothes and clean my teeth.

It is too early to leave for my meeting with Spider, so grabbing the laundry bag I head to the launderette. I sip coffee, which doesn't taste like coffee, from a paper cup and watch the washing rotate. It is a similar to my thoughts, the same idea circling, unable to escape. My father dead ... my father buried in Broomstone forest ... my father dead ... my father buried in Broomstone forest ...

At least when I return to my flat I feel a bit better. Clean sheets, no longer tainted with the lingering stench of Jay.

My return journey to the golf club is slow. As I reverse my mini from its place on the street I nearly bump the car behind. I know my reactions are hampered and crawl along. At the golf club I put on dark glasses, to hide my red rimmed eyes.

I am going up the stairs when a voice calls, "Hey! You need to sign in." I return to the reception area, apologise and go through the rigmarole of signing the guest register.

It is gone ten by the time I reach the dining room. Spider is already there, "I've ordered coffee. Do you want anything to eat?"

I shake my head. "Tell me," is all I can say.

Spider lets the waiter put a coffee pot and cups on the table and leave. Then he pours us each a cup and begins.

"Well, as I said in my message, we found a body. All is consistent with an adult male, and some clothing which, going from our previous investigation, is also consistent with your father."

I let out a muffled cry, and my cup trembles as I replace it. Spider reaches for my hand and squeezes it. "I'm sorry Annie. If there's any consolation at least you now know. At least you don't have to keep wondering whether he's dead or alive."

Daddy is dead. How can I ever be consoled? Another thought strikes me, as forceful as lightening, "Will I have to identify him?"

"No, not after all this time. If there are any particular objects found with him then maybe I'll ask you to identify those."

Spider is squeezing my hand, but it remains cold. "You're in shock Annie. Is there anybody you could stay with for a while?"

"No." I shake my head although it increases the turmoil in it. I have no one. Jay has left, maybe Myrtill ... but I wasn't sure she'd want to see me. I am only employed by Archie, we aren't really friends and then Woody and Ma ... it doesn't bear thinking about. "Will you arrest Woody ... my mother?"

"We've still got further examinations and an autopsy to perform. Formal interviews will come first. I just thought I should let you know what our initial findings were."

"So, it might not be him?" There is a note of hope in my words.

"Annie ..." He could add, 'don't be stupid,' but I insert it myself. "It's likely that when further examination has been carried out we'll be able to determine what might have happened. We need evidence of wrongdoing to arrest anybody. Then we'll go from there."

Spider leaves soon after, saying, "I'll keep you in the loop, Annie."

I sit for a long time; sipping cold coffee and watching people come and go from the 18th green. Some are happy, some cross; all of us going round and round and round, with no apparent aim.

Sometime later a waiter suggests it is time I leave. I get to my car and don't know where to go. Should I return to the Hall or the flat? If I go to the Hall what will I say? I decide another night at home will be the best option. I'll decide if I want to continue with Lorelei's biography.

I have only been back a few minutes, enough time to put the kettle on and remake the bed, when there's a knock on the door.

My mind must still be foggy because I open the door too far before I realise Jay is standing on the doorstep. Before I have a chance to shut it, he has placed his foot in the opening. "Glad to see you're back, Annie. Is that the kettle boiling? Invite us in, won't you?" And with that, he pushes inside and I don't have the strength to repel him. He swings a chair out from the table and sits down, legs splaying out, in the same way he always had when we lived together.

I make two mugs of tea. "Thanks Annie. Now what's up? You've got dark glasses on. Got a migraine? Or are you just trying to disguise yourself? Can't fool me though." He is smiling. I remain silent and glare at him. "You'd better tell me all about it. Who else's shoulder are you going to cry on?" He comes round the table and makes an attempt to hug me like before, but I stand up and pull away.

"No Jay. Whether or not I've got other people in my life is not the point. The fact is, I don't want *you* in my life." I grab his cup of tea and pour it down the sink.

He follows me, standing too close behind me. "Don't be like that, Annie, I'm only trying to help." I can feel the warmth of his body pressing into me. Once, I might have turned and sobbed into his shoulder, then we would end up in my bed, then he would go ... until he was feeling low and needed some company. I can see my reflection in the mottled tap, my dark glasses bulging like an insect. "Go away Jay," I hear the creature say, "Go away now."

Suddenly there is a draught of cool air at my back, and empty space. "Okay, be like that. I'll leave you to live in la-la land … imagining you'll get a better offer. Maybe a prince will come and rescue you." Before he slams the door, he shouts, "Ha fucking ha! You always were a frigid cow."

I hear the thump of his feet as he goes down the stairs. When there is silence again, I return to the table and drink my tea.

By the time I've finished it I have made a decision. I grab my bag and car keys and head back out.

I arrive at Ma's block of flats and sit in the car, one minute removing the key, the next minute replacing it intending to drive away. But eventually I get out, shut and lock the door and head into the building.

I knock, too long and more loudly than necessary in the quiet building. "Okay, I'm coming," I hear Ma call. "Annie," she says as she opens the door, more of a sigh than a word. "Come in." She stands back and I push past her, wanting to turn and hug her, breathe her scent in, remind myself of her sweetness. She doesn't move toward me, so I just go and stand by the window in the lounge.

"Have you heard?"

"Heard what?"

"They found Daddy."

"Oh, Annie …" Ma is beside me, leaning forward and embracing me. She whispers, "I didn't know." I hardly hear her through my tears. She lets me cry myself out, until I am simply weeping silently. Then she leaves the room and returns with a mug of herbal tea and a box of tissues.

Whilst I calm down, she says, "I'll tell you what happened, Annie. I need to explain." She sits on the couch and begins. For a moment I think she's going to say, '*Once upon a time …*'

"I think that something would have happened one day … you know what your father was like. I'd always thought it would be me who'd end up dead though. That night was dreadful. He was in such a rage when he came in, telling me I wasn't good enough and that he was going to leave. He'd said it so many times before that I didn't rise to the bait and just said, 'Where will you go then?' My indifference angered him more. 'I'm going to somebody who wants to be with me, somebody worth a thousand of you.' 'Who?' I asked thinking he had fallen for one of the barmaids at the Linden Tree. I thought he might have come back with somebody; I saw a candle flickering in the woodshed and he stank of sex. I was surprised when he said, 'Lorelei,' though I knew he'd been mooning over her for ages. I laughed. I thought it was funny, a joke. For Lorelei to want a man like him didn't make sense. She was a 'whore', just like your dad once said ... wanted everybody but not long term. Don't get me wrong, I thought when she first appeared, all those years ago, when you found her in the river; that's when I thought I might lose Ryan, but she had a fling with Woody and that was that."

Ma looks at me, to check I'm still listening; I sip my tea and nod.

"Well, me laughing made him lose it. He started hitting out. At me, at the crockery, at the furniture. Combined with the storm in the background I was more frightened than ever before. I thought he would kill me. I grabbed something to protect myself. He lunged at me and I pushed back at him. It was only then I realised I held a knife, the smallest one, but enough to make him scream with pain as it pierced his shoulder. That's when he fell, stumbling backwards and hitting his head. Just catching it on the corner of the piano keyboard. He didn't move." Ma gives a strange sob and covers her mouth with her hand as if trying to keep the truth in. "Annie, he was dead, I didn't kill him but I made him fall. And I didn't know what to do." Ma sits still, her eyes squeezed shut.

"Well, somehow I pulled him into my room and tidied a bit and waited. You probably came in around then. I think Woody must have known something was up. I truly believe he heard me through the forest. Maybe the trees told him. Anyway, the next thing I know is that he's there at the cottage, and I didn't have to explain. We just wrapped Ryan up, 'I'll deal with him,' he said. 'You clear up here.' And that's what we did. I have no idea what he did with him, Woody never told me. I suspected he buried him because his clothes were muddy, his face and hands filthy when he came back. And I'm sorry Annie, but it was when he was getting undressed to get washed that we ended up in bed together. You might not understand, but going through something so huge, so emotional, well we were in a different world. We loved each other, but that was the first time ... I promise you that."

"I wish you'd told me, Ma. You could have said. You'd have been found not guilty; everybody knew he beat you; it would have been self-defence."

"I know, but at the time I didn't think. And once the body had gone and the house had been cleaned, well that changed everything."

"But you planted his boot and the bottle of vodka by the river."

"We just wanted the whole thing to go away. Woody thought that if he was 'presumed dead' that would be the end of it. And it was. Until now."

I shift in the chair. If Ma was capable of covering up killing Daddy, then perhaps she had harmed Lorelei. "What about Lorelei. Did you poison her?"

Ma blinks. "No!" She shakes her head. "How could you think that?"

"The tonic you made that I took to her, when you discovered she was pregnant."

"That was a harmless concoction, and it was meant to be good for her and the baby." Ma is twisting her fingers into the fabric of her dress so tightly it looks as if it might tear. "But when I made it, it was with hate and bitterness, so perhaps that seeped in somehow."

"Perhaps." Ma looks so miserable, the hatred she's had for Lorelei all these years starting to spill out. "She did steal your songs then?"

Ma is crying, the drops running down her face silently. "I didn't want to hate her ... I thought she was Holly, somehow returned to me … Holly, my sister, who I thought had died because of me. I would have forgiven her anything."

"So, Holly did die?"

"I caught measles at school and passed it to Holly. We were both very ill, my parents as well. But Holly, she was too little to survive, or so they told me … they never let me say goodbye."

We sit for a long time our hands entwined, our bodies close, supporting each other. Before I leave I say, "When you tell your story to the police, don't mention the knife."

"Do you think there'll be evidence?"

"I'm not sure, more likely they'll find a head wound on the skull, consistent with a fall."

"Okay, okay, I'll remember that," Ma says, looking at her lap. "When do you think they'll be here?"

"I don't know, but don't tell Woody yet. Best they don't get the idea that you've been colluding together."

I leave her sitting on the couch, statue-still, like a graceful grey sculpture; staring silently at the floor.

….

My predictions are borne out. My father's skull had a large crack, consistent with him falling backwards and hitting his head on a sharp corner. There was no mention of a knife wound.

CHAPTER 45

We make a sorry procession as we make our way to the crematorium. I am travelling in Archie's Audi watching the village fade behind me. The sky is gunmetal with a constant drizzle of tiny droplets saturating everything, making the world silver and insubstantial. It still isn't cold but I cannot feel warm, even in a borrowed coat from Poppy.

As we take our seats there is a commotion at the back, and everybody turns to see Cedric pushing a wheel chair down the aisle. Lorelei looks like a Pierrot puppet, her white face a shiny circle below her silver hair. Her once luminous eyes, just grey depressions. She has been shrouded in a white blanket, and her features remain blank. When everybody has settled the service begins.

It is brief. I know later I'll have to go and collect the urn with my father's remains. I'll probably return to where the old house had been and scatter his ashes in the surrounding wood. I wonder whether all this has been worth it. Finding out about my father's death and burial and then simply returning him near to the place he'd been interred; but with my mother and Woody facing prosecution.

CHAPTER 46

The night before I leave Broomstone, I tell Archie, "I can't write a book about your mother. It's just too difficult." He doesn't seem surprised.

"That's a shame. I thought you'd be the best person for the job ... but I guess a lot has happened." He puts a hand on my shoulder and squeezes. "I'm sorry, Annie."

"It's alright," I manage to say. "In some ways I'm glad I've found out."

I had taken a walk to my old home earlier in the evening and scattered Daddy's ashes. I'd sat on the log and imagined the house as it had once been but saw my mother's family living there and try to envisage Holly's little body being taken out, wrapped up. Rather than the alternative of a tiny girl being dragged away from her home by a witch.

I saw the cottage as it had been when we first moved in and Woody sitting carving in a haze of sawdust. Sunlight catching the particles turning them gold, making it look to me like a place of enchantment. But then I recalled the wood shed with Lorelei and Daddy, making their dark love spell. I even envisioned my mother pushing my dad and heard once again the sounds of dragging and hiding a body, masked by the crashes of a storm. I was holding my head in my hands, my eyes moist when I heard a creak behind me.

"So, she did it ... your Ma. I told you, see. She killed him." It was Ham, not ghosts, and I turned to look at him. He said, "You let him go here?"

"Yes, I scattered his ashes."

"It's a good place for him to be. His home. They don't

mind." He shook his head and then was gone again, vanished between the trunks of trees.

I got up and patted a tree trunk. "Goodbye," I said to the trees, to Daddy, to all that had gone before. And I once more followed the track into Broomstone village, not looking back.

....

Before I leave I need to see Lorelei. I don't tell anybody and simply knock and walk in. She is motionless in the bed. Her head a white dot against the pillows. I stand over her, not certain who she is.

She doesn't open her eyes but suddenly reaches out. Her hand grabs my arm. Her grip so tight that I can't release it. Her fingers are deformed and mottled with age and illness; they look like the roots of a willow. At that instant I am convinced she is a Dryad. With my free hand I drag the bedding away. It slides to the floor. Her legs are old, cream with flaccid flesh. Her toes long and white. Human.

"Annie, what the hell are you doing?"

Archie is beside me, pulling my wrist from Lorelei's grip, so that it leaves red marks. "I was ... I was ..." But I give up trying to explain. "I'm saying goodbye."

Archie is shaking his head. As I am pushed from the room, I'm certain I hear Lorelei speak. "Holly ... I'm Holly ... Holly I'm ..." It sounds like an echo from years ago, when I'd found her in the river and thought she'd said, 'Lorelei.'

Before I get into bed I pick up the 'R' letters and stroke each one appreciating the feel of the grain under my fingers. Woody had been right; these were the only letters the pieces of wood could have made. I wonder whether people are the same, their destiny carved into them at birth. Predicted from the creases of the palm and whorled pattern of their fingertips. It is over thirty years ago that the 'R's' had been carved, and I still have that clear picture of Woody in my head, sitting on his log clouded by wood dust, and my mother's song drifting from the cottage into the glade. I put the book ends back on the shelf sensing a chill running through my bones. Not far from where Woody sat and where my mother sang, Daddy's body was buried. And both Ma and Woody knew.

I don't know what will happen to them. They are still being questioned and sooner or later a case will be prepared against them. Spider says that my mother will go on trial for manslaughter rather than murder. Woody will have charges against him for the unlawful burying of a body. The sentencing will depend on how much my mother can prove about her abuse and fear for her life at the hands of my father. I will have to give evidence. For now, I put it out of my mind and sleep soundly for the first time since being back in Broomstone.

In the morning I contemplate re-visiting the glade, one final time. But now I think of it as a place of death and burial. Just like the tales that have gone before. I pack up my suitcase and laptop and go downstairs, saying a silent goodbye to everything I pass.

At the front door, I give Poppy a brief hug, and Cedric offers a more formal shake of the hand. I embrace Archie though, sensing his taut slender body against mine. Although he tries, he can't hide his anxiety. I smile as I recollect all the times I had cuddled and comforted him as a baby. I am sorry to say goodbye to him. Even Rasputin comes to wind around Poppy's legs as she stands on the top step. They wave me off.

As I leave the boundary line out of Broomstone, I give a great sigh, letting all the stagnant air of the village escape. Let it go. I have left the curse behind me.

Broomstone no longer has the power to hold me in its grip. It is just a village, cut off in some ways, but not from reality. The people in it are real, do real things, good things and bad things. Not a battle of Good vs Evil, but something in between, something normal.

At least I have no need to return … ever.

There are tears in my eyes as I take the familiar road out

of Broomstone onto the bypass, because I can't help thinking about Ma and Woody and what I have stirred up, causing pain to people that I love. I cannot alter the past, just as I can't alter other peoples' actions. All I can do is change my behaviour. And I make a decision … If Jay is near my flat, I won't let him in, even if I have to force him out. I'm not going to put up with his lies and cheating any longer.

I stretch out my finger to click the CD player on, but then stop. I tune into a local radio station instead. As the breeze blows through the open window, I sing along with a recent pop tune, although I really don't know the words. It bestows a feeling of freedom.

....

Epilogue:
Once upon a time there was a witch. Like most witches she was a dual. A mix of good and evil. Two personas blended into one. This witch could not bear children, and as she so desperately wanted a child, she needed to steal one.